Praise for *The Dead of Mametz*

"A superb mystery as well as one of the most moving war novels I've ever come across."
Betty Webb, *Mystery Scene Magazine*

"This satisfying historical debut partners abundant military and battle details with breathtaking spy adventure on both sides of the front."
Library Journal

"A pacey mystery... the writing is excellent, the characters and dialogue very believable... a superb effort."
The Great War Magazine

"Hicks has taken the reader on more dead ends and twists and turns than it would at first seem possible and then, just at the end, when you think you have finally understood his methods and solved the crime at the same time as him, there is another astonishing twist that further hints at the abilities of this very capable author."
Justin Glover

"... need-to-read tension and riveting detail... recommended to all those interested in WWI or who love a great mystery... a great mix of an intriguing storyline and superb historical detail."
South Wales Branch, Western Front Association

"The plot convincingly intertwines itself between the genres of a detective novel and a soldier's-eye account of trench warfare to create a compelling and intriguing hybrid."
Paul Simon, *Morning Star*

THE
DEAD
of
MAMETZ

THE
DEAD
of
MAMETZ

JONATHAN HICKS

The characters in this book are entirely
fictional and are not intended to bear any
resemblance to anyone living or dead.

First impression: 2011
Second impression: 2012
© Jonathan Hicks & Y Lolfa Cyf., 2011

Cover design: Dorry Spikes

The publisher acknowledges the support of the Welsh Books Council

ISBN: 9 781 84771 315 5

FSC

Published and printed in Wales
on paper from well maintained forests by
Y Lolfa Cyf., Talybont, Ceredigion SY24 5HE
e-mail ylolfa@ylolfa.com
website www.ylolfa.com
tel 01970 832 304
fax 832 782

PROLOGUE

7th July 2007

DOWN THE NARROW track came the red Ford car, billowing a cloud of dust behind it as it went. The driver carefully manoeuvred around the deep holes, only too aware that any damage to this hired car would cost him dearly, whilst his attention was drawn increasingly towards the view to his left. He twisted his head as he drove, snatching glimpses of the mass of greenery on the hill opposite. The wood looked verdant and peaceful now but it was not this contemporary view that filled his thoughts.

He cursed as the car lurched in and out of a pothole, his attention distracted by the vision that just entered his mind, the past superseding the present. *Dangerous*. Braking fiercely, he looked for a place to park. Finding none, he rolled the vehicle onto the verge and switched off the ignition. This was not the place for a car to break down and the thought of being stranded here did not appeal.

Silence fell like sleep. Nothing stirred around him and he looked again at the wood. Time had moved on. Even a gap of a few seconds had made a difference to its shape and colour. Now every glance at the object of his visit seemed to be returned by a glower from the army of trees on the low hill opposite.

There was no other visitor here today and for that he was thankful. This was not the sort of experience he wanted to share with anyone, no matter how well meaning, or worse still, how well informed. His recent days walking the battlefields in the area had been blighted by the pontificating amateur experts who gave loud, often erroneous lectures to small groups of bizarrely dressed tourists or, worse still, sullen hordes of iPod-dangling teenagers who yawned and talked as a backdrop to displays of received wisdom.

This was the moment he had been waiting for, something he had forced himself to postpone for several days. He had denied himself this sacred visit deliberately, saving it up for his last day. Now it was his and his alone. Now it was time.

He got out of the car, checked up and down the track to make sure he was alone, then raised his eyes to the mythical beast that stared disdainfully over his head. The eyes looked vacantly over the valley opposite, unblinking, the teeth bared at an enemy long gone. The sun shone brightly on the red scales, making it look Disney-like, almost comical, under its all-seeing rays, but he knew the symbolism here was anything but entertaining or humorous. He studied its contours, its protruding potbelly, the shape of the beast flawed but ferocious, and then made his way up the steps towards the memorial, its frozen anger holding no fear for him.

Oscendale looked at the inscription on the bronze plaque attached to an upright stone which stood alongside the dragon. *The Battle for Mametz Wood.* The text was in English, French and Welsh. A map showed the direction of the attacks and an order of battle listed the regiments involved. *During this action the division suffered over 4,000 casualties and this memorial was raised in 1987 to remember this sacrifice.*

He ran his fingers over the raised letters. Behind these letters were the Fallen. The names might be on memorials elsewhere but here they had died. In this area had ended hundreds of lives, their hopes, laughter and pain, and brought sorrow to the living with their passing.

The old man turned to face the valley and gazed towards

the wood, one hand on the red dragon, fittingly snarling in the direction of what in the summer of 1916 had been the German lines. The sun bathed the crops that were ready for harvesting now and the birds sang cheerfully up above. Jack Oscendale was glad he was the only tourist who had made the hazardous drive down the French country lane to the site. It would have been wrong for anyone else to interfere with his private moment on a day such as this.

But this was not how he had thought he would feel. It was like the funeral of a friend of long ago. It reminded one of the past and the present, and the years in between without contact. It also made one long for the sunny days of the future.

Oscendale stroked his grey hair absent-mindedly and let his thoughts drift back to a time ninety years before. Recalling the numerous books he had read on the subject and the eyewitness account his father had left him, he found no difficulty in picturing the ghastly events that had taken place here. He pictured lines of khaki-clad men advancing over the field ahead. Walking, falling, dying. He heard the noise, the screams, the rifle fire and the shells.

But time had moved on. The land had returned to normal. The fields were now back to their pre-war and proper purpose, raising food for a hungry French population, and the trees in the wood had grown again to provide a perfect pastoral vista. All seemed as it should be today.

Except for the cemetery.

The lines of white headstones stood like rows of perfect teeth grinning across the valley in the sunshine, as if at macabre jokes told amongst the dead – who lay in this French field, so far from home and their loved ones, buried long ago by the hands of strangers. Together the hundreds of souls watched him as he approached.

Everything is superficial, just skin deep, he mused. This valley and wood were merely a veneer of civilisation. Ninety years ago this had been a charnel house, a field of slaughter, where men fought each other in a frenzy, until, exhausted, the battle was called off and both sides drew breath ready for the next encounter. And now, apart from the lines of white stones, all seemed commonplace and serene.

He walked down the path to the cemetery, opened the gate and searched the register for the name he wanted. There it was. Postponing the moment of meeting for a while longer, he allowed himself time to study the comments in the visitors' book. *'A moving experience', 'a link with the past'*, the living attempting to connect with the unimaginable horror that had occurred here. Messages to the dead.

The grave itself was set five rows back on the left. A neatly kept headstone. One of hundreds all keeping watch over the dead.

'Private Harold Bratton
Welsh Regiment
Killed in action 7th July 1916.'

So they still thought that was how he died. In action. And on that date.

CHAPTER 1

September 1914

The earth felt crisp and cold against his cheek, its early morning scent stinging his nose as he struggled to control his excitement. The grey-clad figures moved across the ground like automata, their *picklehaube* spikes glinting in the bright sun. He watched them closely, fascinated by his first glimpse of the enemy. These were not like the Boers, shooting at you from behind cover, unseen death coming from any direction. These were trained infantrymen, the Prussian Guard, pride of the German Army, part of the largest military force in Europe.

And they were coming right at him.

William Vincent rubbed his eyes again to clear them of the night's torpor. He had been fast asleep when the call had come to stand to. Shaking the early morning cold from his bones, he had woken his men and nagged and cajoled them until they were ready to go into action.

His uniform smelt of sweat and dirt, and the endless days of retreat had taken their toll on his boots, never mind his feet. He had realised how out of condition he was some days previously. His strength was still there, kept up by his previous employment, but being back in the army was different. He knew he did not have the endurance he had once had. He was getting old. *Maybe this is my time.*

Tanned and moustached, he still looked every inch the soldier. He was proud of his record and proud to be here again, in the front line. Touches of grey in his brown hair, he thought ruefully, but he knew he could still do his job. Still defend his country.

Vincent looked along the barrel of his rifle, the small metal sight fixed on one individual in the mass. An unknown man. One of thousands, but the one he had randomly selected to die.

He spoke again to the men of his section. "Hold your fire. Wait for the officer."

Vincent looked at the row of men lying on either side of him. Trained men. Good men. The bedrock of the British Army. All regular soldiers, some of whom had served with him in South Africa. Tough, determined men. Determined to drive these bloody Huns out of Belgium.

The Germans were closing but he knew that not a single man would fire in panic before being ordered. They would wait for as long as it took and then the killing would begin.

Vincent fixed again on the German. Why him? Why not the one to the left or right? He wasn't sure. And anyway it didn't matter. They were all the same and all deserved to die. This man was tall, tall even for the Guard and that physical quirk had probably picked him out as Vincent's target.

"Fire!" The command rang out and he was deafened by the volley of rifle fire that erupted all around him. But he was too experienced a soldier to allow the noise to put him off. He squeezed the trigger gently and felt the stock slam into his shoulder as the bullet sped on its way, the crack of the cartridge a harbinger of death.

The smoke from the muzzle temporarily obscured his view but when it cleared he saw the man was lying prone on the grass, his rifle hurled some feet away from him. *Good,* thought Vincent, *that's one of the bastards. Now for the rest.*

"Let 'em have it, boys!" he yelled, caught up in the euphoria of the kill. Watching the figures fall in groups, he jerked back the bolt of his rifle, inserted another bullet, slammed the bolt forward and sighted on another random figure. This time he saw the man tumble backwards with the force of the bullet and fall prostrate on the ground. He repeated the action and saw another figure spin around as the bullet caught him in the shoulder.

After several minutes the advance slowed and stopped, then turned itself around and, to the accompaniment of cheers from Vincent and his men, the Prussian Guard retreated to the cover of the wood from which it had emerged.

"They'll be back, boys. Keep 'em peeled for the next lot!" he shouted above the raised voices. He knew it couldn't and wouldn't last. There were thousands of Germans on the march through Belgium and his group on this hillside were only a few hundred strong. Still, they could hold them back whilst the main body of the army got away. If the French stood firm they might even be able to drive them back. *All the way back to bloody Germany.*

"Sergeant Vincent!" an officer's voice called.

"Sir!" *It was Jamieson, the stuck-up sod. What did he want now?*

"Form a detail and go down and search those bodies. See if you can find out exactly which regiment they are. Might be useful to HQ to determine troop movements."

"Yes, sir. Lewis, Arnold, Jones. Come with me."

Three soldiers followed Vincent down the hillside. He knew that they were dead men if the Huns attacked again. They'd be out in the open and would be cut down like hay.

"Right let's do this quickly, boys, and get back up that hill."

They split up and Vincent took the right flank. He searched through the pockets of several dead men, retrieving identity cards – *soldbuchs* – and other papers before a movement he detected out of the corner of his eye swung him round. One of the Germans was still very much alive.

The man was attempting to prop himself up on one elbow. His other shoulder was a mass of blood. Vincent walked across to him, rifle and bayonet at the ready, and then stopped dead in his tracks as a face from his past reappeared in front of him. The moustache was new but there was surely no mistaking the rest of his features.

"Karl?" he queried. "Karl Muller?"

The German turned a pair of dazed eyes towards him. "*Mein Gott*. William, is that you?"

"Bloody hell!" cried Vincent and placed a hand on the German soldier's uninjured shoulder.

Muller winced with pain as he tried to adjust his position. Vincent dropped to one knee and said, "Here, let me." He unpacked his medical pouch and started to unwrap a dressing.

"Oh God. What a bloody shame eh? You and me meeting here like this," said Vincent, the unreal nature of what was unfolding here in a French field beginning to impact on him.

"The hand of God is certainly playing a trick on us both, I think. White Rock seems a long way from here, doesn't it?" Muller said, his breathing becoming more difficult as he spoke.

"Yes. Good times, Karl. How the hell has it come to this? I can't believe it, you and me here now, in a place like this. I suspected you had enlisted, of course. But here? Damn it!" The tension of the moment overcame Vincent and he dropped the dressing onto the earth. Muller smiled ruefully and shook his head.

"Do you have any water in that canteen of yours?" Muller asked.

As Vincent was fiddling with the stopper of his water bottle, Muller said, "William, you were a good friend to me once. I am dying now but there is something I want you to have. Open my tunic pocket please."

Before Vincent could comply he heard Arnold shout out. "Sergeant Vincent! Here they come again!"

He looked across the field and saw another long line of German infantry emerging from the woods. He looked down at Muller and said, "Karl, I have to go now. Your own men are coming. They'll take care of you."

"No!" said Muller fiercely. "It will be too late. Take what is in my pocket, please. They must not have it." He grasped Vincent's arm and his face took on a look of steely determination that shook the British soldier.

Vincent looked puzzled for a moment and then unbuttoned Muller's tunic pocket and removed a piece of paper. A shot cracked in the distance and a bullet whizzed over their heads.

"Go, William! Be quick now!" said Muller, his manner relaxing now that Vincent had complied.

Vincent needed no extra bidding. He said goodbye to the German soldier and called out, "Right, you lot. Let's get out of here!"

On his command the four men raced back up the slope towards the British positions and it was not until very much later that Sergeant William Vincent had the opportunity to take out the piece of paper his old workmate Karl Muller had given him.

CHAPTER 2

26th June 1916

THE NIGHT WAS clear and calm. No wind blew across the field tonight but even so it was bitterly cold. Private Harold Bratton shuddered as the chill of the night air cut through his uniform. He sucked again on the cigarette, after looking left and right to ensure that he wasn't being watched. Smoking on guard duty was not a good idea but what else was there to do on a night like this? Nothing was going to happen. It never did. The Germans were miles away so what was he supposed to be guarding? His mates? They were all sleeping soundly in the nearby hut, warm and comfortable, while he froze out here. *Where was his relief? Bloody late again.*

In the distance he could hear a low murmur of gunfire but all seemed quiet in this sector tonight. *It was somebody else's turn*, he mused. *About time too.* Aged nineteen, Harold had seen enough killing to satisfy his teenage curiosity and knew now that it was just a matter of survival. 'King and Country' he'd signed up for, but after the last two years it was more 'Harold and Mates'.

Two years. Nearly two years ago he had walked away from his job as a coal trimmer on Barry Docks and signed up for the army. He had queued with the others at the Drill Hall in Barry, waiting his turn patiently.

"How old are you, son?" a moustachioed recruiting sergeant had asked him.

"Eighteen, sir!" he had lied enthusiastically, desperately trying to make his round teenage face look older by sucking in his cheeks.

The sergeant had eyed him suspiciously. "Well go and walk around the block until you're nineteen," he had responded.

So he had. He was back at the desk in fifteen minutes and the same question had been asked.

"I am nineteen, sir!" he had lied again. The sergeant had nodded and Harold Bratton learnt that service to his King and Country had depended on a lie.

And he'd been lying ever since. He had lied to get in and had lied to stay in. And courage too was a lie. In reality the whole war terrified him. When he had gone home on leave he had lied to his former workmates about conditions at the front.

"What's it like then, Harry?" they had asked him in the Windsor Hotel in Holton Road as he downed another free pint of beer. *Beer for the hero.* What was he supposed to say? *More horrible than anything you can imagine. My mates of two years ago are not my mates this month because they're dead or wounded. I've seen sights a young man of nineteen should never have to see. But I have to go back and that's the strangest thing of all. I don't want to desert, I have to go back. I will go back. And do you know what? I'll do it though the next grave might be mine.*

He thought about home, his mother and father carrying on their endless labours. Dad on the docks, working all the hours God sent, and Mum working from light to dark just to keep the family going. And after it was all over, after the Hun had been beaten, would it be back to normal? Back to the docks, working until he married, settled down and became just like his father? Was that it then? Was that his future – if he was allowed to have one?

He was startled from his thoughts by an unmistakeable sound: a rifle shot.

Bratton clutched his rifle to his shoulder and looked in the direction of the hut where the rest of his section was asleep. The shot seemed to have come from in there. *Impossible. Not unless the Germans had entered unseen and were killing his mates in their sleep.* His mind pulsated. Germans here, behind the lines? A raiding party maybe, intent on taking a few prisoners. *Okay, come on then you bastards. Harry Bratton's waiting for you.* He focused on the door of the hut, breathing quickly, ready to shoot the first German soldier who entered into his sights.

Suddenly the door to the hut was flung open and a figure stumbled out and began to run towards him. *Khaki uniform. Don't shoot, Harry, it must be one of the lads.* The darkness of the night hid the man's face and it was not until he had covered twenty yards that his features became clear enough for Bratton to recognise him. It was Corporal Vincent. Vincent had been his sergeant until he had been demoted last month.

One of the older soldiers in the battalion, Vincent had been a mentor to him at first. A sort of father figure to the younger soldiers, showing them the ropes, keeping them out of trouble until they were experienced enough to look after themselves. Bratton had joined the company in February, green and brash. Eighteen months of training and boredom in Blighty had made him impatient for the front line. Impatient to be here, to be part of the killing.

Bill Vincent had knocked him into shape, as he had promised to on their first meeting, turning the keen young boy recruit into a soldier, teaching him the tricks and keeping him alive, until it was his turn to die. Teaching him the different sounds of the German shells, when to duck, when to run, when to sigh with relief at still being alive.

Then Vincent had changed. He had started to drink more heavily and became sloppier in his duties. Bratton saw how

Jackson and Howells, the other NCOs in the section, had it in for him. They'd snitched on him to the officers and Vincent had been up on a charge which saw him lose one of his three stripes. Vincent had become more withdrawn and morose as a result.

Vincent looked back over his shoulder several times as he stumbled towards Bratton, his Lee Enfield rifle clattering on the ground as his movements became more uncoordinated. Then he saw Bratton and stopped. His eyes were glassy and Bratton wondered whether he had been drinking again. His brown hair was dishevelled and his tunic was unbuttoned and his thin lips hung open in surprise.

Then his movements changed. He suddenly became still and calm. He lowered his rifle, reached into his pocket and extracted a piece of wood. Calmly he placed the rifle between his legs, placed the muzzle to his cheek and, using the wood, pushed the trigger.

There was a loud crack and in an instant his head jerked backwards, the rifle falling noisily to the ground. Bratton stood transfixed by the sequence of horror that was playing itself out in front of him. Vincent lay on his side, blood pouring from his mouth, the left side of his face an oozing mass of blood and tissue.

Bratton was paralysed. He had seen terrible injuries and death before. He had held one of his pals as he bled to death in front of him. But the shock of the whole event had left him staring in horrified fascination at the twitching man. Then he realised that the movement was Vincent stretching his left hand towards him. Horrific gurgling noises were emerging from where his left cheek had been and still the trembling hand was coming towards him. Bratton at last recovered some power of movement and reached forward to touch it. A small piece of paper was pressed into his palm. Vincent nodded once and lay back on the damp earth.

Harold Bratton opened the piece of bloodstained paper and by the light of the moon quickly scanned the contents. Through the shock of the last minute's events, a clear path began to emerge – a way forward. He now understood the opportunity presented to him by the dying man. Stuffing the paper into his trouser pocket, he fired three shots into the air and shouted for help before making his way towards the hut from which Vincent had emerged.

CHAPTER 3

28th June 1916

THE TOWN OF Albert was an artery of activity. The narrow French streets were crowded with columns of marching British soldiers whose passage was marked by the tramp of their feet into the dust of the roads. Long lines of military vehicles crowded into the town square and out of it again, all intent on a single purpose: the preparations for the first stage of the great offensive that would win the war after two years of fighting. Confidence permeated the air. This was the moment. The hour had come. The momentum seemed unstoppable. How could the Germans rebut such a weight of men and equipment?

Along the streets they marched and passed the golden statue of the Madonna that had hung precariously from the spire of the cathedral since the great battles of 1914. When the virgin fell, the war would end, they said. *Well, there are plenty of fallen virgins in this town,* thought Assistant Provost Thomas Oscendale as he watched the lines of soldiers from his office window.

He caught sight of his reflection in the glass. *Older and more lined by the day. Dark shadows under the eyes as well. You need to start looking after yourself, Tommy boy,* he mused.

So this was it then. The Big Push. Oscendale could not share the enthusiasm of his fellow officers as they talked endlessly in the mess of how many miles of enemy territory would be taken soon. His time at Gallipoli the previous year had taught him the folly of overconfidence and he took the minority view that this war would last for years until one side collapsed, exhausted from the attrition of the fight. Then the complex issue of the peace would have to be sorted out.

Oscendale watched messengers running to and fro between the buildings around the square that housed the brain of the British military operation on the Somme. The activity never ceased of late and neither did the cases it was his job to investigate. He turned from the window and resumed his seat at his desk. Traffic control rotas and files of petty crime lay in ranks for him to investigate, tick off and file. The endless lot of the military policeman.

The telephone rang, providing a welcome excuse from the task of sifting the files and he lifted the receiver to his ear.

"Oscendale," he opened, his voice displaying the remnants of his father's Cornish accent.

"Ah yes, Oscendale. Probert here. Now look, it's about the chap you haven't sent me yet. I ordered this to happen some weeks ago. Where is the blasted man?" The officer's irritation was evident and would probably escalate as it had done before. Oscendale ran his hand through his hair, leaned back in his chair and allowed himself to enjoy the next two minutes of his life.

Major Alexander Probert of the Welsh Regiment was of the opinion that members of the Military Foot Police were nothing more than annoying midges to officers who dealt with the real purpose of the war: killing Germans. As such they could be utilised for any duty, including acting as Aides de Camps – ADCs – to middle-ranking officers. Probert had informed him some weeks ago of his request, a request that Oscendale had patiently refused to accede to.

"Good morning Major Probert. It appears that your request for an extra member of staff has become lost in the system. Would you care to resubmit it?" he said, unable to keep a hint of sarcasm out of his voice. That was enough to set Probert off. Oscendale pictured his florid face and decided this was good sport. He really should do it more often.

"Now look here, Oscendale, I've had just about enough of your delaying tactics. Your bloody glorified coppers should be put to better use than snooping about after my men."

Oscendale took a deep breath and responded. "Probert, one day you will be ringing me to ask for the services of one of my men, and it will be for something more than acting as your bloody manservant. Let us hope it will not be for murder."

Before Probert could respond, he replaced the receiver on its cradle.

Oscendale smiled to himself. Irritating regimental officers was a real pleasure sometimes, he decided. He had joined the Military Foot Police at the start of the war, naively eager to do his bit. A policeman by profession, he knew that crimes would not just be committed against the Germans. Criminals would join up and soldiers would be driven to crime by a whole combination of circumstances. These would need investigating and justice would need to be served. A lawless army was a danger to its friends as well as its enemies.

He turned his attention to the memorandum in front of him. *Corporal William Vincent, aged 37, a career soldier entering his twelfth year of service, plus several years on the reserve list. Committed suicide 26th June 1916. Suspected of murdering two fellow soldiers in their bunks on the same date.*

War did strange things to people he mused, but the callous killing of two erstwhile colleagues whilst they slept? The Provost Marshal said it could have happened as the result of neurasthenia – shell-shock. After all, the battalion may have just come back from the hell of two weeks on the front line and from what Oscendale knew of it that was enough to drive anyone to madness. But still, enough to kill two men in cold blood? It didn't seem likely.

There was a knock at the door and his assistant, Sergeant North, entered. Hard-faced and bullish, North was a military policeman of the old school. His loyalty to the British Army was without question; his loyalty to Oscendale unfortunately was.

"The bastard's service record, sir," said North. Red-cheeked and flaccid, he was a bully by nature and Oscendale had had to work hard to keep him in check. Over the preceding few months there had been a battle of wills which Oscendale hoped he had now won. But he was not convinced.

Oscendale's face adopted a pained expression as he grimaced at the terminology. He stared into North's eyes, hidden deep in folds of skin. "His mother might dispute that with you, North."

"Don't expect the bastard had one, sir," replied North before he turned on his heel and left, closing the door firmly behind him.

Oscendale stared at the door and pondered the prospect of the Military Foot Police ever having a different image with men like North in it. Still, the man was efficient at what he did, typing reports and making tea, but any real detective work was well beyond his limited intellect. That was Oscendale's job.

The service record was the standard format: date of attestation, which in Vincent's case was in 1899, physical details and then a list of home and overseas postings. He had left the army and worked in a copperworks in Swansea before being recalled to the colours in August 1914. It was all fairly routine until the previous month when his slow progression up the ranks had been reversed.

Beneath it was the transcript of the Court of Enquiry:

COURT OF ENQUIRY

Proceedings of a Court of Enquiry assembled at Albert on the 27th June 1916 by order of the G.O.C. 38th Infantry Division for the purpose of enquiring into the circumstances under which 62115 Sergt. Jackson, 34516 A/Corporal Howells and 2783 Cpl Vincent all of Welsh Regiment were killed on 26-6-16.

PRESIDENT   Captain M. S. Draper K.R.R.C.

MEMBERS   2/Lieut. Davies Welsh Regiment.
                     Lieut. C. B. Smith K.R.R.C.

IN ATTENDANCE   Nil

The Court having assembled pursuant to order, proceeded to take evidence.

1st Witness

Capt. Jesser Morgan, Welsh Regiment stated:

On June 26th 1916 at the Transport lines Welsh Regiment I was called by Pte. Turner at 4.20 a.m. He reported to me that he had heard three rifle shots and that Sgt. Jackson and A/Cpl. Howells had been shot dead and that Cpl. Vincent had shot himself dead but that he had not seen him. I went out and inspected the hut and found Sgt. Jackson dead in his bunk shot through the head. A/Cpl. Howells was also dead in his bunk shot through the chest. About 40 yards away in the wagon lines Cpl. Vincent was lying dead shot through the mouth.

I had sent in a charge against Cpl. Vincent on June 23rd 1916 of refusing to obey an order. The order had been given by Sgt. Jackson and A/Cpl. Howells and they were the chief witnesses against him.

Cpl. Vincent had been my sergeant and had been reduced for drunkenness the previous month.

2nd Witness
No. 57941 Private H. Bratton, Welsh Regiment stated:
Between 4 a.m. and 5 a.m. June 26th 1916 I was on guard duty and I heard a rifle report. Very soon afterwards a door slammed and Cpl. Vincent was running towards me and as he was running he was looking back over his shoulder. Directly he looked to his front again he saw me and stopped dead. He then turned about, bent down and keeping the butt of the rifle on the ground and his head close to the muzzle, fired the rifle and fell down. I went straight up to him and found he had shot himself through the head and was dead.

3rd Witness
No. 54706 R.Q.M.S. W. Evans, Welsh Regiment stated:
At about 4.30 a.m. on June 26th 1916 Pte. Turner came to my hut and reported to me that Cpl. Vincent had shot Sgt. Jackson. I at once got up and proceeded to the hut where Sgt. Jackson slept. Sgt. Jackson had been shot through the head and was dead. I then ascertained that A/Cpl. Howells had also been shot and was dead. I then left the hut and proceeded down the lines for a short distance of about 30 yards where I saw the body of Cpl. Vincent and lying by his side was a rifle and a piece of wood which I produce* and which had obviously been used to fire the rifle against himself. I picked up the rifle and opened the breech. An empty cartridge case was in the breech and two live rounds were in the magazine. In the meantime I sent a mounted orderly for the Medical Officer and another orderly to report the matter to Capt. Morgan.

* The piece of wood was shown to the 6th witness Pte. Barnes who recognised the shape and the notch in the end.

M. S. Draper. Capt.

4th Witness
No. 5238 A/Cpl. J. Cooper, Welsh Regiment stated:
Between 4 a.m. and 4.30 a.m. on June 26th 1916 I was woken by what I thought to be a rifle shot in the hut where I was sleeping. Directly after the shot I heard someone rush out of the room and shut the door of the hut but was not sufficiently awake to see who it was. About two minutes afterwards I got up and shouted for the stable-picquet after having seen that Sgt. Jackson had been shot through the head. Pte. Turner answered my call and I sent him to R.Q.M.S. Evans with the news.

5th Witness
No. 56650 Pte. E. Johnson, Welsh Regiment stated:
At about 4.30 a.m. 26th June 1916 I was roused by a rifle shot in my hut. I got out of bed and later saw that Sgt. Jackson and A/Cpl. Howells had been shot and were dead. I know nothing more about it.

6th Witness
No. 51380 Pte J. Barnes, Welsh Regiment stated:
About 5.30 p.m. on 25th June 1916 as I was lying in bed I saw Cpl. Vincent carving a piece of wood and cutting a notch in the end of it. I did not ask him what he was doing it for.

7th Witness
No. 52838 A/Cpl. J. Chadwick, Welsh Regiment stated:
About 4 a.m. on June 26th 1916 I was awakened by what I thought

to be a rifle shot in the hut where I was sleeping, followed by a further shot a while later. I didn't see anything else.

8th Witness

No. 54008 C.Q.M.S.C. Ramsden, Welsh Regiment stated:
On June 25th 1916 I marched Cpl. Vincent in front of Capt. Morgan on the charge of refusing to obey an order. After the charge and evidence was read Capt. Morgan asked him if he had anything to say to which he replied that it was pure spite and very hard on an older man to be brought up on a charge by two young N.C.O.'s, meaning Sgt. Jackson and A/Cpl. Howells.

9th Witness

Capt. J. S. Thomson R.A.M.C. stated:
On the morning of June 26th 1916 I received a message to attend some wounded men in the Welsh Regiment transport lines. I sent an ambulance down which came back empty with a message to say that all the men were dead. I went down myself at 10 a.m. and saw the bodies of Cpl. Vincent, A/Cpl. Howells and Sgt. Jackson, all of the Welsh Regiment. Sgt. Jackson was shot through the head – his death must have been instantaneous. A/Cpl. Howells was shot through the chest – his death must have been practically instantaneous. Cpl. Vincent was shot through the head and his death must have taken place shortly after the wound.

I am of the opinion that 62115 Sgt. Jackson and 34516 A/Corpl. Howells both of the Welsh Regiment were shot by 2783 Cpl. Vincent, Welsh Regiment on 26th June 1916.
The murders were intentional and premeditated.

C. D. Bryant. Brig Genl. Comdg. 38th Inf. Division.

Witnesses? More like witlesses, thought Oscendale. Not a very convincing Court of Enquiry, although he had known of worse. Sometimes military men were out of their depth when attempting to replicate the protocol of the law. Yet military law was often something else again, he ruminated. Why hadn't they interviewed Corporal Chadwick properly as he was the only man to have heard more than one shot? If Jackson and Howells had been shot wouldn't the other soldiers in the hut have heard both the shots? In a confined space like a hut the noise would be unmistakable. Presumably the court had assumed they were dead to the world after a night's drinking. The irony of his last thought made him smile briefly. And if Vincent had killed them both, why did Private Bratton report that he kept looking backwards as he ran from the hut? What was he afraid of?

He looked again at Vincent's service record. The man had enlisted at twenty years of age. On the attestation form he had listed his trade as that of a copper worker. His home was 26, Sea View Terrace, Mount Pleasant, Swansea. Vincent had elected to join the Rifle Brigade and after completing basic training at Winchester he had been posted to South Africa as part of the British forces fighting the Boer farmers. After serving there he had spent some time serving at home before being demobilised to the reserve. He had been called up as a reservist at the start of the war, assigned to the Welsh Regiment, re-assumed his previous rank of sergeant, and had served in France and Belgium ever since.

Oscendale leaned back in his chair and rested his eyes on the window once more. *'2783 W. Vincent'. What drove you to do that, Corporal Vincent? What dark thoughts were playing inside your head that night?*

CHAPTER 4

29th June 1916

THE TELEPHONE JARRED Oscendale awake. A woman murmured softly at his side and he spoke quietly into the receiver so as not to disturb her. She had arrived late that evening, worn out again by a twelve-hour shift tending the hundreds of wounded pouring into Advanced Dressing Station Number 11. The strain was beginning to tell on her, he knew. She was less talkative than usual and seemed detached whilst they ate their evening meal together in a local café. When they returned she had thrown off her shoes and had fallen asleep in a chair within minutes. He had undressed her and put her to bed then sat at the window when the puzzles of this latest case came again to torment him and deny him sleep. After an hour he had reached a brick wall in his mind and gave in to the arms of Morpheus.

"Mmmm, yes, what?" he mumbled, cursing himself at once for not responding in a manner befitting an officer. Sometimes he forgot.

"Oscendale? Avate here. Are you awake?"

I bloody well am now, sir, he thought but said, "Er yes, sir. What time is it?"

"Three-thirty. Listen, I know you're up to your eyes in this suicide case but the local gendarmerie have just discovered the body of a dead Frenchwoman."

Oscendale frowned. "What's it got to do with us, sir? Can't the local police look into it?" He knew he sounded ratty and realised that the frustrations of this latest case were getting to him.

"Well normally they would, of course, but unfortunately there's a link to one of our chaps so I'd like you to take a look."

Oscendale was fully awake now. "Where's the body, sir?"

Avate replied, "Let me see. It's 14, Rue St Juliette, in the south of the town. I'll send a car round for you in ten minutes."

"South? Isn't that where one of the battalions of the Welsh Regiment is billeted?"

"Yes, them and the Royal Welsh Fusiliers. Get over there, examine the body and poke around a bit. Tell me what you come up with. If it's what I think it is, this won't be great for Anglo-French local relations, if you catch my meaning."

Oscendale knew exactly what Avate meant. The murder of a local French prostitute by British soldiers was not unknown. He had investigated several similar cases and knew the bad feeling they stirred up amongst the local populace. A tart was a tart, but a dead tart was a different matter altogether.

Dressing quickly, he felt as if he had aged ten years since the war began, most of it occurring lately. *Still,* he considered, *you wouldn't have it any other way Tommy Boy.*

After a bone-rattling ride through the streets of Albert, the driver eventually found Rue St Juliette. It was a typical French street: high-sided buildings of grey stone loomed overhead and seemed to squeeze each passer-by. Shutters were closed at this time of night and people tried to sleep despite the ever-present sound of gunfire in the distance. Oscendale spotted two gendarmes standing guard at a doorway and indicated to the driver to stop.

Telling the soldier to wait, he got out of the car and looked up and down the street. Nothing out of the ordinary and certainly nothing seedy. Quite the opposite in fact, he decided. It certainly didn't look like an area for prostitutes – unless this woman had been very special.

It had rained on the way and he pulled his cap down low over his eyes. As he hurried towards Number 14 he spotted several sets of net curtains twitch as curiosity overcame good taste and the locals peered out at the activity occurring in their street.

He showed his identity card to one of the gendarmes and was permitted to enter. A gaslight flickered on the wall of a narrow hallway, an ancient piece of furniture acting as the sole welcoming note. More gendarmes were in the hallway and one pointed to a room on the right. Oscendale spoke briefly to the man, who thought for a moment and then answered his question.

He entered a room with a large table in the centre. Lying on the floor was a woman, her arms extended either side of her. Her dress had ridden up to expose pale thighs and a red circle of blood lay on her stomach like a target. A slightly-built plain-clothes policeman stood nearby, conversing with a British officer. Both men ceased talking as he entered and turned towards him.

"Assistant Provost Oscendale," he said. "And you are?"

The French policeman nodded curtly but said nothing, his bald head and black goatee beard giving him a somewhat sinister air. The officer saluted and said, "Lieutenant Price, Welsh Regiment. How do you do, sir."

The speaker was polite but nondescript. Probably the latest in a long line of family soldiers, Oscendale decided. Over here and over promoted. Bit old to still be a lieutenant but maybe his lack of intelligence was holding him back. He needn't worry too much though; there would be plenty of gaps in the officer ranks when this latest show was over.

Price continued, gesturing at the policeman, "This is Inspector Valère of the Albert Gendarmerie." Oscendale offered his outstretched hand to the policeman who hesitated and then shook it. Oscendale stared back into the man's eyes.

Yes, thought Oscendale, *probably hates the sight of British soldiers at the moment.* A murder in his town would be tricky to solve and local angst would need addressing too.

"I understand there is a suspected military link?"

Price replied while Valère bent down near the body. "We found a general service button in the woman's left hand. Must have been one of our chaps who did it."

"What's her name, Lieutenant?" Oscendale said irritably; he disliked the way the woman was being anonymised already. Several hours ago she had been a living person, with her own secrets and desires. A good copper had told him that once and he had never forgotten it. Her face looked calm and peaceful, but the blood had drained from it and rigor mortis was setting in. The bloodstain on her stomach had dried to the colour of good wine. He bent over her body and studied her clothing.

"Um, don't know. Inspector?" Price turned to Valère.

The French policeman replied in heavily accented English without looking up. Oscendale saw his presence was clearly annoying the man.

"Jaulard, Madame Catherine Jaulard. She owned the local boulangerie." Valère continued to scrutinise the dead woman and Oscendale noted the way the man's experienced eyes scanned every inch of the corpse.

"I see. Who found Madame Jaulard?" Oscendale forced

himself to control his irritation with the French policeman who had barely acknowledged his presence since he had entered the room.

"One of her employees. When he arrived at the boulangerie to begin the baking he found it locked. That was unusual. Madame Jaulard never missed a day's baking so he came here and found her. He is in the other room." Valère's English was excellent but his anger was barely below the surface. He rose from the body, stretched out his hand and passed an object to Oscendale.

Oscendale saw that it was a military general service button currently in general use amongst the Kitchener recruits. *Could be any man from any regiment. Not much to go on.*

"Have you searched the room, Inspector?" he asked.

"Of course," Valère replied, fixing Oscendale with a look of annoyance that said *don't try to teach me my job.*

"And did you find anything unusual?" Oscendale persisted, determined to be part of this investigation whether he was wanted or not.

"Nothing out of the ordinary. The button indicates that one of your soldiers killed her, probably because she was a decent woman and refused his advances." Valère's anger had broken free now. "So I suggest that you and Lieutenant Price find out which of your men returned to his billet with this woman's blood on his uniform."

"Was the carpet damp?" said Oscendale quietly.

"What?" said Price, bemused. Oscendale ignored the officer and spoke again to Valère.

"If you had checked it before your gendarmes started treading all over it, you'd have been able to ascertain what time she let the murderer in. It started raining at around two o'clock one of your men told me. So if you had checked it you'd have known."

Having seen that he was not dealing with a fool, Valère nodded politely in deference.

"We did not check the hallway carpet, Captain Oscendale, but there are damp footprints on the carpet in this room."

Oscendale continued. "So why would a respectable businesswoman, dressed in her evening clothes, admit a British soldier after two o'clock in the morning?"

Valère nodded. "Madame Jaulard was no fool. If she let a man into this house tonight it was by arrangement. It was someone she knew."

"Or someone she thought she knew," murmured Oscendale. "What do we know of her social life? She was a widow?"

"Yes, she was a widow but there had been a man in her life, according to Etienne Laurent, the baker who found her. He was a British soldier who used to come into the boulangerie but he stopped coming when the preparations for the great offensive began."

"Does Laurent know his name?" asked Oscendale, his pulse starting to quicken.

"No," said Valère consulting his notebook. "But he remembers it sounded French."

CHAPTER 5

29th June 1916

Etienne Laurent sat slumped in a chair in Madame Jaulard's front parlour. He looked up as Oscendale and Valère entered.

"Monsieur Laurent, Captain Oscendale would like to ask you some questions," said Valère in a somewhat brusque manner. Oscendale knew that he had not completely won Valère over but at least he was thawing a bit.

Oscendale pulled a chair up next to Laurent. The man had a thick mat of black hair above dark, suspicious eyes and a physique that told of many years spent in manual labour. At the end of fifteen minutes Oscendale had established that Madame was a good employer who treated him well. She was hard-working and had taken over the boulangerie when her husband had been killed at Neuve Chapelle the previous year. Laurent had worked for her for three years. Many British soldiers came into the boulangerie to buy bread and, as Madame was an attractive woman, many men had tried to flirt with her. One man she had taken a particular shine too, though. He had a French sounding surname and she had joked that with a name like that he should be fighting with the Poilus – the French Army. The man had been a regular visitor over the next few days and Madame would often step outside onto the busy street to talk to him. Oscendale pressed him on the man's name but he seemed genuinely unable to recall it. After all, he was a baker and did not concern himself with Madame's private affairs.

He had arrived at the boulangerie at his usual time that

morning, 3.00 a.m., ready to begin the first bake of the day. Madame Jaulard always arrived before him. She would unlock the door and begin the process of heating the ovens. Today it had been raining and he was keen to get inside quickly; he nearly broke his wrist, he said, when the door to the boulangerie refused to give way. He had knocked on the glass and peered inside but had seen nothing. He had then walked the short distance to Rue St Juliette to see if, for once, his employer had overslept or if she were ill. Either case was unlikely, he said, as Madame had the constitution of an ox and the timekeeping of a high-quality clock so he was suspicious even before he arrived at the front door of number 14.

The door had been open. Again he had knocked but after receiving no response to that or his calls, he had tried the door handle and found it unlocked so he had entered the house. The hallway light had been lit, yes. He had found poor Madame where she lay. He buried his face in his hands. She had looked so undignified, lying there with her dress like that, but he was afraid to touch anything for fear of being implicated in the crime so he had ran to the gendarmerie and reported what he had seen.

"The clothes that Madame Jaulard is dressed in. Were they her work clothes?" asked Oscendale.

Laurent looked up, his face running with tears. "Non, monsieur. Madame would not have worn such fine evening clothes to fire up the ovens."

Oscendale nodded. It was as he thought. Madame Jaulard had been expecting a visitor or had just returned from a night out. But such a punctilious woman, endeavouring to continue her husband's business after his death, would not have allowed herself the luxury of a late night out during a working week.

No, it was more likely that she had been expecting her killer and had admitted him or her sometime after 2.00 a.m.

"Did Madame Jaulard have any relatives or close friends? Someone who might know the name of the British soldier you mentioned?" said Oscendale.

Laurent thought for a moment. "Oui, mon Capitaine. Her sister, Madame Veronique, who keeps a café on Rue Lamartine."

Oscendale stood up and he and Valère walked back into the other room. Catherine Jaulard's dress had been lowered to cover her modesty, for which he was grateful. By all accounts she had been a good woman who did not deserve to be the subject of emotionless speculation by professional men while she lay dead on her own carpet in such an undignified state.

"Inspector Valère, can one of your men show me the way to Rue Lamartine? Perhaps Lieutenant Price and I can go and tell her sister the terrible news while you continue your investigations here."

Valère frowned suspiciously then shrugged. "Certainly, Captain Oscendale, but I fear you will have to carry out the unpleasant task by yourself. Lieutenant Price was called away urgently."

It was now Oscendale's turn to frown. "Called away? By whom?"

"I do not know. While you were interviewing Laurent he told me that he had to leave but that you would give him a full report into the case later today."

Oscendale knew that this was not standard procedure. The MFP would carry out their investigations in secret, only informing the regimental officers concerned when their work was complete. A thought occurred to him.

"Have you met Lieutenant Price before, Inspector?" he quizzed.

"No," replied Valère. "He arrived after I did, introduced himself and said he had been sent over by Regimental Headquarters as soon as they heard about the discovery of the body."

Oscendale thought for a moment. "So you would routinely contact the local HQ when you come across a case such as this?"

"Only where there is suspicion of a British soldier having perpetrated the crime," Valère countered.

"And how long after your arrival did Price get here?"

"Some five minutes or so after I telephoned the local British headquarters."

"Then he couldn't have come from Regimental HQ. It's in north Albert and that's a good ten minutes drive away; I didn't see a military car outside when I arrived."

Valère looked like he had been insulted. "I know the geography of my town, Captain Oscendale. I assumed he had been billeted in the vicinity and a call had been placed to him."

Oscendale was not convinced but decided to keep his thoughts to himself. If Lieutenant Price was with the Welsh Regiment then he was the Kaiser's uncle.

CHAPTER 6

29th June 1916

"MADAME VÉRONIQUE ROBERT? My name is Captain Oscendale and I am a military policeman. Can I come in? I am afraid I have some bad news for you."

The woman who answered the door to the café had brown hair, tied back with a bow. Her white nightdress was covered with a check dressing gown and she was still bleary-eyed with sleep. The sight of the gendarme at Oscendale's side quickly swept aside all vestiges of rest and she stood aside to let the two men in.

She indicated one of the café tables and they sat while she lit a candle lamp and brought it to the table. The pale, flickering light gave their faces an eerie glow and Oscendale used the intervening moments to rehearse how he would break the news of her sister's death to the woman. He had gone through the act many times before, in small, terraced, red-bricked houses in Barry to inform yet another woman that her labourer husband had been found drowned in Barry Docks or killed in a fight outside one of the many public houses that littered Dock View Road.

This time, though, it was different. He was already deeply troubled by the circumstances of Madame Jaulard's death and was not at all sure that sinister forces were not at work.

The routine came first. "You are Madame Véronique Robert, the sister of Madame Catherine Jaulard?"

Fear came into the woman's eyes. "Is it Paul? He has been wounded?"

Oscendale guessed this was reference to her absent

husband who was probably serving with the French army, as her brother-in-law had done.

"No, Madame. It's your sister. She was murdered this morning."

There was never an easy way to break the news so he had found through bitter experience that it was best to get it over with and let the bereaved woman's tears come.

Madame Robert sat stunned for a second or two and then gave a huge sob, while bringing her hand to her mouth. Oscendale and the gendarme sat and squirmed uncomfortably while the woman wept. He was not the type to put an arm around a grieving woman's shoulder and evidently the gendarme was of the same ilk. After a time she recovered her composure and began to speak.

"What happened to her? Was it the *Boche*?"

"At the moment, Madame, we are unsure. Tell me, did your sister have a man in her life?"

He realised at once that he had made a mistake. The woman took her hand away from her mouth and gave him a look of outrage.

"A man? After her poor Charles died last year? No, Monsieur!"

"But there was a British soldier she used to talk to a lot. A man she met at the boulangerie."

The woman stopped sobbing and thought for a moment, fixing him with her cool, blue eyes.

"You mean William? But he was just a passing friend. They would talk and he would make her laugh. There was nothing more than that."

"So she mentioned his name to you?" he persisted.

"Of course. He cheered her up. But that was all," she ended fiercely. Oscendale knew that Madame Robert was a woman of considerable pride and strength and wondered if her sister had been from the same mould.

"So his name was William. Did she tell you his surname? It was French-sounding I am told." He knew he was getting closer and felt his heart pounding.

"That is true. He said he was of Huguenot descent and his ancestors had settled in Cornwall."

But I think they moved further west than that, thought Oscendale.

"And his name, Madame?"

"Vincent. His name was William Vincent," said Madame Véronique Robert and continued her outpouring of grief for her dead sister.

CHAPTER 7

29th June 1916

THE QUAYSIDE AT Boulogne was packed with the casualties of the recent fighting. All along the wharf lay hundreds of stretcher cases, while RAMC orderlies and VAD nurses walked up and down the ranks of the wounded and maimed, tending to those who clamoured for attention. Others lay still and quiet, waiting calmly for death or deliverance.

Oscendale sat at the window of a café and watched as the stretchers were slowly lifted aboard the army troopship *Brighton* in preparation for the Channel crossing. More cases for the overworked hospital staff at home. More pain and suffering to be hidden from the British public.

They came in a variety of guises, bandaged in a myriad of ways, but each one seeking the solace of home. A warm bed, a comforting hand and an escape from the terror of the trenches – a 'Blighty'. Oscendale had seen hundreds of wounded men being evacuated at Gallipoli and during the battles of 1914, but this was on a much larger scale. He wondered how the people at home would react to seeing the hospital trains disgorging their distressing cargoes at stations the length and breadth of the land. How the great wave of patriotism would founder then, smashed against the jagged rocks of the stark reality of modern warfare.

It was warfare that none of them had expected. Truly terrible in its materiel and propagation. The preconceptions of 1914 had been swept away. No great cavalry charges sweeping the enemy from the field. No set-piece battles where men lined up in ranks in brightly coloured uniforms and fought for glory until one side ran away. This was different, a hard unremitting slog to wear down the enemy by fair means or foul. And the consequences lay in front of him: shattered human beings who welcomed a spell away from it all. But many of them would be back, he knew. The monster of war would not be placated yet.

Boarding the ship, he presented his identity card and was waved through by an agitated sailor. The decks slowly crowded with men who lay or stood according to their condition and eventually the ship made its lumbering way out of the port.

Leaning on a rail, Oscendale lit a cigarette and mulled over the detail of the case thus far. He was certain now that the two cases were in fact one. He still had nagging doubts about the circumstances of Vincent's death. On another day it could have been viewed as an unusual case of suicide brought on by bullying NCOs, except that William Vincent had been one of them until recently, one of the group. Something had gone on between him and Jackson and Howells which had led him to take such drastic action. But what was it? They apparently had some sort of a hold over him and in Oscendale's experience such behaviour usually hinged on information that the victim did not wish to be made public. It seemed to have happened fairly recently too, judging by Vincent's behaviour over the past few weeks and yet Vincent had not wished to share his problem with anyone, except possibly with Catherine Jaulard.

What did Jackson and Howells have to gain from their behaviour? Power? Control? NCOs usually had enough of that over the other ranks. No, it had to be something far more basic. Something soldiers never had enough of, besides sex. Money. And most of the time the two went together, he knew. He had been due a few days' leave anyway and so deciding to pay a visit to Vincent's family home had not been a hard decision to make. Perhaps the answer would lie there. It was as good a place to start as any. And anyway it gave him the chance to have a few days to himself. Time to think. To think about him and Kathleen. *And a dead Frenchwoman.*

As the sea wind whipped across his face, he let his thoughts move away from the obscurities of the case to his own life. And in the way that our daily experiences often trigger off similar thoughts, his mind went back to other sea crossings he had made. His first crossing to France in the autumn of 1914. The excitement of a foreign war and the nervousness he had felt at the prospect of transferring his police skills to a military stage.

And now here he was, going home. But he had nothing at home. His work was his home, his refuge. Who was he kidding? He was going home to work. He flung his cigarette into the foaming water and turned away from the receding coastline of France.

The Great Western Railway train stood hissing at the platform, its dark green livery giving it a military air. The platform was crowded with men in uniform, some going home on leave, others with nurses and doctors in attendance. This latter group were at the far end of the platform in an attempt to keep them away from more sensitive eyes than his, whether in uniform or not.

The compartment was stuffy and hot. Smoke hung in the air and the musky smell of the dirty seats hovered around his nostrils. A soldier on the seat opposite him slept deeply, mouth hanging open. Oscendale placed his forehead to the cool glass of the window and looked out as the English countryside slid past. He closed his eyes and tried to sleep but failed. A group of soldiers played a noisy card game across the compartment and he thought better of asking them to keep their voices down. This was their relief from hell and they were welcome to make as much noise as they liked. They had earned it.

The countryside was much changed since he had last been home. That had been when he was wounded the previous year, but then he had been lying on a stretcher in a mail coach and had seen nothing for hours except the dark sky and grey fields scuttling past a dirty window pane.

Now fields and villages, glorious in the heat of a British summer, rolled by, each one seemingly untouched by the havoc that was being wrought across the Channel. Yet each settlement hid sadness behind its façade. News of a death or a wounded son, brother, father or husband had affected each one, and if the growing casualties on the Western Front were anything to go by, there would be more bad news for the foreseeable future.

He looked back inside the compartment once more. The soldier opposite him was still asleep and the card game was progressing to the accompaniment of raucous cheers and the swapping of insults. At last he dozed fitfully until a change in momentum woke him. The train had halted at a station. A man in a suit walked along the corridor, took one look inside the compartment and moved on to find another, quieter place to pass the journey. A soldier slumped into the seat next to him after placing his kit bag in the netting above his head.

The others had paid little attention to Oscendale's MFP badges, but this man was different. At first he ignored Oscendale but after shifting heavily in his seat a few times, he lit a cigarette and said with beery breath, "Military Foot Police, eh sir?"

"That's right," replied Oscendale and wondered how far the man would go. He was in no danger; striking an officer was a court martial offence and every soldier in the British Army knew it, but the man could be an irritation for the rest of his journey.

"Yes, the Military Foot Police." The soldier drew out the words in exaggerated fashion. "The force of law and order. Never see any Military Police in the front line, though, do you, sir?" the man pressed.

Oscendale bit hard on the bait, his patience already at an end. "Actually, private, have you read today's *Times*?" and he motioned towards the paper he had discarded on the seat.

"No, sir, why?" the man asked quizzically.

"Because you will see that a corporal of the Military Foot Police has just been awarded a posthumous Distinguished Conduct Medal."

The card game had ceased and he had the attention of all the soldiers in the carriage except the private in the corner who continued to sleep.

"For what?" the man replied cynically, "directing the traffic?"

He expected a laugh or two from his peers across the compartment but was rewarded with silence. The other soldiers knew the value of a DCM and knew it was not lightly won.

"Actually no," said Oscendale, picking up the newspaper and opening it. "There's a photograph of him. Corporal Robert Jay, aged 35. Killed at Ypres 20th May. Even has an account of his deed. Do you want me to read it to you?"

The man said nothing and sucked heavily on his cigarette, sensing defeat.

"I'll take that as a yes then." He began to read. "'On the night of 20th May Corporal Jay went out alone into no-man's-land to retrieve a wounded man. Unfortunately, he was hit by shellfire on his return to our trenches.' It even gives an account by his officer of his death and I'll read that to you as well. 'As soon as I heard that he had been wounded by shellfire I went to see him at the dressing station but he was unconscious and died three hours later. He was bold and fearless under shellfire and set a fine example of courage and devotion to those under his charge, creating in them a feeling of confidence and safety by his coolness when in danger.'" Oscendale paused for effect before adding, "I expect he was also very good at directing traffic."

Oscendale closed the paper and placed it back on the seat. He turned away to look out of the window. The man finished his cigarette, stood, retrieved his kit bag and went to seek another compartment.

CHAPTER 8

30th June 1916

NUMBER 26, SEA View Terrace, Mount Pleasant in Swansea. A nondescript terraced house with a view over the sprawl of Swansea Docks. Oscendale agreed that you could view the sea – just – but the drizzling rain and the yellow clouds from the several copperworks nearby meant that it was a struggle today at best.

Two-up and two-down. The motto of the industrial poor. Its windows gazed with dead eyes over the industrial scene beneath its feet. Railway lines and sidings extended like a spider's web, their intricate patterns of rail and sleepers passing trains from one area to another as the great machine of industry ground on.

Alongside the lines ran the river Tawe, its dark, polluted depths stained by the blood of industry. It murmured its discontent as it flowed to spill its filthy contents into the waters of Swansea Bay. On the way it cleaved the jagged metal and stone of Swansea Docks where ships sat patiently, waiting to be filled with the black gold from the mines further up the valleys and the copper from the workings that jostled for business on the outskirts of town.

Hunching deeper into his army overcoat and drawing up the collar, Oscendale knocked again at the door of the Vincent family home. This time a shuffling inside indicated that he had been heard on his second attempt and he waited patiently as a bolt was slid back and a key turned.

A woman with the uncertain age of someone who has worked too hard for too long gazed vacantly at him, a baby cradled in her arms. The smell of damp vegetables assailed his nose.

"Mrs Vincent?" he enquired. "Captain Oscendale, Military Foot Police. I've come about your husband."

The woman drew a short breath and stood aside, her eyes on the floor, so Oscendale went into a narrow, dimly lit passageway and removed his cap. He stood expectantly but quickly realised that this was not a household that stood on ceremony so he let himself into the front parlour.

The room was shabby in its best parts, but best was always a relative term in an industrial working-class home. A weather-beaten mirror reflected more gloom back into the room. The carpet had lain for many years, its stains testament to a lifetime's use. A settee and two armchairs ringed the room. Their original pattern was indiscernible as blankets now covered the upholstery in an effort to eke out yet more life from these victims of time and long use.

Mrs Vincent passed the baby to a small girl with dark rings around her eyes who suddenly appeared at her elbow and vanished as quickly as she had come, and the two of them were left alone to pick over the bones of William Vincent's life.

The drawn curtains and thin gaslights gave the room an ethereal quality and Oscendale hesitated, wondering whether he was to sit in one of the armchairs or not.

At last Vincent's widow spoke. "Why the police?" she said. "I've had the letter, you know. Did he desert or something?"

"No, he didn't desert, Mrs Vincent. I just wanted to ask you a few questions about William."

The woman sighed. "Do you know what happened? All the letter said was he'd died. Was it the Germans or an illness of some sort?"

What was he to say? That her husband had blown his head off with a .303 bullet seconds after murdering two British soldiers? Hardly a war-hero story and the repercussions could stay with the family for generations.

"How long had you been married, Mrs Vincent?" He tried to deflect the uncomfortable subject.

Thankfully the woman let the topic drop. *Probably still in shock*, he thought.

"Seventeen years. Course I haven't seen him for much of those seventeen years. Spent most of the early part of our marriage time in South Africa. Then it was the army, nothing but the army. Always was. But he was a good man, sir, and we got lovely kids."

Oscendale looked around, expecting more to appear but the woman smiled and said, "Not here, sir. The oldest is in a copperworks in the Hafod and the others are in school."

"Did he write to you recently?"

"Yes, sir. Got his letter here on the mantelpiece." She rose and picked up an envelope from behind the clock above the fire, which was now making Oscendale uncomfortably hot.

"May I see it?" he asked.

"Don't see why not. There's no lovey-dovey in it. Wasn't given much to that sort of thing was my Bill. Here."

She passed him the envelope and Oscendale removed a piece of paper and began to read William Vincent's last communication with his wife.

Dear Bea,

Well love it has been a while since I wrote last but to tell the truth things have been so busy here that I have not had the time.

You may have read in the paper about the Big Push. We are to be part of it though I can't say where. I will do my duty as I have always done and hope I can come home safe to see you once more.

Things have been bad with the two I wrote to you about before.

They know some things that have made things hard for an old soldier like me. But it won't last. If all my plans come off we won't have to worry any more. Our lives will change and I know you and the little ones will be happy.

I won't say much more other than White Rock. You might know what I mean by that if you remember Karl.

I shall keep my head down and hopefully come through it all. Unless I get a Blighty one of course and then I'll be home sooner!

Your husband,

Bill.

P.S. I have sent some silk postcards for our Ruby. I haven't been able to get so many this time as we're far from a town, if you get my meaning.

After gleaning nothing further from the widow over the next twenty minutes, Oscendale left Mrs Vincent to her grief and stood for a while surveying the septic view below the road that the terrace stood on. He rested his hands on the low stone wall that separated the housing of the workers from their places of work and mulled over the contents of Vincent's letter, as drops of rain began to fall once more.

White Rock. The key to Vincent's optimism seemed to centre around White Rock and Karl. When he had asked Vincent's widow what she thought White Rock referred to she had informed him that the only White Rock she knew was the name of the copperworks where Vincent worked before the war, and where her eldest son now worked. It was about half a mile away along the valley. As for Karl, she said she had no idea, but Oscendale sensed she was holding something back. The woman was loyal and stoic, he surmised, and her lips were sealed.

CHAPTER 9

30th June 1916

THE RAIN FELL lightly as he left the depressing row of little houses. As he walked his spirits sank further as he watched a pale yellow cloud drift down the valley, across what was left of the view over the town of Swansea. Gas. But this was the gas of industry which held fewer horrors than the sort he was accustomed to seeing. It spread slowly in a huge swathe of hell-like waste and left him with a sense that men seemed determined to destroy all that was clean and fresh and natural. He turned left and made his way along a curved road until it dropped into a closely-packed set of houses before ending at the still, black waters of a canal.

Oscendale walked along the canal towpath, watching the low, slim barges piled high with coal as they moved along the water, pulled by taciturn, sombre horses guided by tough-looking men with flat caps and dirty jackets.

The rain beat at the surface of the black water now, dimpling it, whilst around him the oddly shaped factory buildings grew in height and number. Tall brick chimneys lowered over him. He passed over a grey stone bridge while another barge slid under his feet.

His uniform attracted two kinds of responses, cheers and claps from the majority, curses and shouts from those who recognised a military policeman's hat. But he was never ignored. A military policeman this far from France meant trouble for someone. It was just a question of whom.

After a while the rain began to soak into his clothing and

he sank deeper into his greatcoat, until at last he reached the site of the copper workings. The smell of sulphur was now pungent and his thoughts raced back to the horror of the gas attacks he had witnessed. No gas masks here, though they were desperately needed.

The collection of copper factories squatted on either side of the valley in a bleak vision of industrial power. Smoke belched into the sky from dark chimneys and hung there, trapped by the rain clouds. Mile after mile of buildings ran up and down the valley. Hell's furnaces to feed the devil's war.

He found the White Rock copperworks on the east side. One of the smaller factories, its bleak buildings spoke of hard labour and death. *White Rock*. It sounded like a piece of romantic coastline, sunning itself under a burning sky. But this was no idyllic retreat, just a dark industrial complex that glowered at him as he approached.

To reach the manager's office it was necessary to pass across the works floor itself. The cavernous, steel-girder-framed building opened up in front of him as he stepped through the doorway. It was like being inside the skeleton of a huge dinosaur, he decided. The ribs projected in all directions, holding up a vast roof from which little heat escaped. The temperature hit him like a boiling wave and for a moment or two he found it hard to catch his breath. Memories of the heat of the Dardanelles seized him and he slowed his footsteps until the madness passed.

The copper worker detailed to be his guide looked at him with the superiority of one who had spent his whole life working in such conditions, as his forebears had done before him. Solid and square, his lined, flushed face spoke of years battling against the heat.

"Always gets you, first time," he grumbled and they began the long walk to the far end of the building. Furnaces glowed and hissed on either side as they were fed, and men hammered out discordant, rhythmless tunes on steel benches. To add to this din men bawled at each other over the cacophony, while in the centre of the room a vast H-shaped press slammed down with relentless precision on metal inserted from below. All around stood buckets of water to which men made regular trips to ladle liquid down their parched throats.

Oscendale coughed as the sulphurous air began to irritate his lungs. This time the copper worker did not turn round in disdain but continued his regular, sidling gait towards the door that meant escape from the inferno.

Young boys scurried to and fro, fetching and carrying, and Oscendale wondered how many of the adults present had begun their working lives here in such a manner. He looked at their faces, not yet stained green like the satyrs who tended the furnaces all around them.

Vast open vats of molten metal stood at the far end and more men stood unprotected above them, stirring the contents with pieces of wood stained emerald green by the process.

As they reached the sanctuary of the door and were at last about to leave the demonic images behind, Oscendale turned to his guide and asked him how difficult they found it to recruit workers in such conditions. The man smiled grimly and said, "The wages are good and to some that's all that matters. If their chests survive the first six months all they need to worry about is accidents."

"And do you get many of those?" asked Oscendale frowning.

"Let's just say we are recruiting all the time. Bit like you lot really, sir," he added.

Oscendale took the point and decided it would be better to remain silent until he met the manager. A working man never liked an outsider criticising his place of work, in the same way as a man never liked others to know how much he earned; it showed how little he would settle for in life.

He was directed to the manager's office and his guide scurried away. A thin-faced woman in a precisely fitted black dress sat behind a desk with the designation *secretary* placed in front of her. She smiled briefly as he stated his name and his business. Flitting through an inner door, she emerged some seconds later to inform him that Mr Llewellyn was free to see him.

A crisply suited round man in his late fifties rose to greet him, obviously thrilled at the sight of a war hero in his establishment.

"Captain Oscendale, how are you? One of our heroes at the front, eh? How are things over there? Giving the Boche hell, are we?" The man beamed and Oscendale knew it was time to burst his bubble.

"Actually, sir, I'm a military policeman and I'd like to interview one of your employees."

The smile dropped from the man's face like a trench mortar shell. This was not what he expected. *One of his employees in trouble with the police?*

"Who is it? I mean, what has he done?" By now the man was clearly flustered and either the heat of the furnaces or that of the situation was affecting him. His cheeks glowed a ruby red.

"Rest assured, Mr Llewellyn, he has done nothing wrong. I just want to talk to him about a case I'm investigating in France."

"Right, right," said the man, clearly not convinced. "Miss Turner, come in please."

His secretary glided back into the room and stood patiently waiting for her next task.

"What's the man's name, Captain?"

"Vincent, John Vincent."

"Miss Turner, please ask Wilkins to find John Vincent and bring him here please."

The secretary was gone with a click of heeled boots and an uncomfortable time passed as Llewellyn endeavoured to engage Oscendale in small talk, without listening to any answers. The minutes seemed to turn into hours.

At last a young man in his mid-teens was shown into the office, removing his cap in due deference as he did so. His filthy clothes and the odour of sweat spoke of many long hours tending the blast furnaces which fuelled the copper workings. His face was strained and dirty, and Oscendale felt some sympathy for his plight. With a widowed mother, he was now the sole wage earner and the head of the household. *Too much responsibility too soon.*

"Now then, Vincent. The policeman here wishes to speak with you. Mind you tell him no lies." Llewellyn waved an admonishing finger at Vincent, like a teacher with a naughty pupil.

Vincent raised his eyes from the fat man behind the desk to the policeman and Oscendale sensed it was not his first discussion with an officer of the law. Llewellyn showed no signs of leaving so Oscendale pressed on.

"I'm investigating the death of your father and I'd like to ask you a few questions."

The youngster shifted uncomfortably, but whether this was a reaction to his father's death or the presence of a policeman, Oscendale wasn't sure.

"How long have you worked here, John?"

The simplicity of the question took the young man by surprise and he looked relieved.

"Two years and four months, sir."

"And what is it you do?"

"Furnace man, sir."

Oscendale pictured the work. Ten hours at the foot of a blast furnace shovelling coal into the monster's mouth, fuelled by regular intake of liquid. And more on the way home.

"Your father was a furnace man too, wasn't he?"

"Yes, sir. Before he joined the army."

"And he worked here at the White Rock works, didn't he?"

"Yes, sir." A look of suspicion came over the young man's face so Oscendale pursued the theme.

"So is that why you tried for a job here?"

Vincent shot a look at Llewellyn and then back to Oscendale.

"I… I think so, sir. Mr Llewellyn was good enough to take me on here."

Oscendale paused. Was there something there or was the tiredness he now felt after the long journey making him overreact?

"I see. And the last time you saw your father was when?"

"Last time he was home on leave, sir. Six months ago."

"How did you get on?"

Vincent shrugged. "Okay, I suppose. Never really seen much of him. Being in the army, like."

Oscendale let the lie go.

"Did your father ever mention a change in his circumstances to you?"

The young man coloured beneath the dirt of the foundry.

"How do you mean, sir?"

"I don't know. Perhaps coming into some money or something?"

"No, sir," the young man replied. But Oscendale sensed the same feeling of familial loyalty that he had detected when the boy's mother responded to his questions.

Perhaps the boy was learning to lie as well as tend a blast furnace. Two lies?

"Right, I think that will be all. Thank you, John."

"Back to work, Vincent," said Llewellyn.

When the boy had gone, Oscendale turned back to Llewellyn. The man was nervous, shifting uncomfortably in his leather chair, his fingers playing constantly with a pen.

"Do you remember his father, William Vincent?" he asked the fat man.

"Bill Vincent? Yes of course. Good foundry man. Very dependable. Rarely late."

"And what about a man named Karl? Did he work with him?"

"Karl?" Llewellyn echoed. "No, can't say we've had anyone here called Karl."

Oscendale shook hands with Llewellyn and made his way outside, still puzzled by the lies Vincent had told him. Why had he denied seeing his father regularly when according to his service record he had been home several times on leave last year? And the topic of money had caused the young man to lie for a second time. Vincent must have told the family that he had plans to come into a substantial sum of money. But from whom? The letter Mrs Vincent had received had hinted at something. Did the boy and his mother understand the coded message?

As he watched the military policeman walking away from his office, Gerald Llewellyn lifted his telephone and spoke.

"Listen. John Vincent. Works in B Building as a foundry man. Get rid of him. Yes, today. I don't know, but he's mixed up with the police over something and I want him out."

CHAPTER 10

1st July 1916

KATHLEEN HAD ALREADY gone to work when he returned to his room after the long journey back to France. The bed was untidily made, evidence that she had departed in a hurry after yet another restless night. The dawn was just breaking; blood-red slashes that cut across the lightening sky. The rumbling gunfire that had gone on for days suddenly ceased as he washed his face in a china bowl on an ancient table. He paused, stunned by the silence. Then came the dread at the thought of the thousands of men leaving the relative safety of their trenches and going over the top at that very moment into the hell of German bullets. In a few hours' time there would be more young men for Kathleen to tend as they lay wounded or dying on camp beds in the big marquee that constituted her dressing station.

The thought of so much impending death troubled him, paralysed him momentarily as he realised it was happening now, at this very moment. And if he became part of it, if he were killed, what would the future hold for Kathleen? Would she always remember him or would she seek solace with an amusing soldier who turned her sorrow into laughter lines? Would she move on until he became just another man in her past, as transient as the dawn?

The water dripping down his face brought him back to the moment and he loosened his tie and lay on the bed. He could still smell Kathleen's scent and saw the crinkles in the bedclothes where she had lain without him. Oscendale dismissed his melancholy thoughts and endeavoured to close his eyes and sleep before the hubbub of the day began again. Surprisingly, he thought later, he fell asleep almost immediately as the warmth of the room enfolded him and the horror of death gave way to the thoughts of the warmth of a woman's body.

He awoke a short time later as the sounds of an army on the move echoed up from the street below. Shaving quickly, he dressed and made his way to his office on the square. He reported in and then began typing up his report for Avate. The words did not flow and he swore several times and threw balls of screwed up paper into his wastepaper bin until the report emerged: factual, concise and devoid of the emotion he had felt at seeing the widow spread-eagled on the floor, dignity and life both obliterated.

North knocked hard on the office door. His boss was probably staring out of his window again, lost in some deep contemplation. He had given up knocking softly, then louder the second time. Recently he had jumped to the second, louder knock without bothering with the first. *Got results quicker, that did.* The captain was a bit of a dreamer but he seemed a good copper. Mysterious though. Nobody seemed to know much about him, although office gossip had it that he had been wounded at Gallipoli last year. Anything like that earned North's respect but he just wished the bloke would be a bit more army-like. Too arty for North's liking.

"Come in!" Oscendale called, somewhat irritated again by North's brusque manner. Why couldn't the man move around the place quietly instead of stomping around in his size-ten army hobnailed boots? When he had time he would have to see about getting a less irritating office assistant.

"Post, sir." North proffered the pile of mail and Oscendale took the letters and began to read the envelopes.

"Thank you, North. Have this report sent round to the Provost Marshal immediately, would you?"

"Yes, sir. And there's this one, sir. The reply from Swansea you've been waiting for." North winked and clumped off. Oscendale stared after him. How did North know that? Maybe there was more to the man than he gave him credit for.

Oscendale ditched the pile of envelopes and immediately opened the small, buff-coloured envelope North had saved till last with a dramatic flourish that was new to him. *Might be hope for him yet*, mused Oscendale then dismissed the thought as being too ludicrous to pursue.

Inside was a typed letter on police-headed paper. It read:

Dear Tom,

Greetings from the white feather brigade to our heroes at the Front! Oh and a hello to you too.

Oscendale smiled. Phillip Morris of Swansea Police had not lost his sense of humour, despite the blackness of the age. Oscendale had written to him when Vincent's link with Swansea first came to light just in case he missed anything on his own visit.

I have been to Ludwig Richter's White Rock copperworks as you requested and managed to dig out some information from one of the older foremen. Took me a few pints in one of the local hostelries, though, which you owe me for by the way. Let's hope it's not too long before you are in a position to repay me.

A sentiment with which Oscendale heartily agreed but doubted very much would come to pass in the near future. He had, after all, avoided making contact with Morris when he had been in Swansea for a reason he could not quite define. Was it because he felt different to how he had been before the war? More remote, more detached. Too distant from his old friends to seek them out again when he could. A different man now.

William Vincent was employed at Richter's for about three years. Nothing remarkable. Late a few times and one falling out with his foreman but nothing major. Seemed a good employee. They remember him coming in one day, handing in his notice and saying he was off to rejoin the army. Figured as he was a reservist that he would be called up anyway so he might as well jump as be pushed. The chap I spoke to had the feeling it was marital difficulties. Wanted to see the world again and dump the missus. You get the picture.

Oscendale had visions of the tired woman in the dingy terraced house in Swansea and tried to empathise with Vincent, but the man's selfishness left him cold.

The letter continued: *One other strange thing this chap said was that Vincent struck up a friendship with a German engineer who came over to help with something at the works. Couldn't remember his name but recalled the two of them spending a lot of time together socially. He left around six months before Vincent quit to join the army.*

Anyway, that's all that came out of it, except that I'm now an expert on the process of making copper. A second career in case I never make inspector!

Keep your head down and come back to South Wales for some real detective work when it's all over, not that bullshit you get involved in over there.

Regards, Phil.

Good man, Phillip Morris, thought Oscendale. Could well make inspector if he pleased the right people. Interesting letter too. So Vincent had known a German engineer before the war. Was that person the Karl he wrote about in his last letter to his wife? It seemed likely. And was that when the friendship ended or had they continued it through correspondence? Without any evidence it was impossible to say. Perhaps he had meant to send letters to his old friend but never did.

He pictured the friendship. A middle-aged ex-soldier who thinks he has deserved some peace and quiet but has to keep working to keep the wolf from the door. An army pension did not amount to much, he knew, so Vincent had taken the job in the local copperworks. One day a group of German workers arrive to help with the installation of a new piece of machinery or to assist with a new process and the two men strike up a conversation and a friendship. Then the powers that be decide to go to war and Karl returns to Germany to take part in a conflict to destroy his erstwhile friend and his country. He sighed with the absurdity of it all. Two international friends had become part of an international war, but on opposite sides.

So that was the link, thought Oscendale, *but how had it led to Vincent's death?*

A while later, having now dispatched his report, he decided to pay a visit to the Welsh Regiment's headquarters. If Catherine Jaulard's murderer was a British soldier then perhaps he could ascertain something of the regiment's troop movements over the twenty-four hours prior to her death. He passed his details to a clerk and sat outside an office for half an hour until he was allowed in to see the man whose nameplate adorned the door. Nothing new in being kept waiting, he knew. The stock of the MFP did not ensure immediate access to anyone.

Major Ferris was a round, white-faced, career army man

whose current sedentary lifestyle could well prove hazardous to his health. He did not rise from his neat and orderly desk as he motioned Oscendale to sit.

"Good morning, Captain Oscendale. Not often we have dealings with the Military Foot Police at present. Far too busy involved in the Big Push, don't you know." The slight was unsubtle and he looked for a reaction which Oscendale disappointed him by refusing to give. Such matters were puerile and he stared back with indifference. There was really no point in comparing his own experiences with a desk johnny like this whose closest contact with the front line was watching the ranks of real fighting men walk through the square each morning.

"Good morning, Major Ferris," he said with a pleasant smile on his face. "Yes, I am sure it's a busy time for you at present." He opened a palm and gestured to the latest sheaf of papers awaiting the desk-bound major's attention. Ferris followed his hand and a slight grimace of annoyance came over his face. Whether it was the boredom of the impending paperwork or the fact that Oscendale had highlighted his minor role in the offensive he was not sure – but he did care.

Ferris reached for a box on his desk and offered Oscendale a cigarette, which he declined. *An unguarded moment of good manners. Tut, tut.* He must have hit a nerve with this cadaver of a man.

"I suppose you're here about the murder of this French tart. Bad business, what?" Ferris paused to light a cigarette he had taken from a wooden box that now opened only towards him.

Oscendale bristled. The undignified final image of the young woman came back into his mind. "Actually, she owned a thriving bakery and her husband was killed last year at Neuve Chappelle."

Ferris looked hard at Oscendale and sucked heavily on his cigarette.

"Yes, well, quite." He changed tack. "I understand from my clerk that you think she was murdered by one of our men?"

"It's possible. Were any of the men from your regiment in town that night?"

"No. They were going back up the line that afternoon so there was no leave the night before."

"I see. Would it have been possible for a soldier to break camp and go into town if he had wanted to?"

"That is always a possibility; you and I know that, Captain Oscendale. All I am saying is that officially there were no soldiers of this regiment in town that night."

Oscendale rose. "Thank you, Major. Just one more thing. When was your office told of the discovery of the body of Madame Jaulard?"

Ferris remained seated. *No respecter of military policemen, this one*, thought Oscendale.

"About breakfast time on the morning of 29th June. Why?"

Oscendale left the question hanging in the air and let himself out.

CHAPTER 11

1st July 1916

THE ANTEROOM WAS stuffy and hot, the closed windows taking no account of the summer sun and his mind drifted back to the previous summer and the baking sun on the beach at Seed-el-Bahr. The Gallipoli case had replayed itself in his mind several times recently and he knew, despite his best efforts, that its intricacies and bloody consequences would never leave him.

His musings were interrupted by the harsh tones of a MFP sergeant. "The Provost Marshal will see you now, sir." He was led into the modest office of Provost Marshal John Avate. Avate was a thick-set, bespectacled man in his early fifties and he remained seated whilst Oscendale walked to his desk.

"Good morning, Tom. Just finished reading your report. So you think the French police were meant to think Catherine Jaulard was murdered by a British soldier?"

"Somehow, yes I do. It may have been a local man but I'm not convinced of it as yet. She became friendly with William Vincent but with Vincent dead on the 26th someone else must have killed her," replied Oscendale.

"But someone must have wanted her dead for a reason," said Avate, removing his spectacles.

"And someone was there to make sure she was dead," added Oscendale.

"Ah yes, the mysterious Lieutenant Price. Any news on him?"

"Ferris's clerk showed me the list of officers in the Welsh

Regiment. Plenty of Prices but no Lieutenant Price and certainly no-one matching his description. Our man is not an officer with that regiment."

"Who do you think he is then?" Avate's brows met as he realised the significance of this last fact.

Oscendale sighed before replying. "I'm not sure, but I'll wager he was military intelligence come to make sure that she was dead and that a French police inspector saw what he wanted to see and allowed all his anti-British sentiment to get the better of his detection skills and police training."

"Hmmm," said Avate. "Then you turn up instead of some thick-headed military copper and he goes scuttling back to tell his masters they've got a problem."

"Could be. But it still doesn't bring me any closer to proving who killed Catherine Jaulard. The only motive I can come up with is her friendship with Vincent, but it wasn't even a close one according to her sister."

"Was her house ransacked?"

"No, and although we were meant to believe she'd been sexually assaulted, I'm not sure that she was. Her body could have just been laid out like that deliberately. Something else to put us off track."

"The French report is not in yet so we can't be sure either way. So what next?" Oscendale saw from Avate's raised eyebrow that his boss knew that Oscendale had something he was keeping back.

"Well, sir. It's this Lieutenant Price again. You see, it rained that night and was still raining when I arrived at 14, Rue St Juliette. I had a raincoat on, as did Inspector Valère, but Price didn't."

"And his uniform was dry?" added Avate.

"Yes, sir. Bone dry and no sign of a coat. I checked with

the gendarmes and they said that they never saw him with one on."

"And he must have got wet if he was outside," concluded Avate.

"That's my point, sir. None of the gendarmes remembered seeing him arrive. The first time anyone remembers seeing him was in the room where Catherine Jaulard was found murdered."

"So you think he was in the house all the time?"

"Exactly. I think he murdered Catherine Jaulard, went to button up his coat and realised that a button was missing. He then wasted precious minutes searching for the button on the floor of the room, not thinking to look in her hand. At this point Etienne Laurent enters the house looking for his tardy employer. Price makes himself scarce and waits for him to leave. He can't leave without the button so he resumes his search only to be disturbed once more. He hears the gendarmes arriving, takes off his coat so as not to be rumbled and hides somewhere until he can join the group surreptitiously."

"So the button is not a red herring?"

"No, sir. Maybe I'm getting too suspicious, I don't know, but my first thought was that the murderer was a jealous Frenchman who wanted to put the blame on a British soldier, but Valère's conclusion suited Price down to the ground and before anyone could explore another avenue he was gone into the night."

"So that means that his overcoat may still be in the house somewhere."

"And I'm going back to find it. If we have it, we may have the killer."

"And how was Madame Jaulard killed, Tom?" enquired Avate.

"With a knife, sir. No noise."

"But that means her killer must have been allowed to get very close to her without arousing suspicion."

"Yes, and if you add that to her evening attire, then we have a woman who had arranged a rendezvous with someone she knew or trusted, and was relaxed enough in their company to allow them to get close enough to stab her in the stomach."

"So was it Price she had arranged to meet?" asked Avate.

Oscendale shook his head. "No, but I think it was Price who appeared at her doorway that night. Whether she or someone else let him in I'm not sure. Maybe he broke in. At any rate she wasn't expecting him. Nobody knew anything about a relationship between her and a British officer. And my bet is that if anything was going on between them, her sister or one of the employees in the bakery would have known about it. You can't keep something like that quiet in a small community. Too much of a scandal and far too interesting a piece of gossip to keep to oneself. No, I think she was expecting someone she knew quite well. Someone that her sister and her employees knew. For a respectable woman like Catherine Jaulard to be dressed in her evening clothes just hours before going to work that morning indicates to me an assignation with a good friend."

Avate frowned. "But the only name that's come to light so far is that of William Vincent."

"Exactly, sir. Perhaps she arranged to see Vincent. She changed into her finery and answers the door to him."

"But Vincent is already dead."

"Yes, but she doesn't know that."

"So someone uses Vincent's name to get her to see him?"

"Yes, it's the early hours so there's no-one around. When she answers the door to someone she thinks is Vincent but isn't, then there's no one to see him enter the house."

"But she would have recognised the man as not being Vincent. Why would she let him in?"

"Don't forget, sir, that this chap Price is a skilful liar. Probably told her that he had some bad news about William Vincent. That he'd been killed in action. She opens the door, lets him in and he kills her."

"But why kill her?"

"So that she couldn't tell anyone about him and his visit."

"And what was he looking for?"

"Information. She knew something about William Vincent, or at least that's what Price thought, so he quizzed her about it. She probably grew suspicious. Remember this woman was a local businesswoman and no fool. He decides he's heard enough or that she knows nothing, then he kills her."

"And assaults her?" asked Avate, his disgust evident on his face.

"That's the bit I'm struggling with. He may have wanted to make it look like a sexually motivated crime to throw us off the scent or there may have been a more sinister, even baser motive. She was an attractive woman and Price is a man."

Both men fell silent as they contemplated Price's actions in killing the defenceless woman.

Avate spoke at last. "Bloody callous sod this Price to stay in the house and then stand over the body of the woman he'd just killed while you and Valère go about the investigation."

"Probably had no choice, sir. He couldn't get out of the house after the gendarmes arrived and decided to bluff it out.

Still, I agree he did show a certain, how shall we say, warped fortitude in standing there looking at the body of Catherine Jaulard."

Avate nodded. "He seems a cold, calculating character, Tom. You watch out for this one."

Oscendale nodded. "I intend to, sir, but I am going to catch the bastard."

Oscendale left Avate mulling over the news he had brought. He walked out of the building and into the July sunshine. The damp of the night air had long gone yet puddles lay in the gutters that ran along the sides of the square. He shivered involuntarily and for an unknown reason looked behind him.

There was no one there apart from the drivers waiting outside for their next journey, smoking cigarettes and sharing rumours about the progress of the Big Push. He shook his head and told himself to relax. *Not enough sleep last night,* he thought, *or this case is already getting to you.* His driver jerked to attention as he approached.

"Where to, sir?" he asked.

"Rue St Juliette, Jones. And mind the potholes this time, eh?"

CHAPTER 12

1st July 1916

CATHERINE JAULARD'S HOUSE stood quietly in its allotted place, the late morning dew disappearing from its frontage in wraiths of vapour as the sun arrived at last to shine on the narrow, dark street on which life went on again as it always did. French townspeople made their way to and from work and went about their business as if the greatest war mankind had ever seen was not going on in earnest several miles away. *The resilience of the human spirit*, thought Oscendale as he briefly surveyed the scene. *Whenever this bloody war ended these people would carry on with their lives, each bearing their own personal tragedy from the conflict.* But it wouldn't end there, he knew.

Who would tidy up the mess? This wouldn't be a quick post-repast clear up. There would be bodies, thousands of them, lying in the soil until it was turned over by the farmer's plough. A hand. A head. Each day a part of a man would emerge like a ghoul from the ground, crying out for a named burial and relatives to mourn over him.

The trenches would be filled, the wire taken away and the world would carry on. But there would always be the reminders: the tunnels with their deadly hoards of explosives, and the concrete blockhouses the Huns constructed so fiendishly would not be disposed of easily.

And the munitions. Oscendale knew from his observations that not all shells went off. Some buried themselves deep in the mud or the woods, lying in ambush for the unwary of the future. Who would clear them up? It could take years and years to make the rich countryside of northern France safe to till again.

But that was the future, to be sorted out when the killing had stopped. Other matters now began to occupy his thoughts.

The gendarmes were still outside the house, new faces but performing the same duty. *Ils ne passeront pas.* He showed his identity card and was permitted to enter.

Oscendale walked along the hallway once more and through into the reception room. The body had gone and nothing seemed out of place since his previous visit so he began the search for Price's overcoat. Such a bulky item would not be easily hidden and as the man had probably acted swiftly, he could not have moved very far away from the scene of the murder.

Suddenly, he felt uneasy and experienced a sense of being watched. Stopping his search, Oscendale stood up straight and looked around the room. Nothing. No-one. He was alone. But the feeling lingered. The spirit of the dead woman? Forever to haunt the place of her passing?

Leaving Catherine Jaulard's soul to eternity, he walked through a doorway into the kitchen at the rear. Another door led back onto the hallway. Price could have left the room through either door and re-emerged into the reception room while all eyes were fixed on the body. A quick introduction and he would be accepted as having just arrived. Why would anyone check with the gendarme at the door unless they were suspicious? And who would suspect a British officer anyway? *British officers did not commit murder.*

Oscendale began opening the cupboards in the kitchen but found nothing other than the daily paraphernalia of an ordinary life. He frowned as his search came to an end. He was sure he was right; the overcoat must be here somewhere. Then he remembered the heat of the kitchen the night he had first come here, how it made him consider removing his own overcoat. And the smell of Madame's cooking stove. Cooking. *In the early hours of the morning when she was going to work?*

Then he realised. He rushed across the room and flung open the door of the range. The remains of Price's overcoat lay on a heap of cold ashes. Using a pair of wooden laundry tongs which lay in the sink, he carefully removed the fragments that remained and examined them. The thinnest parts had gone but part of the thicker collar material remained. Turning it over he found what he was looking for, the regimental laundry mark and next to it, sewn on a white strip of cloth, a number.

There was a sound in the hallway, voices talking in French. Quickly putting the fragment of collar into his pocket, he turned to see Inspector Valère in the doorway. How much had he seen? The policeman gave no indication of having witnessed anything he deemed suspicious and Oscendale wondered for a moment whether he had got away with his subterfuge or not. For a reason he couldn't quite establish he did not wish to share this newly gathered information with the Frenchman. This was a British matter and he decided that it was probably better for the British Army to solve it. Besides, he did not give much for Valère's chances of catching a rat like Price.

"Bonjour, Captain Oscendale," Valère opened. "You have come back to examine the scene of the crime for more clues?"

There was a twinkle in the man's eye and Oscendale realised that he had seen what he had done, or at least the end of his movements. It seemed that he had no choice other than to share the information but he didn't have to tell him everything.

"Inspector Valère. I wondered whether the contents of the stove could yield any information. I found this burnt collar and a laundry mark attached." He held it out to Valère who took it and held it up to his face. He sniffed it like a suspicious dog and turned it over, examining it closely.

"A laundry mark? What can that tell us?" he asked. The emphasis was on the 'us' but Oscendale was not quite sure whether he meant himself and the rest of his force or whether Oscendale was being invited to remain a part of the investigation, despite having attempted to go off on his own. He decided to try to be deliberately obtuse.

"Is it a local laundry mark?" he asked. There was so little left of the coat collar that perhaps Valère had not recognised it as a British Army one.

"Perhaps," the detective said noncommittally. "There again it could be a British Army mark," he added slowly, fixing Oscendale with a stare.

Oscendale smiled and said, "No flies on you, Inspector Valère. I think it's a British Army coat and I believe it was left here by Lieutenant Price."

This time Valère frowned. "The British officer who was here on the night Madame Jaulard was murdered? Bon sang. So you think he was involved in this in some way?"

Oscendale was prepared to share a little. He was still curious as to why Valère had re-appeared at the crime scene today.

"It seems that he left his coat here and endeavoured to destroy it. He also left the house without telling either of us and hasn't been seen since."

Valère rubbed his chin thoughtfully. "I have some news

for you, Captain Oscendale. The doctor has examined the body of the unfortunate Madame Jaulard. She was killed by a stab wound to the abdomen, that much I think you already suspected. However, the doctor says that she was also sexually assaulted." The distaste was evident in his voice and Oscendale knew that such behaviour was anathema to men of such dignity as Valère. He turned to leave the room, the conversation obviously at an end.

"Before or after she was killed?" Oscendale asked.

Valère stopped and turned to face him again. "The doctor cannot be sure but the two events were not far apart, that much is certain."

"Tell me, do you think a British soldier committed both crimes?"

Valère sighed. "Captain Oscendale, I am under great pressure to solve this terrible crime. You tell me that a British officer was behaving suspiciously at the scene of the crime. I met the man and cannot believe that he would have raped and killed Madame Jaulard and then stayed at the crime scene until we arrived. No, I think we are looking for someone who knew Madame Jaulard very well, who could gain her trust to allow him entry to her house in the early hours of the morning. I think they made love, had a lovers' argument, and he killed her with a knife, probably from the kitchen."

Oscendale was horrified. "A local man! But haven't I just given you an alternative? There was a British officer's coat burning in the stove. The laundry mark is still attached. All we have to do is track the coat back to the owner and we have the man who was present during the night of the murder."

Valère's voice rose and suddenly Oscendale understood. "And what do you think that would do for Anglo-French relations, *monsieur!* At such a critical time of the war, when a large-scale offensive is underway that could end everything, you want me to put a British officer on trial for the rape and murder of a pillar of the local community! No, these crimes were committed by a local man I am sure, and I intend to find out whom!"

Valère was now red-faced but Oscendale knew that the man did not believe what he had just said. He had been ordered to find a local man guilty and to conclude the matter as soon as possible. There were more important events occurring and a murder had to be solved, the murderer dispatched to the guillotine, and the war proceeded with.

Oscendale tried one last time. In a more subdued tone he said, "Inspector Valère, I understand what you are saying but if you give me some time I am sure that I can bring the guilty man to justice."

"Justice? Is that what you call it? Captain Oscendale, I may be a small-town police inspector but I understand the way of the world. I will do my job, you will attempt to do yours, and the British Army will look after its own. I will find a local man and he will be charged with Catherine Jaulard's murder. Then the case will be closed."

Oscendale began again but Valère held up a hand and looked at the floor. "No, Captain Oscendale. I can see you are an honourable man, but this case does not bode well for men such as you and me. We are cast adrift on an uncertain sea and we must ensure we do not drown. Do you understand me?"

Oscendale nodded. He understood perfectly well what this wise Frenchman was telling him about the way power worked. He fell silent and Valère turned and left him standing there with the piece of cloth in his hand, his faith in humanity once more greatly challenged.

CHAPTER 13

2nd July 1916

"PRICE? YES, SEEMS a good man. Joined us three or four days ago." The speaker was a captain with the Welsh Regiment. Pale and thin, his pristine, tailored uniform spoke of the man's obsession with detail, his complexion of many hours behind a desk sifting the minutiae of a regiment's *raisons d'être*.

"Can you describe him for me?" pursued Oscendale, anxious to close the gap that seemed to be expanding between him and his chief suspect.

"Describe him?" Oscendale wondered whether the man prefaced every reply with a question of his own. "Well, about average height, clean shaven, brown hair, pretty nondescript really." This brief description seemed to match his own recollection of the man he had seen at Madame Jaulard's house. *Nondescript.* The perfect description for a man who didn't wish to be noticed as he went about his work.

"And where would I find him now, captain?"

"Probably supervising rifle practice at the butts. All the junior officers are down there."

Oscendale made his way through the bustling camp, glad that the irritating interview was over. He had followed his copper's nose on this one. It seemed unlikely that Price would stray far from his home; he had not yet found what he had searched for in Catherine Jaulard's house, what indeed had led to her murder. Ergo he could not afford to leave the area just yet. Oscendale reasoned that he would resume his duties, an officer hidden amongst many other officers – a tree in a forest.

Clapboard wooden huts stood in rows on either side of a parade ground. The soldiers of the Welsh Regiment might be near the front line but there was no excuse for not marching and drilling. He watched one section go through their paces under the critical gazes of several sergeants and wondered how many would return in a few weeks after they had been thrown into the mincer of the Somme.

The news he had heard in the local *estaminet* the previous evening of the first day's attack boded well: numerous German casualties and thousands of yards of ground taken. The trouble was that Kathleen's absence from their bed that night had meant only one thing: numerous British casualties and a medical system that was evidently struggling to cope.

He found the laundry room down a narrow row of huts, smoke billowing from a chimney. Walking inside he was greeted by the odd mixture of stale body odour and pungent army-issue detergent. A soldier in a vest approached him, sweating heavily.

"Yes, sir. Can I 'elp you? Picking up your laundry?"

"No. I wonder if you could take a look at this number. Ever seen it before?" He held out the fragment of overcoat collar with the laundry number he had retrieved from the stove at Rue St Juliette.

The man studied it for a second. "Yes, sir. That's one of ours. Give me a sec and I'll tell you whose it is. Looks like he'll be drawing a new overcoat, state of that!"

The man laughed at his own joke and disappeared into a makeshift office, emerging with a ledger book. He ran his fingers down a page until he arrived at the number he was looking for. "There we are, sir. P/4633. Lieutenant Price. That's the number of all his laundry." The man beamed at his own success.

Oscendale thanked the soldier and emerged gratefully into the cooler, certainly cleaner, air of a July morning. He walked between another row of huts, ignoring the sullen stares of the men who sat in shirt sleeves polishing their equipment in the morning sun. The row opened out onto green fields which were becoming overgrown through lack of attention. He heard the cracks of volleys of rifle fire and headed in that direction. He crested the brow of a small hill and saw below him the rifle range.

A line of soldiers lay on the ground, their Lee-Enfield rifles cradled to their shoulders. They flinched from the recoils as bullets sped towards targets some 200 yards away in front of a small mound. Oscendale smelt the acrid odour of discharged bullets and watched as the NCOs walked up and down the line, occasionally bending over a man to correct his body position or to tap his shoulder for encouragement.

He approached without being noticed and looked at the officers who sat in a gun pit with raised binoculars. If Price was in there he didn't want to scare him off. He walked into the pit and waited patiently until the rifle detail had finished and the men lowered their binoculars.

"Good morning, gentlemen," he said to their backs, "Captain Oscendale, Military Foot Police."

The officers turned to face him but none even resembled Price. A tall, grey-haired lieutenant spoke first. "Good morning, Captain. Lieutenant Windsor. Come to see how well our boys are shooting? The answer is that I hope the Huns stand still and wait to be shot because at the moment they'll be into our trenches before we hit any of them!" The man's dissatisfaction with the quality of his latest batch of Kitchener recruits was immediately apparent.

"I'm looking for Lieutenant Price. Have any of you seen him? I was told he was here."

"Down in the butts," replied one of the other men, "helping out with the targets."

Oscendale left the men and, taking advantage of a rest period, he made his way down the side of the range until he reached the edge of the long, narrow trench which hid the men who worked the targets from the rifle fire above them. He jumped in and walked towards a group of men who were replacing a shot-out target. An officer stood side-on to him and he immediately recognised him as the man he had met in Catherine Jaulard's reception room.

"Lieutenant Price?" he said quietly.

The man turned to face him. The reply was jovial enough but Oscendale noticed an almost imperceptible stiffening of the shoulders.

"Captain Oscendale! We meet again. Any luck with discovering the murderer of Madame Jaulard?"

"Yes, I've made some progress. Actually it was you I wanted to speak to next."

Before Price could reply a telephone rang in a dugout cut into the bank of the trench and a voice shouted, "Request for the All Clear, sir!"

"Excuse me, Oscendale," said Price and ducked into the dugout.

A few seconds later, to Oscendale's horror he heard the crack of rifle fire. Before he could take cover a bullet hit the target above his head, ricocheted into the bank in front of him and zipped past his cheek to embed itself in the sand by his left ear. He threw himself down onto the floor of the trench just in time as other bullets sang and whined all around him.

Oscendale rolled onto his side and saw Price emerge from

the dugout. He just had time to draw himself into a ball as Price's boot connected with his shins. He gasped with pain and looked up to see Price heading off along the trench.

In a flash he was on his feet, his head pulled in as the .303 bullets continued to rip into the targets above his head. Price was moving quickly and was almost out of the trench. Oscendale gave a despairing dive and managed to tap one of Price's ankles. The man stumbled and fell but was quicker to his feet than Oscendale and was up and out of the trench before Oscendale had fully recovered from his own fall.

Price ran round the back of the rise at the rear of the targets and disappeared from view. Oscendale sensed caution might be the order of the day. He drew his Webley pistol from its holster and walked slowly round the corner of the mound.

Price was nowhere to be seen. Before him at the foot of a short slope a wood rose up. He could hear nothing above the continuous crackle of rifle fire so could only assume that Price had entered the undergrowth at the edge of the wood. He threw himself on the ground, realising that even now Price may be training his own revolver on him.

Raising his head above a tussock he scanned the border of the wood. He thought he detected some movement off to the right but couldn't be sure. The trees stood cool and welcoming as the sun beat down upon him and the day warmed up. He knew that Price now had a huge advantage. If he waited, Price would escape. If he stood up and approached the wood he could be shot down.

He decided that he had to take the chance and began a stooping, zigzag run towards the first line of trees. No shots rang out so he assumed that Price was already deeper into the wood. Oscendale took stock of the situation as the trees engulfed him, letting his eyes adjust to the gloom all around him.

While he did so he began to mull over the implications of this latest train of events. Price was obviously guilty of at least some involvement in the murder of Catherine Jaulard. His actions of the last few minutes indicated that he didn't want to be cornered by Oscendale. He hadn't even had a chance to explain why he was here before the man had deliberately attempted to kill him. But why had Madame Jaulard been killed? Oscendale suspected that she knew something, possibly told to her by Vincent before he killed himself. But what would he tell a casual acquaintance in a foreign land?

He forced himself to concentrate. *Focus now, Tommy boy, otherwise you'll never have another thought on this case ever again.*

A light wind began to stir the branches of the trees, and the sun's rays began to dance in a section of the wood thinned out in front of him. He raised his revolver and began to edge forwards. He felt exposed and truly in danger. Price could be anywhere, far away by now or close at hand ready to put a bullet into his brain.

A sound off to his left indicated that Price had not fled the scene. He turned towards it and a bullet cracked into a tree trunk nearby. *Not a patient man*, he thought and drew heavily on all his strength of will to drop down into the undergrowth and sit still, waiting for Price's impatience to get the better of him.

Minutes passed and he began to regret taking his own advice. Price could have fired to slow him down and even now could be out of the wood and gone. Gone where though? Oscendale realised with a cold shiver that Price's cover had been blown. He couldn't reintegrate himself back into his regiment but neither could he settle in elsewhere while

Oscendale was on his trail. He had to eliminate Oscendale to be safe.

Then he saw him.

A figure moved quickly between two ash trees and began to fire. The shots were random, scattered, intended only to provoke Oscendale into returning fire and exposing his position. He held his fire and counted. On the fifth shot he raised himself and levelled the Webley at Price who by now was only twenty yards away.

"Drop it, Price!" he ordered.

Price turned to face him. "Captain Oscendale," he replied. "I see you have the better of me."

"Drop the gun and put your hands up."

Price didn't move; he held his gun at his hip, the barrel pointed towards Oscendale.

"You really shouldn't have been the one who answered the call out that night, you know," said Price.

Oscendale was intrigued. "Why not? It's one of my duties."

"Because you are the only man who could make the link with William Vincent."

So it was about Vincent.

"So why was she killed, Price?"

"That's for you to find out. Perhaps you can ask me again one day, if you get stuck."

Then came the retort of the revolver. The bullet zipped into Oscendale's arm like a red hot dart and he span around with the impact, dropping his own gun. He saw Price turn and run deeper into the wood and knew he would get away. But how had he done it? Where had the extra bullet come from? Price had fired six rounds; he had counted them!

Then he cursed himself for underestimating the man. He

had planned his tactics off to a tee, firing one bullet and then reloading, guessing that Oscendale would not show himself until he was certain Price was out of ammunition.

Oscendale examined his arm. He guessed it was a flesh wound, no more. It would hurt for a few days and be an inconvenience, but more importantly it slowed him down enough to resist the temptation to pursue Price further into the wood. The chase was over. For the time being.

CHAPTER 14

2nd July 1916

THE DOG BIT hard on his arm and Price's demented face shouted encouragement as the animal sank its hot teeth deeper into his flesh. Its rancid breath entered his mouth and made him retch. The pain swirled like a cloud around his body and he felt himself falling forward.

Oscendale opened his eyes and found himself bathed in sweat. A dream, but the pain in his left arm was no figment of his feverish imagination. He tried to raise it from the bed and found it hurt like the devil so he lay still and tried to come to terms with his surroundings.

A sombre-looking VAD nurse saw him trying to move and scuttled away to an office at the end of the ward. Seconds later a sandy-haired doctor with round-rimmed glasses was bending over him taking his pulse.

"So you've decided to rejoin the land of the living, Captain Oscendale."

Oscendale recalled being shot and the pain in his arm but remembered little else. Then it came back to him. Price had escaped and for some reason he had decided not to follow him. Fear of the man? Sound common sense? He didn't know.

"Where's Price? How did I get here?" he babbled.

"Price?" the doctor answered calmly. "Who's Price? And as for how you got here, well, I know you caused quite a stir as you came staggering over the mound at the rear of the rifle range. Luckily for you our men decided not to shoot you as a German but to bring you here instead. Lie still now."

"But I felt all right after I was shot. I remember it," he said, puzzled at the doctor's description of his movements thereafter.

"Delayed shock, old boy. Often happens. Chap gets shot, feels fine, then keels over. That and the loss of blood, of course. Anyway, no more questions just now. Couple of days and you'll be out of here, I should think. In the meantime, rest and recuperation are my orders."

Oscendale gave in and slipped off into sleep once more: an unsettled sleep where men in gas masks pursued him through streets and woods.

He was glad to wake several hours later and immediately felt better. He saw the reason why at the side of his bed. Kathleen was dozing in a chair, her face illuminated by the electric light hanging above her head, her black-stockinged legs stretched out in front of her.

He reached over and prodded her. "Where are my grapes, nurse?" he asked.

She yawned and countered, "Only heroes get grapes. Idiots who walk into woods pursuing men with guns get bread and water. And it's matron to you, Captain Oscendale."

He smiled and she smiled back, her face hospital-pale beneath a mass of jet-black hair.

"Look, Kathleen, I can't afford to be laid up here for several days. I have an investigation to continue. Can't you give me something to get me back on my feet and get me out of here?"

She frowned. "Don't be ridiculous, Tom. You have a gunshot wound to your upper arm and have lost a lot of blood. Besides which you're suffering from shock."

"Very well. I'll stay here until tomorrow and then I'm leaving. And don't try and stop me."

"Or what? You'll leave when Doctor Stephens tells you and not before."

Oscendale fell silent and fumed inside. He still felt woozy it was true, but whether that was as a result of the medicine he had been given or the blood loss he wasn't sure. He felt himself slipping backwards again and just had time to decide on his next move before sleep overcame him, like a wave of warm water.

When he awoke it was still light. Kathleen had gone and for a moment he felt a pang of separation. The nurses were busily going about their work on the ward. He had been so light-headed earlier that he hadn't really surveyed his fellow patients so he spent some time stirring his brain into life by trying to determine a man's character from the faces in the beds that he saw around him. He soon grew tired of the game and was relieved when his meal came and he was able to eat it without feeling nauseous.

The soldier in the next bed to him was sitting up with his head bandaged. He was recounting a story to the man in the next bed along.

"… so I went down the trench and peeked round one of the traverses. Next thing I know some Hun has hit me on the head with his rifle butt. I staggered backwards and he came at me with his bayonet aimed at me wotsit. I deflected it with my rifle and then we're on the ground wrestling in the mud. Luckily, one of my mates finished him off. Stuck his bayonet right through his back. 'Oi,' I said, 'you could've had me and all!' but I was glad he did it. I looked down and it seemed like my left hand was just blood. He must've caught me with his bayonet and I didn't notice until after he was dead. Then I passed out."

"So what happened next?" asked the other man.

"Well I've gone and lost three fingers here," said the soldier holding up his bandaged left hand, "and I've got a fractured skull and all, and do you know what the surgeon asked me before he treated me?"

"Go on," said the man, obviously enthralled by the story.

"He said 'Are these wounds self-inflicted, private?' Bloody hell! I spend three hours trapped in no-man's-land, so cold my face turns blue, I lose three fingers and I crack my head open just to get into this hospital bed. Likely story innit? So I says to him 'That's right, sir, we have a history of self-inflicted wounds in the Welsh Regiment.' By the look on his face I can see that he wonders if I'm joking or not. So as I don't want to be up on a charge I says, 'No, sir. These wounds were received through contact with the enemy.' Then he looks happier and decided to treat me after all. So here I am."

The soldier laughed bitterly and immediately wished he hadn't as his free hand rose to his injured head and he grimaced with pain.

Doctor Stephens came onto the ward later the following morning and, somewhat sceptically, pronounced Oscendale fit to return to light duties. Oscendale left the field hospital that afternoon, his arm tightly strapped and a box of pills in his pocket.

His first stop was his room for a wash and brush up, essential to get the smell of the ether out of his hair and throat. He then paid a visit to Avate who was surprised to see him and chastised him for not taking more time off. Oscendale brought him up to speed on the recent developments in the case and ended with his account of the pursuit at the rifle range.

"But why would a British officer kill a French bakery owner? To shut her up?" Avate asked.

"Could be. Vincent may have told her something, something she didn't even realise she knew. Or he may have given her something, something that Price was looking for."

"Do you think he found it?"

"No. I think it could still be there. Valère placing gendarmes at the door is an inconvenience to Price but I'm sure he'll try again."

"So where do you think he is now?"

"I'm pretty sure he's arrogant enough to try once more, even though he now knows I'm after him. He's biding his time until he can try and get into Catherine Jaulard's house again. If I were him I would go to ground, blend in somewhere I wouldn't be noticed."

"And where would that be?" Avate's eyes twinkled as he guessed the response.

"Where all officers should be. With other soldiers."

CHAPTER 15

3rd July 1916

WAS THERE ANY finer architecture than Louis XIV baroque? thought *Hauptmann* Michael Bernhofer of Department IIIb. *Particularly when it evolved to encompass rococo styles as well.* He followed the smooth, flowing reliefs around the room, their subtle, intricate lines entrancing him as he became more and more absorbed. The ornate ceiling seemed to defy gravity and the gold shimmered as he twisted his head to survey the whole room. The whites and pastels calmed and soothed him as he lost himself in a world of elegance and beauty.

'Rocaille' and 'coquille', he pondered. The rock and the shell that gave their names to this divine expression of art. He considered the furniture as his gaze fell to the gravity-bound objects on the floor. It was all so carefully crafted, sculpted even, to match the setting of the room it served. All so perfectly interlaced, one form entwining with the other.

"The trouble with you, Bernhofer, is that you're such a man of culture. You have far too much imagination to make a career in the military." The speaker was a thin-faced officer with piercing blue eyes. Bernhofer immediately bristled and prepared himself for what he knew would be an awkward next few minutes.

"My dear Stoltz. That is precisely why I joined the Intelligence Branch. I fear, however, that this is the closest you will come to intelligence." He smiled at his fellow officer. Wilhelm Stoltz had the ability to get under his skin quite like no other human being he knew.

The man's narrow lips clenched momentarily but then a

watery smile emerged. "Tut, tut, Bernhofer. I do enjoy these little spats of ours but sometimes you are too cruel."

Bernhofer's response was cut off by a voice calling the men to assemble around the table. He took his seat and surveyed the other officers called to this meeting. They were a mix of the German aristocracy, well schooled in the traditions of the German Army. And now they were here for real, doing what they had both been trained to do.

A serious-looking general major opened the meeting. "Gentlemen, as you are aware the British offensive on the Somme has caused considerable alarm. The first day was a disastrous one for the British. Our intelligence sources put the British casualties as high as 60,000." He paused for effect and a murmur of conversation began around the table.

"We were, of course, aware of their intentions from our observation of their build-up. The week-long artillery barrage which pounded our first line trenches gave further notice of an attack. However, this failed to penetrate our deep dugouts and when the barrage ceased our men were able to re-enter our trenches, set up their machine guns and strike the British as they advanced. The assault lacked the necessary speed and we were able to inflict heavy casualties."

Astonishing, thought Bernhofer, and he pictured the lines of heavily clad British soldiers advancing at a walk through no-man's-land and being mown down by artillery and machine gun fire. He knew that they themselves were now fighting a defensive war and had prepared their positions well, but the British had no imagination and had relied on brute force in their attempt to smash their lines.

"There was some minor loss of ground but on the whole it was a great victory. However, we cannot be complacent. The British will try again and we must be ready for them."

Bernhofer looked around the room again and wondered why he had been ordered to attend. So far this appeared to be a standard planning meeting and the role of his branch of service in such discussions was extremely restricted.

"The ground that has been lost will be retaken. We cannot afford to lose any territory, particularly that which gives us a height advantage. To this end I can announce that we will be launching a counterattack in the Yellow Sector tomorrow morning at 5.30 a.m., codenamed *Zieten*."

At this point most of the officers in the room were paying rapt attention to the speaker. However, as Bernhofer let his eyes continue their journey around the décor of the room, they met those of a shaven-headed, monocled *Oberst* who was ignoring the briefing and instead was staring at him. The man nodded curtly and smiled even more curtly before holding Bernhofer's gaze. Bernhofer surmised to be the figure as a rather too well-fed career officer who evidently knew the details of the briefing already and was wondering why Bernhofer was present – a question Bernhofer was beginning to find not a little irritating himself.

The rest of the meeting centred around preparations for the attack and ended some two hours later, during which time Bernhofer paid polite attention to the finer details of the plan and greater attention to his surroundings.

As the meeting broke up, his arm was grasped by the officer he had seen looking at him earlier. "*Hauptmann* Bernhofer, my colleagues and I would like to speak with you – privately."

He was ushered into an anteroom and the door was closed behind him. Two other senior officers were seated on padded chairs and had begun to light cigarettes. No names were exchanged and Bernhofer was not invited to sit.

"Sorry to appear underhand, Bernhofer. You probably wondered why you were told to attend that meeting. The truth is that I ensured your name was on the list because we wanted to speak with you afterwards."

The other men stared keenly at Bernhofer. As a *Hauptmann* with Department IIIb of several years standing he was not inclined to be intimidated easily and he stared back at each one in turn. A red-haired *Oberstleutnant* with a facial scar laughed suddenly and said, "He is no pussycat, this one. You were right to choose him."

The monocled *Oberst* smiled without humour and spoke again. "*Hauptmann* Bernhofer, you are patently aware, no doubt, that we have been fighting a defensive war since the Schlieffen Plan broke down in 1914. Our intention is to hold the ground that we took then for as long as we can or until the enemy is worn down by their efforts to dislodge us and sues for peace.

"This strategy has taken an enormous toll on our country's people and its resources. We are already making cutbacks in the quality and quantity of our soldiers' equipment in order to save resources. But this can only be taken so far without affecting the capability of our fighting men. Our ill-advised U-boat policy will also anger many other nations who are currently neutral and the danger of provoking the Americans cannot be underestimated.

"To that end, we have either to sue for peace or find fresh ways of resourcing our war effort. And as it happens an opportunity has presented itself, which is why we need your help."

Bernhofer was intrigued. He had rarely heard such open criticism of the conduct of the war and was aware by inference that these were men of high standing and influence.

"I would do anything to help my country, *Herr Oberst*," he replied cautiously.

"Good. I am glad to hear it. Now, we have kept you standing long enough. Excuse my bad manners but we have to be sure you are with us."

It was time to decide. Bernhofer let his natural curiosity get the better of him. His father had told him that men who read the signs were the ones who would get on in this world. He nodded in assent and was motioned to an empty chair. The officer removed the monocle from his eye and fixed Bernhofer with cold grey eyes.

"Tell me about this agent you have been running behind the British lines for the past year."

Bernhofer looked up, startled. The agent, codenamed 'Hapsburg', had been a closely guarded secret, even from his superiors. Bernhofer had learned early on in his career in Department IIIb that it was a good idea for an ambitious officer to have his own private enterprises which need not be made known to the rest of the department. In doing so, he would gain access to privileged and fresh information which could then be brought into the light of day at the appropriate moment. The kudos of imparting such information meant advancement and favour. He was therefore surprised and then moved to anger by the man's blunt remark, indicating his knowledge of such an underground operation. It was, of course, not a good idea to let such furtive plans become public knowledge and he wondered for a moment if this were the end of a promising career. His instinct told him to be cautious and so he framed a neutral reply.

"I do not think, *Herr Oberst*, that such information can be imparted in such a public forum. You are all strangers to me and therefore have the advantage. I am sure you would deem it incautious of me to divulge details of such an operation – if indeed it existed at all."

While he spoke he thought quickly. These were obviously men of high rank and no little influence and power, but they had only hinted at their designs so far. He decided to play this game very tentatively.

The *Oberstleutnant* spoke next. "Bernhofer, your natural caution, even scepticism, does you credit. I would expect nothing less of a man with your reputation. You are aware that you are highly regarded within your branch of service and that is the reason why we wished to speak with you this evening." He turned to the primary speaker and said, "It is time, I think, to take Bernhofer into our confidence. Tell him about it."

The monocled *Oberst* nodded in agreement and looked at Bernhofer over clasped hands before speaking. "Very well. You are no doubt aware that in times of war it is not paper currency that carries any value. Such a unit of monetary exchange can be far too susceptible to the vagaries of the market and, dare I say it, too dependent on whichever side wins. It is too volatile to make it a solid, substantial investment."

He looked at Bernhofer for an indication of a response but Bernhofer remained motionless. He still had no idea where this conversation or briefing was heading. The officer continued.

"Two months ago we received intelligence that items of great value lay buried in Mametz Wood. One of our soldiers came into possession of a map locating the exact spot some time during the first months of the war. He foolishly lost possession of the document but has been able to make a copy. However, it appears that the man, who is now an officer by the way, has had his memory affected by his experiences since then. Our pioneers have dug in the spot indicated on his map but without success. The current British attack in this sector has proved, as you can imagine, something of a hindrance to our work. It is vital that we retrieve these items before they are either blown to pieces by artillery shells or the British seize the ground and make it impossible for us to continue our quest."

During his speech the man's eyes never left Bernhofer, boring into them for a sign of weakness or contradiction. Bernhofer looked away, beginning to tire of the man's attempt at intimidation. He saw the discarded monocle on the table shimmering in the candlelight and Bernhofer felt drawn deeper into the heavy atmosphere of the room. Not a man spoke or even moved as the *Oberst* continued his exposition.

"We are aware from our sources that the original map of which I speak was passed to a British soldier sometime in 1914. We had given up hope of seeing it again until information reached us recently that the owner of the map had been identified and, as luck would have it, or divine providence perhaps, was in this area of the Front. However, our plans to recover the map have hit a small snag."

The man paused and looked around at his companions, as if seeking their approval to continue. A dark-haired officer who had so far not spoken nodded curtly and he continued.

"We have discovered that the man has met an unfortunate demise. However, it seems highly probable, given the circumstances of his death, that the map was with him when he fell. We believe it was passed to another individual. Your job, Bernhofer, is to find out whom."

There it was then. No discussion. He had been taken into their confidence and now this circle of officers expected him to comply with their instructions. But how would this sit with Bernhofer's own superiors in Department IIIb? Heavily involved in espionage and counterespionage work, he was used to working independently. But this mission was something else. *Who else knew about this inner circle?* he wondered.

The officer was speaking again and his words dragged him back into the room, away from his troubled thoughts. "Of course, we do not believe in putting all of our eggs in one basket so we have asked *Hauptmann* Stoltz to devise a plan for the recovery of the map as well."

Bernhofer turned to see Stoltz, who stood smoking against a wall, one arm placed behind his back. *A metaphor for the performance of your duty so far, my dear Stoltz,* thought Bernhofer. So there was to be an element of competition. Furthermore, he deduced that Stoltz had evidently already been briefed. So was he, Bernhofer, an alternative or a second choice? Whichever way it was, his natural competitiveness came to the fore and he knew what his answer would be.

He replied, "*Herr Oberst*, I would be honoured to carry out your instructions. What additional information can you give me?"

The officer smiled. "Good. I have always thought that competition amongst junior officers was healthy and I am sure that an appropriate reward will await the successful man. In terms of additional information, no, we have nothing more. Your job is to find the map and bring it back to us. Then we can excavate the correct area." There was a note of irritation in his voice, born of frustration at wasted time, and it did not escape Bernhofer's notice.

Bernhofer was dubious as to the real motives of this assembled group. What would be the result of his finding the map and whatever information it contained? Was this group of men really seeking to bolster the Kaiser's coffers? Or did they have a more selfish purpose in mind? War made many men rich in a variety of forms and he studied the faces but could discern nothing of their true motives. Nevertheless, it was his duty to obey his senior officers so he resolved to recover the map and worry about the motives and consequences later – if he could.

There was more. The *Oberst*'s voice cut into his musings once more. "I need hardly remind you, Bernhofer, I am sure, that what you have been requested to do is highly confidential." The piercing eyes burrowed deep into his again. Requested or ordered? Bernhofer knew it was the latter but the use of the term was interesting. Were these men acting independently? It might explain the veil of secrecy that was obviously being drawn over the whole affair. So he was to discuss it with no one. Not even his own department. He assumed Stoltz had had the same instructions and wondered if he could keep his mouth shut. What little he knew of the objectionable man was not good, but he knew he was a killer, so sentiment would not stand in the way of his pursuing the goal to its conclusion.

Bernhofer stiffened. "I am well used to similar work, sir. You may rely on my discretion." He felt slightly annoyed at the implication but worked at not letting it show.

"Good. We are aware of your record of service so far, Bernhofer, and that is why you have been chosen for this mission. Go to your task now and I will contact you in a few days to discuss the progress of your work."

With that a silence descended on the room and Bernhofer knew it was time to leave. Emerging from the anteroom, he bade a silent farewell to the elements of the room that had so fascinated him and was ushered out of an ornate door, closely followed by Stoltz, who said nothing as they crossed the marble-floored entrance hall and emerged into the warm night air. A gentle rain was falling and Stoltz turned to him as he pulled on his gloves and said, "The hunt is on then, Bernhofer, and to the victor the spoils. Let us hope there are no casualties when we hunt down the boar."

"There are always casualties, Stoltz. You know that," replied Bernhofer and felt Stoltz's anger bore into his back as he walked towards his waiting car.

It had been an interesting evening. At last he felt he was on the cusp of something big, something that could be his crowning glory, or if that was too fanciful, at least a chance to make himself known to higher circles and to enter the world of the elite he had craved for so long. Promotion would follow this and who knows what else? And anyway, British Intelligence had been quiet for so long that he was bored with reading the results of prisoner interrogations, looking for some germ of interest amongst so much trivia. His routines would now change and as he left the ground of the château he resolved to seize this opportunity with both hands. Hapsburg was the key and it was time to make contact again.

CHAPTER 16

3rd July 1916

MATRON KATHLEEN MORRISON of the Voluntary Aid Detachment woke with a start.

Alongside her a man sniffed quietly and she turned to see he was fully awake and staring towards the window.

"What's the matter? Troubled dreams again?" she asked, her mind still full of the fog of sleep.

The man rolled onto his side and she saw his face bathed in the moonlight. Her stomach ached as her eyes played over the drawn, tired features she knew so well. He was troubled by his latest case, she knew, and seemed as far away as peace when a puzzle was playing around inside his head.

She raised her hand and began to massage his scalp.

"It won't go away, will it?" she asked.

Oscendale closed his eyes and shook his head. Never mind the military code of secrecy, he didn't want to worry her with the details of this case. Something was wrong, terribly wrong.

He got up and walked to the window. Looking down on the road that ran alongside the hotel, he saw there was still movement of men and munitions even at this time of night. *More meat to the grinder.* He thought back to the activity he had seen at Verdun in the spring. La Voie Sacrée. Thousands of lorries that conveyed replenishment, soldiers and weapons.

That case had been difficult, not least because of the initial resentment of the French authorities, but this quite different. The nature of Vincent's death had not troubled him – he had seen too much to lie awake at night worrying about that. However, he was still struggling for a motive. And exactly how did it fit in with the murder of Catherine Jaulard?

He heard a movement behind him and Kathleen was standing next to him, her body wrapped in the silk dressing gown he had bought for her. She slipped her arm through his and together they looked at the clouds skittering across the face of the moon.

"The weather is changing," he murmured. "There's a storm coming and it'll play havoc with our next attack. The ground will turn to a swamp and our men will die in it, one way or another."

He fell silent for a while and she knew better than to interrupt his train of thought. At last she could bear it no longer and spoke.

"Would it help to talk about this case, Tom?" She nuzzled into his side and he felt her soft body move against his. She aroused him like no other woman he had known and he hesitated now. He was duty-bound to keep the details of the case to himself and he had rarely discussed his work with the other women in his life. Some hadn't cared what he did and showed not the slightest interest in his police work. Others had been intrigued until he had told them some exaggerated gory details of a murder he was working on, a description of the state the body had been found in, for example. That was usually enough to sate their curiosity and they never asked again.

This time, though, the intricacies of this case as it was unfolding were keeping him awake at night, puzzling over the variety of explanations for Vincent's final behaviour and his link with Catherine Jaulard. Suddenly, he felt the need to share his thoughts with another person. Jack would have been there in the past and they would have bounced ideas off each other until the facts all came together to make a complete picture. But Jack was gone and his only companion in the MFP was North – and that scenario was obviously out of the question. He could go to Avate, of course, but he always liked to present his boss with solutions rather than problems, or 'issues' as he had once heard one smart fellow officer describe them.

No, he needed to unburden his thoughts to someone he knew, and Kathleen, with her military knowledge, might be able to help him. So he lay back on the bed and began to recount the details of the case thus far and some of the ideas he had come up with. She listened in silence for the most part, occasionally interrupting him to clarify a point. At the end of half an hour, she rose from the bed and crossed the room to the table, her silk dressing gown caressing her body as she moved. Opening a box on the table, she lit a cigarette before speaking.

"The thing is, Tom, it appears to me that you don't have enough information yet. You have a man who has murdered two of his fellow soldiers, then committed suicide. Then this Madame Jaulard is brutally murdered and you think there's a link. You say you've spoken to some witnesses and the ones you want to interview next are preparing to leave for the front line. I think you're speculating too much at the moment. Without more information you don't have anywhere to go. You need to be patient. Something else will turn up and you'll be off again. I also think you're letting this Lieutenant Price get under your skin. You're in danger of making him the focus of your attention. You'll come across him again, I know you will. In the meantime I think I know just what to do to send you back to sleep."

She moved back to the bed and lay down by his side. She began to run her fingers through his hair and to massage his scalp again. Within minutes his eyes had closed and the problem of William Vincent receded from the forefront of his thoughts.

Ever the pragmatic Kathleen. He began to wonder what the future held for them. Time was passing and the war dragged on. Would there ever be peace? Presumably something would end the killing and they would all pack up and go home. But to what? He could not see himself back in his tiny office in Barry Police Station. The squat, solidly built building, which sat looking over the Old Harbour and seemed to symbolize all that was dependable about justice and the law, had been his life for several years before all this began, as he dealt with the minutiae of police work, its successes and failures, triumphs and tragedies, and all the vagaries of human behaviour.

He saw again the cells with their odour of vomit and urine, the pathetic, weeping wife who begged him for her husband's release so he could work in the docks to earn money to feed the family; the urchins who stole food simply because they were hungry; and the suicides and murders, the gas oven and the kitchen knife, the razor cases whose sad lives he was obliged to delve into in the company of distraught spouses.

Sometimes he had closed his office door behind him at the end of his spell of duty and turned right instead of left towards his lodgings. His path had taken him to the Old Harbour itself, now decaying and silting up, made redundant by the opening of the main docks some twenty years before. He had stood and looked at the few fishing boats that sat bobbing in a desultory fashion on the dark, mud-stained water. Its time was over, overtaken by the march of industrial progress.

He knew now that he could never go back. Back to his lodgings with Mrs Regan and her cosy front room, the silence of his bedroom as he had lain awake in the early hours agonising over the details of his latest case. He had seen too much, felt so deeply, that his life, and indeed his vision of life, had changed irrevocably. He had seen how cheaply human life could be valued and knew that he was as damaged as any shell-shock case. It was just that he was fortunate enough to be able to control it. For a while at least.

Kathleen moved again at his side, her warm, scented body stirring under the sheet. She had helped. Had helped enormously. From the moment he had first asked her to set aside the daily horror of the hospital to spend some time with him, he had known she would act as a welcome balm for his silent suffering. And if he could do the same for her then he would be happy. She seemed so strong, so determined. Determined to save a life if she could and to ease a passing if she could not. And yet it never reduced her to tears, as he was sure it would him if the roles were reversed. She bore it all stolidly, only occasionally telling him about a case that had touched her more than the others – a last letter home she had written at the bedside of a dying man, the empty bed when she returned to duty. Each combined to alter her, he knew, but the change was almost imperceptible. It was only as the months passed that he began to notice the subtle changes in her where the war was leaving its mark.

On their first evening out together they had talked late into the evening and he had felt that instant rapport a man sometimes feels with a woman, that feeling of mutual understanding, of a shared knowledge, of the unity of being of two strangers whose whole lives have led them to this one moment. Fanciful stuff for a military policeman, he knew, but then perhaps the war was changing him in other ways as well as those he recognised.

Their relationship had deepened until the evening they had made love in his hotel room, the intensity of the moment taking them both away from the horrors of the outside world to somewhere safe, peaceful and yet only temporary – something of which they were both all too well aware. The time, the place, the feeling all combined to leave him feeling closer to her than any other woman he had known. The pleasure of their lovemaking put all the dying and the suffering to one side for a time, but in the early hours the thoughts always came back to him – and to her, he knew, from the stifled murmurings she uttered in her deep sleep. The abject misery of all this would never leave them. Perhaps all they could hope for was a brief moment of solace in a world of death and destruction from which there seemed no escape. If so, then it was enough. For the present anyway.

She moved again and reached for him. He moved to her, seeking an escape from the troubled thoughts that again wracked his night-time hours. "Can you give me something for the pain?" he asked and she smiled and pressed her moist lips to his.

CHAPTER 17

4th July 1916

THE WOOD WAS cold and damp. It was early, very early. Pockets of mist rose from the ground as the early morning sun attempted to stir the vegetation into life. Wisps of vapour appeared like genies, slowly twisting their way through the branches. Dark green leaves oozing dew reached into and out of the ephemeral mist. All seemed quiet and still.

The khaki-clad soldiers moved cautiously forward, treading carefully. One wrong move now, one misplaced foot could cause a branch to snap and a noise like a rifle shot ring out in the still morning air. Their eyes stared keenly into the first light of the day, endeavouring to pick out movement and a threat, but nothing stirred.

The officer was out in front, his revolver held high as he peered into the gloom. He knew that their quarry was close. The intelligence reports were certain that they were in this part of the wood, though as of yet there was nothing to indicate this.

Men kept their breathing regular and silent, fearing that the noise would travel too quickly and alert their quarry to their presence. This was the juncture of life and death, the time that determined whether a man lived or died. A lack of caution now could mean a bullet wound or sudden death.

Just a few more yards now and they would be upon them. The tension in the air was palpable. Men sweated in serge uniforms as their excitement mounted. Rifles were held steady but inside men trembled.

The officer leading the way suddenly dropped to his knees

and motioned to the soldiers behind him to halt. Instinctively they responded, glancing nervously around to see if there was anyone on their flanks. The man pointed to a gap ahead and the dark smoke of an early morning campfire was clearly visible, rising between the trees. A figure was attempting to force the fire to catch, blowing hard at the base. His back was to the group and the officer was sure he was unaware of their approach. On either side of him stood a hotchpotch of tented accommodation – stained and faded army tents mixed with groundsheets slung from tree branches.

The officer motioned two groups to spread out to his left and right. The men moved into position and when he was sure they were ready he took the trench whistle from his breast pocket and raised it to his lips.

The piercing blast shrieked clearly in the still air and immediately cries rang out as the soldiers charged into the clearing, their rifle barrels catching the morning sun's rays.

Men staggered wearily from the tents, their slumbers disturbed first by the whistle and then by the shouts of the attackers. Some attempted to defend themselves against rifle butts and punches but most raised their hands sullenly and stood still.

Within minutes it was over. The captives were lined up, their eagle-eyed attackers watching for any sign of resistance. Oscendale walked forward and shouted, "Who's your leader?"

A bedraggled man with a beard stepped forward. His filthy overcoat contrasted starkly with Oscendale's own. "I lead this group of men," he said.

Oscendale eyed the deserter. Dark-rimmed eyes and sallow features looked back at him. Oscendale had seen many types of deserters over the past two years and he attempted to surmise what category this man fitted into. Some were scared, some shell-shocked, some were conscientious objectors who had not been recognised as such. Sometimes they had been wounded and refused to go back, while others cited political objections to the war, as the reason for leaving their pals behind.

"Has anyone joined your group over the past two days?" he asked the man. He was met with sullen defiance and normally Oscendale would have welcomed the battle of wills. This time Oscendale was after a bigger fish and, irritated by the delay that now presented itself, he tried again.

"I asked you, has anyone joined your group over the past few days?"

The man did not respond. His dark eyes became more confident and he stared back at Oscendale with resentment. Old impatience took hold and Oscendale turned to one side.

"Right then. Sergeant Taylor?"

A hefty NCO stepped forward. "Sir!"

"Have your men search the tents. We're looking for a man of average build with brown hair, probably dressed in a lieutenant's uniform, though he may have discarded it."

Taylor called a small group of men to him and began to search the tents and shelters. Oscendale never took his eyes from the face of the man he had originally spoken to. *There it was.* The man had looked quickly to a poncho slung from a tree branch at the edge of the clearing. Out of the corner of his eye, Oscendale saw a flash of movement.

"Taylor!" he shouted and pointed but Taylor had already spotted a figure come out of the shelter and sprint for the cover of the trees. He raised his rifle and fired. A cry rang out and the figure fell to the ground.

Oscendale raced across the clearing to where the figure lay face down on the grass, a scarlet bullet hole in his left calf.

"Good shooting, Taylor," smiled Oscendale.

"Thank you, sir," replied the NCO. "Didn't fancy chasing the bastard through the woods."

Oscendale turned the groaning figure over; it was Price. He opened his eyes and glared at Oscendale.

"You will regret this, Oscendale," he spat. "You should learn to keep your bloody nose out when you're told."

"Oh I don't think so," Oscendale countered. "And I'll be telling your boss Vedmore the same thing later today. Lock him up, Sergeant Taylor. Charge him with desertion in the face of the enemy."

Taylor's face beamed with delight at the prospect of arresting a bogus officer and as Oscendale turned away Taylor kicked Price twice in the ribs before he was lifted roughly to his feet, handcuffed and marched away through the trees.

CHAPTER 18

4th July 1916

BREAK OF DAY *in the trenches. Almost poetic that,* thought Oscendale as he made his way along a communication trench with a corporal who guided him skilfully forward.

The message had been waiting for him when he had returned from his visit to the deserters' camp.

'German officer taken in a trench raid near Mametz Wood. Interrogate and report. Avate.'

It was routine, of course, but this time it was a welcome distraction from the machinations of the Vincent case. *The Vincent case.* Was he over dramatising something that was so ordinary? Why couldn't he see it as just a simple case of murder and subsequent suicide? Yet still he could not get the image of Catherine Jaulard's dead body out of his mind.

He cursed as he stumbled over a rum jar which sent him sprawling onto the duckboards. He got up, flicked wet mud off his trousers and continued the hunched trot along the trench, the corporal making no allowance for his fall and continuing to hare along in front of him. *Come on, concentrate,* he said to himself, *it's far too bloody dangerous here to be thinking about other things.*

Eventually he rounded a corner to see the corporal standing grinning in front of him.

'In there, sir. And an arrogant sod he is too.' He motioned towards a dugout entrance cut into the side of the trench, a sheet of waxy material acting as a flimsy protection against the weather – and a gas attack.

Oscendale stooped to enter a dimly lit, damp-smelling

earth cave and, as his eyes adjusted to the dark, he became aware of two figures sitting on wooden bunks on either side.

A British soldier sat pointing his SMLE rifle with bayonet fixed directly at the German officer and he looked up in relief as Oscendale entered. The young man must have thought the Hun was going to leap on him at any moment.

The German attempted to stand but managed only a crouch owing to the height of the dugout roof. The soldier flinched as if this was the assault he had been dreading and jabbed his bayonet at the man, but Oscendale asked the German to sit down and the young man sighed with obvious relief.

Oscendale sat on a vacant bunk and drew out a packet of cigarettes. Lighting one for himself, he paused then offered one to the German who accepted. Leaning over to light the man's cigarette he caught the faintest whiff of sweat. A front line officer then, unwashed in days. He sat back and studied the man.

A *Bavarian* according to the rampant lion on his buttons. Probably a conscript as he didn't have the weather-beaten face of many years of military service. Not young, probably early thirties, unusual these days. Cleanish uniform too, little trace of mud or filth. There had been a slight stiffness in his movement as he had reached across for the proffered cigarette. Rheumatism perhaps? Oscendale began to speculate as to the set of circumstances that had led him here.

He began the list of routine questions using his pidgin German but the officer volunteered nothing more than his name and rank so Oscendale turned his attention to the man's possessions. These had been collected in an unused sandbag when he was captured and placed on the bunk beside him.

The German watched him intently as Oscendale sifted though the detritus of the man's life. A *Soldbuch* with the photograph of a bespectacled man stared back at him and there were also photographs of a woman Oscendale took to be the man's mother.

And a piece of folded paper. Oscendale noticed the man stiffen slightly as he picked it up and began to unfold it. It was a map of Mametz Wood, but not a military map with trench systems marked in red and blue and the small black crosses of barbed wire. This was a pre-war map showing the surrounding farm buildings and the château now blasted to something less than rubble by the artillery fire. It showed the paths through the woods and the various huts used by the gamekeepers for storing equipment.

Was this anything more than a planning map used for the construction of defences? He might have dismissed it without further thought had he not noticed a small square drawn onto the map between two woodland paths. It was in black ink and otherwise indistinguishable from the rest of the map's details and would have passed unnoticed to a less suspicious eye, but there was something about this unnecessary addition to a pre-war map that aroused his curiosity.

"What is this?" he asked the officer in German.

The man shrugged and shook his head but Oscendale detected a flash of concern pass across his eyes before the gesture was complete.

"What is it?" he persisted, his voice rising. Still the officer said nothing. Oscendale turned his attention back to the *Soldbuch* and read again the man's name – Franz Luntz. He looked again at the picture. A bespectacled picture of the man in front of him.

Or was it? The man was similar, but perhaps not identical.

"Is this you?" he asked holding the photograph in the *Soldbuch* up to the man's face. The German looked away and Oscendale knew he was on to something.

"Corporal, go and get me a pair of spectacles."

The corporal looked at him askance. "Spectacles, sir?"

Oscendale sighed, "Yes, spectacles. Go and get me some from one of your men."

"They won't have any, sir," said the man plaintively.

"Yes, they will, corporal – reading glasses. Any glasses. Just go and get me a pair."

The NCO disappeared and was back in five minutes with a small leather case which he handed to Oscendale. "Spectacles, sir," he said redundantly.

Oscendale took the spectacles out of their case and held them up to the German. "Put them on," he said in German. The officer slowly unfolded the spectacles and placed them on his face. Oscendale alternated his gaze between the German and the photograph. At last he was certain.

"This isn't you," he said, pointing at the photograph. The German shrugged. "So if you're not going to co-operate I'll have my men take you outside and summarily shot as a spy."

The man furrowed his brows and licked his dry lips. *Good*, thought Oscendale, *he's thinking about it.*

"So I'll ask you once again. Who are you and what regiment are you from?"

The man shook his head and looked at the floor of the dugout. Exasperated, Oscendale decided to call the German's bluff. "Right, private, you look after him while the corporal and I organise a firing squad."

"You wouldn't dare, captain," said the German in perfect

English. "I am a captured German officer and should be treated in accordance with the Geneva Convention."

Oscendale spun round, delighted that he had been correct in his suspicions. "No you're bloody not; you're a German spy and will be shot outside." He motioned to the corporal and they left the dugout.

CHAPTER 19

4th July 1916

THE YOUNG SENTRY stood over the body in a state of shock.

'I couldn't help it, sir. Honest. He just went berserk. Threw himself at me. Tried to get me rifle. I was just defending myself. Christ, I never seen so much blood!'

The German officer lay on his back, his eyes staring vacantly at the corrugated iron roof of the dugout. In the centre of his stomach a hole oozed blood onto his field grey tunic and ran between his fingers where they had vainly attempted to stem the flow. His face was already draining of colour but his lips still twitched slightly, indicating that his life was not yet over.

Oscendale had been making his way back along the communication trench and had gone no more than thirty yards when shouting had drawn him back to the dugout. After pushing his way in through the already assembling crowd of soldiers, he was now witnessing the German's final moments of life.

He noticed that the officer's lip movements were following the same sequence and he realised that he was trying to say something. Bending closer, he placed his ear next to the man's mouth and discerned a single word.

Soon afterwards all movement ceased and the struggle was over. The man was dead.

The guard was now outside, being consoled by his mates, and Oscendale heard the approaching voice of an officer, come to see what all the fuss was about. Quickly, he began to search the dead man's clothing and found what he was looking for sewn into the lining of his tunic.

Bernhofer was aware that he may have made an error. How serious it was remained to be seen. Returning to his quarters after the meeting at the château he had pondered on his next move.

The agent the monocled *Oberst* had referred to had been of use several times over the past year, particularly with regard to troop movements during the build up to the latest British offensive. However, finding out what had happened to the map after the British soldier had died could prove to be like finding the proverbial needle. That was not going to deter him, though, and he had mulled over his first move in the game that could see him being well-rewarded for emerging the winner.

The following morning he had found out the name of the German officer alluded to at the meeting. It was always helpful to have contacts at Headquarters and the name of the officer had been passed to him by mid-morning. The man was currently posted to the area around Mametz Wood and Bernhofer was not surprised by this apparent coincidence. Nothing that the group of men he had met did was done without careful planning and he knew that the posting was deliberately engineered to focus the officer's mind on recovery of whatever object of value was buried in the woodland.

He was incensed to learn by lunchtime, in response to his request to interview the man, that he could not be found. Worse still was his temper an hour later when he was informed that the officer had been captured and taken back to their lines by the British.

It seemed to Bernhofer that this was too much of a

coincidence and led him to the conclusion that the British had somehow learned of the officer's secret and had targeted him for removal. Either that or Lady Luck was certainly piqued at something he had done recently. Whichever way it stood, he knew that decisive action was called for, and quickly, and he thought he knew exactly what was required.

Leaving the dugout once more, Oscendale followed the twisted route along the front line trench and was so deep in thought that it was some seconds before the frantic clanging sound registered.

Rounding a corner of the trench he saw a hooded figure beating a artillery shell case with a piece of metal and gesturing frantically at a group of men to his left, all of whom had risen from their attempts at slumber and were now urgently ripping their gas hoods from their satchels and donning them.

Several men turned towards him as he approached and each pointed over his shoulder to something behind him. Turning backwards, he saw a yellow cloud creeping towards him and he realised that he had been so preoccupied by what he had found on the dead German that he hadn't switched on the internal warning that had kept him alive for so long in this war.

The gas shell had fallen some yards behind him and he hadn't even heard it. He stopped and tore his gas hood from the satchel hung across his chest and pulled it over his head but not before he had taken his first breath of the foul-smelling vapour.

The world outside disappeared momentarily and he became withdrawn and detached from his surroundings, his rasping breath as he inhaled and exhaled the only sound he could hear. In his mouth he could taste the gas and fought hard to resist the temptation to cough. He swallowed hard and his throat burnt and his stomach was on fire but he forced himself to stay calm.

He surveyed the scene around him. A whole race of alien-like beings was passing him, the huge eyes of their gas hoods giving them a frighteningly anonymous appearance. He pressed himself against the wall of the trench and let them go about their business whilst he concentrated on maintaining a steady flow of air through his gas hood tube valve.

Without warning a huge weight fell on his shoulders and he plummeted helplessly to the bottom of the trench, his head hitting the wood of the duck boards, nearly knocking him out. He lay there stunned and the weight left him. He shook his head and turned to his left to see dozens of grey-clad figures, gas hoods obscuring their features, leaping into the trench.

The storm troopers had used the gas attack as cover for their final rush to the British trenches. Oscendale was aware that the distance between the two opposing front line trenches was not large, but he still couldn't understand why they hadn't been spotted by one of the sentries on duty. He could only assume that they had hidden in the shell holes of no-man's-land during the night and had waited patiently for their artillery to open fire with the gas shells that now leaked their venomous contents all around him. More were still falling: a soft plop followed by a hissing as the greenish-yellow fumes leaked out into the air and poisoned everything they touched.

Oscendale hated the use of gas by either side. Being shot at and killed or wounded was one thing, but the aftereffects of breathing in poison gas he had seen at close hand: the struggle for breath, the rasping rattle as the fumes ate away at a man's lungs and throat, the eyes that bulged with the terror of being burnt from within, and the vomiting as the poison seeped down into the stomach. Men survived gas attacks but were often left blinded and with hacking coughs that continued for months, permanently damaging the lungs and throat. Death was not quick with gas; it was a hateful, lingering ordeal.

All around him soldiers were fighting viciously. He saw a German run a Tommy though with his butcher bayonet, the man's eyes wide in terror and incomprehension as he looked down to see blood pouring from his chest cavity. The German withdrew his bayonet then fell dead as his helmet was dislodged by a bullet fired at close range from a Lee Enfield rifle. Two men wrestled with each other on the floor of the trench, each seeking the opportunity to plunge his trench knife into the other. Elsewhere there were standoffs as men prodded cautiously at each other with bayonets mounted on the barrels of their rifles, waiting for the other to make a mistake.

Oscendale watched the dances of death, transfixed. He had been part of close-quarter fighting many times before, but never through the lenses of a gas hood. He was detached, a figure rising above and beyond the bloody encounter, an observer who could walk away at any time.

Then he saw the German running towards him. He was a solidly built character whose bulging eyes displayed the blood lust that was upon him. He had evidently dropped his rifle somewhere and now rushed at Oscendale with his bare hands, hurling him backwards into the trench wall. The gas hood made his vision slightly blurred and he had misjudged the distance between them. His breathing was strained inside the hood and he resisted once more the overwhelming sensation of choking as the vestiges of the gas burnt his throat.

The German's hands closed around his throat and he struggled to loosen the man's grip. He raised his knee but the man was wise to the move and he connected with his outer thigh instead. He pulled and tore at the man's arms but felt the trench begin to move beneath his feet as his brain lost its blood supply. He felt helpless in the face of the man's strength and the eyes behind the glass panels of the German's gas mask showed the effort he was expending.

Then Oscendale did the only thing he could do. With a colossal effort of will he took his hands away from the German's and immediately felt the pressure increase. Instead he reached for the man's gas mask and ripped it away from his head.

At once the pressure ceased and the man started backwards. Terror came into his eyes now as he turned to see where Oscendale had thrown the mask. It was lying in a crumpled heap on the duckboards at the foot of the trench and as he reached for it another German fell into him, his hands clasped to his stomach. Oscendale felt his head clearing and he lurched forward and kicked the mask further down the trench. The German turned to him with a reddened face and Oscendale saw he could hold his breath no longer. As the man opened his mouth to take the breath that might kill him, Oscendale kicked him hard in the chest and he fell to the floor.

Gasping now with the effort of the fight, Oscendale tried to regulate his breathing. Looking to his left he noticed two Germans entering the dugout where their dead comrade lay. Forcing himself to come to his senses, he stumbled towards them, intent on seeing why a British dugout should hold such an attraction to them. Under normal circumstances a hand grenade would have been considered sufficient to dispatch any occupants during an attack on enemy trenches. Why were the two men taking their lives in their hands by entering a dark British dugout? Did they know what lay inside?

The British soldiers were winning the fight now and more were arriving from the junction with the communication trench in response to the alarm being raised. Oscendale saw the two Germans emerge from the dugout and look up at an officer who was crouched on the parapet; one of them shook his head. Glancing around them, they quickly discerned that the fight was going against them. German soldiers could be seen climbing out of the trench and heading for their own lines. Others lay in death embraces with British soldiers.

The two Germans started to climb the trench wall but Oscendale leapt forward and grabbed one by his belt. The man grunted and fell backwards on top of his assailant and for the second time in a short while Oscendale again had the wind knocked out of him. With a savage thrust of his elbow the German caught Oscendale full on the jaw and the glare of the sun shone full in his face as the German rolled off him.

The officer waved his pistol towards the German lines and the men scrambled up onto the parapet and followed him out into no-man's-land. The other German storm troopers who were still engaged in the desperate fight in the trench saw this and endeavoured to join them. One or two succeeded but the remainder fought until they were bayoneted or shot.

Oscendale crouched against the wall of the trench, gasping for breath as he surveyed the whole nightmarish scene. The gas cloud still hung in the air and bodies were concealed and then revealed in turn as the gas wafted slowly around in the almost stagnant air. The exhausted British soldiers sat slumped on the fire step, hunched over, with their rifles between their knees. The hoods made them look like condemned men about to be dropped from the scaffold, but once again Oscendale was amazed at the fighting spirit of these former clerks, teachers, labourers and myriad other occupations that had preceded their enlistment in the British Army.

He thought back to what he had just witnessed. The Germans had attacked with the express purpose of getting into the dugout. They had done it well – these were no conscripts but elite storm troopers who knew their deadly business well. To use such men and treat them as expendable meant that the prize they were seeking was extremely valuable and worth the risk. The two men who emerged from the dugout had obviously been looking for the dead German officer. Finding him, they had made no attempt to remove his body so they were probably looking for something he had on him at the time he had been captured – the map or perhaps the letter Oscendale now had in his tunic.

CHAPTER 20

4th July 1916

THE BRITISH ARMY'S postal service was unquestionably one of its most efficient elements. A letter posted in Britain on one day would arrive in France the following day and be in the hands of the recipient within hours.

It also kept records of every letter sent to every serviceman.

The bespectacled, greasy-skinned clerk was a jobsworth of the first order. Oscendale had to wait behind a grill and fill in a form in triplicate before the man would even deign to discuss the name of the man he had enquired about. That done, he scratched his chin and asked for identification and, having duly obliged, Oscendale was asked for evidence of the authority requesting the information.

At that point Oscendale resorted to a tactic he used very rarely but one that had served him well on occasions in his former career. He leant forward so that none of the other clerks could hear and hissed, "If you don't co-operate now I will bring back half a dozen military policemen and go through your storeroom looking for any envelopes or packages that have been opened. And if I find one, just one, missing any money, cigarettes or even a pair of knitted socks I'll bang you up in the glass house and feed you bread and water for a month. Got it?"

The clerk turned puce so quickly Oscendale thought his glasses were going to steam up. He nodded vigorously and pulled out a set of keys. Opening a door to the side, he invited Oscendale into the storeroom.

He opened a filing cabinet and pulled out a ledger marked 'Welsh Regiment'. Within seconds he had found the name 'Vincent, William' and underneath the dates and postal districts of all the letters and packages he had received.

Oscendale scanned the list and soon found what he was looking for. On the 24th June Vincent had received two letters: one from his mother in Merthyr and another from his wife in Swansea. So Mrs Vincent had replied to her husband's last letter. What plans had they been making for their future? His instinct that she had known more than she had let on during his visit had probably been correct. She had understood the message contained in the letter and had replied immediately. That was a lead that could be pursued further if required.

Leaving the sweating clerk, Oscendale strolled back to the car, whistling as he went. Things were looking up. Now for Lieutenant Price.

The room was stuffy and hot. Stale cigarette smoke hung in the air. There was no natural light; instead a single light bulb attempted to illuminate the area of Interview Room Number Two.

Price sat on one of the two chairs in the room, his hands clasped, elbows on the solitary table while smoking a cigarette with obvious disdain for the whole proceedings. Occasionally he flinched as he adjusted his position, the now bandaged bullet wound to his leg causing him some discomfort.

Oscendale watched him for a while through the peephole in the door, endeavouring to read some signals that the man might give out inadvertently. There were none. He gave up and ordered an MFP corporal to open the door.

Price raised his eyes lazily to meet him as he entered and said, "Ah, Oscendale. I thought it might be you peering at me. Quite the little voyeur, aren't you?"

Oscendale knew it was a crass attempt to needle him before the interview began and forced himself to shrug off the insult.

"It's Captain Oscendale to you, Lieutenant Price – if indeed you are a lieutenant in the British Army."

He paused, raised an eyebrow, and awaited Price's response, but the man was far too good for that, he knew. Price merely smiled and took another pull on his cigarette.

Oscendale continued, "Because if you're not then you will be tried as a German spy and shot. That is, if you don't hang for murder first."

Price showed no sign of fear. "A double killing, Captain Oscendale? Does it really matter what a man dies for?"

Oscendale pounced. "So you don't think that killing a defenceless woman is a crime?"

"This whole war revolves around killing, captain. Hundreds of men will die today. There are enemies everywhere and you kill your enemy wherever he is."

"Or wherever she is?" pursued Oscendale.

Price smirked again. "Really, Captain Oscendale, you *are* clutching at straws. You have no proof that I killed anyone or that I am a spy."

Oscendale took a manila file from his briefcase and laid it on the table. Price ignored it and continued to hold Oscendale's stare.

"A list of the officers in the Welsh Regiment. One or two Prices, as you would imagine, but no Lieutenant Price. Would you like to explain that?"

"An administrative error. I only joined the battalion a

few days ago. My papers haven't arrived yet, that's all," Price countered.

"An officer in the front line without any verification is a suspicious thing in a time of war," challenged Oscendale.

"Ridiculous. You're clutching at straws again. My papers will turn up in the next day or so, you'll see. Anything else?" Price raised his eyebrows enquiringly.

Oscendale changed tack. "Why were you at Catherine Jaulard's house that night?"

"Because I was ordered to attend the scene as a representative of the army."

"But why you?"

"Because I was in the town and could attend immediately."

"Who gave you that order?" Oscendale began to increase the speed of his questioning.

"A note arrived for me when I was in my billet."

"Can you produce this note?"

"Of course not. I'm not in the habit of carrying bits of paper around with me like some sort of walking filing cabinet. For God's sake, man, I'm an infantry officer not a glorified military clerk like you."

Oscendale refused to take the bait. "So why did you leave the scene of the crime so suddenly?"

"To start my own investigation of course and to report to my commanding officer. If there was a military link he would want to hear of it."

The man was proving unflappable.

"If you had nothing to hide then why did you run from me at the rifle range and why were you hiding out in a deserters' camp?"

For the first time Price delayed his response. This time the answer to the question did not flow as fluently as the others. He took another pull on his cigarette to give himself time to think then spoke.

"Listen, Oscendale. A jumped-up little copper like you is useful enough for investigating petty military crime but you're into something you don't understand." His voice had changed to a snarl and he wasn't finished yet. "You're working on your own on this one, no-one to protect your back if you get into difficulty. I'm sure you don't want to be seeing your pal Jack Parry sooner than necessary."

Oscendale felt his mouth go suddenly dry. How had Price known about Jack Parry? The events in Gallipoli were known only to a select few and Jack Parry's death had passed almost unnoticed. Unnoticed by everyone except Oscendale who had felt his former assistant's loss acutely. The wound in his arm seemed to flare up in sympathy. If it hadn't been for Parry he knew he would have died. He struggled to control his anger and realised that Price was good, very good. He knew exactly which lever to pull and that sort of knowledge had to have been acquired somewhere.

Nevertheless, he felt shaken by Price's remark. His head began to swim and he knew that he wasn't fully over the wound he had received at Price's hands recently – the hands that had killed Catherine Jaulard. He folded the covers of the file with as much dignity as he could muster, rose and left the room, feeling Price's eyes staring into the back of his throbbing skull as he went. Outside he leant against a wall until the dizziness had passed.

CHAPTER 21

4th July 1916

My Dear William,

As you have not replied to my previous letter I can only assume that you never received it. Perhaps your censor has confiscated it. Either that or you do not wish to help me out.

Kathleen paused. "It's terrible to think that these two men were being trained simultaneously in how to kill each other more effectively." She shook her head. "This is a ghastly time, Tom, for everyone."

Oscendale raised his head from the bed. He rubbed her back softly. "Go on," he said. "I need to know what else it says."

In a way I understand but I call upon your recollection of our friendship in the Hafod to assist me now.

Kathleen continued her reading of the letter Oscendale had found on the dead German officer. "That's all it says, Tom. Incomplete and unsent. How's the arm now anyway?"

Oscendale smiled weakly. "Hurts like the devil. And my jaw. That bloody German had elbows of steel. So this dead officer was the Karl that Vincent knew in Swansea before the war."

"How can you be certain?" asked Kathleen.

"The Hafod. That's near the district in Swansea where Vincent's widow lives. In his attestation papers it said that he worked in a copperworks in Swansea. I'll bet my last shilling that this Karl is the one who came over from Bavaria to work in the copperworks with other Germans recruited before the war. He met Vincent and when he returned to Germany they continued to correspond."

"Seems a bit far-fetched to me," said Kathleen.

"Why not?" said Oscendale, slightly irritated by her scepticism. "Many foreign workers with a background in the copper industry were recruited to Swansea to set up the copperworks. There were several of them crowded into just one place, the lower Swansea valley, during the last century. Apparently it was just like a Turner landscape, the sky would glow red at night from the heat of all the furnaces. God knows, it's bad enough now. The air would stink and the pubs in the area used to do a roaring trade, probably still do. After a day's hard work in that kind of environment men would need to rehydrate by the gallon."

"So William Vincent was employed in one of the copperworks there?"

"Yes, and his father before him, I expect. They lived nearby and the work is tough but regular, so they carried on in the family tradition, as Vincent's son does now. Why work anywhere else, even if they could?"

Kathleen shuddered. "The way you describe it, it seems a hard, monotonous life."

"Yes, but don't forget what three regular meals a day has done to those men since they joined the army. Most of them have put on weight and developed to what they should have been before the war." Oscendale had seen the effect of army food, regularly served, on young men from the industrial areas of Britain. Men who had joined the army undernourished and underdeveloped would gain weight and fill out once good food and physical training had the desired effect.

She bristled. "So the war has been a good thing? All this killing and maiming?" She got off the bed and stood with her hands on her hips. "I'm surprised at you, Tom Oscendale. You've always wished for an end to all this." *Her Irish accent became more pronounced the more irritated with him she became,* he thought. Their disagreements had become more frequent of late and he knew that long hours and the experience of seeing yet more young men dying today were affecting her.

He contemplated his answer, knowing how prickly she could be about the war and decided to err on the side of caution. A flaming row at this time of night would do no good at all and he did not want to spend the night with him on one side of the bed and her on the other and a yard of space between them. "Not at all. All I'm saying is that the army looks after its recruits. After all, a half-starved man is not much use in a battle, is he?" He raised an eyebrow and she mellowed.

"Hmm. All right. I'll let you have that point. But if you saw what I see every day you wouldn't be so precious about your three meals a day theory. A man with his arm missing is the same man whether he's a copper worker or a soldier."

He could not let it go and before he knew what he was saying his mouth uttered, "So after this lot is over, we all go back to being what we were. A man goes back to his factory or his mine and carries on. One day he has an accident. A coal truck runs over his leg or a pitcher of boiling copper splashes his face. He wasn't wounded in the war but he's maimed or disfigured at home and what does he get? Come on, Kathleen. At least the army takes care of its wounded. It has people like you to do the best for the poor sods and they get proper hospital care. Free I might add. If they're working at home they may get some paltry compensation, if they're lucky, and off they go. No medal, no war badge, just another injured ex-miner or ex-copper worker looking for work.

And imagine the comments. 'Did you get that in the war, chum?' 'No, in a copperworks.' 'Oh well, bad luck.' The war heroes will get the attention afterwards, not the injured working men."

He paused. She had turned away from him and had put her face in her hands. She began to sob quietly and he knew he had gone too far. He reached for her but she twisted and brushed his hand away. He let the sobbing fade and then said quietly, "I'm sorry, Kathleen. It's just I don't see a way out of all this sometimes. It makes me angry. It all makes me bloody angry and I don't know whether it's better to be over here or back home. It's all confusing and messed up."

She turned and faced him. She brushed her hands over her eyes and he reached for her again. "Tell me about today," he said, but she shook her head. He tried again. "Please, I want to know."

She sighed and lay down alongside him and was silent for a time. When she spoke it was in a low whisper that held him entranced. "This morning they brought in the wounded from the fighting. Tom, there were scores of them coming into our dressing station alone. God knows how many more were sent to the other ones. And these were the ones that had either made their way back to their own lines or had been brought in by the stretcher-bearers. There are still many more out there in no-man's-land tonight."

She paused again and shook her head, her eyes staring unfocused across the room as she watched the picture in her head. "They were all in pain. The ones that were awake and alive that was. I saw one of the doctors shake his head as they unloaded one stretcher case out of the lorry and onto the ground. Some of the soldiers standing around were weeping and they were all talking quietly. Nobody shouted, not even the orderlies directing the stretcher-bearers. One or two cried out as they were brought into the marquee we have erected outside the château to cope with the increasing number of casualties. And do you know what, Tom? What the pity is of all this? They had ordered the marquee set up on the lawn *before* the offensive even began. They knew there were going to be hundreds, even thousands of wounded boys and they got us all ready for it."

The bitterness in her voice came out as she almost snarled the final phrase and he lay quietly, not wishing to disturb her flow. This all needed to emerge, he knew, and he could help by being still and not interrupting her.

"I have a score of boys to look after. Three are unconscious and haven't yet come round since they arrived. I have to check them regularly and I'm terrified I'm going to check the next one only to find him cold and gone. They just lie there, all of them, so grateful to still be alive and so thankful for anything we can do for them. All except one. Private Andrew Lawless. Dark brown eyes. Sad eyes. Gunshot wound to the stomach. They brought him in, laid him on the bed and I made him as comfortable as I could. Doctor Timpson came round and examined him. Didn't take him long. Then he drew me to one side and said, "Make his passing as easy as you can, matron. He won't last more than 24 hours." And that was it. He just walked away to the next one, leaving 11633 Private Andrew Lawless to die. I gave him morphine as instructed of course, and he just stared at me with those sad brown eyes. I did my rounds and called back to check on him every hour. Four times I checked and four times he was still alive, looking at me as I approached his bed. The fifth time he was still looking at me but there was nothing there. He was gone. I closed his eyes, kissed his forehead like his poor mother would have done, and pulled the sheet over his head."

She stopped and sunk her face deep into her hands and sobbed again. Oscendale let her cry until the pain was out then held her in his arms until sleep took them both away.

CHAPTER 22

4th July 1916

OBERST MARKUS SOLLNER of Department IIIb took the news with all the ingrained stiffness of the Prussian officer class. Inside he was screaming.

"Are your men sure it was not there?" he demanded of the rigid junior officer who stood the other side of the table from him.

"Certain," Bernhofer replied. "They had long enough to search the body and found a tear in the lining of his tunic. The map had been removed."

"But how did the British know it was there?" Sollner asked incredulously. "Only the people in this room and Karl Muller knew of its existence. Someone has been too garrulous with his mistress after a few schnapps I think." And he scanned the faces of the other men around the table but they just looked away. Apart from one.

"No-one has broken the secret, Markus," said *Oberst* Georg Barhoff. "The British probably got lucky during a body search."

"If Muller had been watched more closely, as I suggested, then we wouldn't be discussing this problem!" shouted Sollner, his fist dropping to the table as he did so.

"What was he supposed to do? Blunder around Mametz Wood looking for the spot? Don't be ridiculous!" responded Barhoff with irritation. "He needed that map."

Sollner leaned forward across the table. "*We* needed that map – and the original," he hissed.

"Then we need to get them back," said Barhoff. "Stoltz, who is your best undercover agent?"

Wilhelm Stoltz leaned forward on the table. He had been watching the argument with some interest and ensured that his entry into the proceedings was as well-timed as an actor's. "I have anticipated your request, Herr *Oberst*. There is a person waiting outside I would like you all to meet."

5th July 1916

The star shell burst brightly high up in the night sky and began its slow, lazy, contorted descent to its demise. The battlefield took on a nightmarish glow as stumps of trees, lines of barbed wire, shell holes and corpses were each lit up in turn by the harsh, unforgiving glare. Shadows flitted and danced like spectres around the normally static, immobile objects, which now seemed alive in the white light. The smashed trees became cloaked figures that pointed at him in the darkness, the wire a prison and the shell holes a reminder what artillery did to the good earth. And the bodies. Lying out here in the open. Unburied and abandoned. The shells of men.

All around him dozens of pairs of eyes peered out and probed the fractured landscape for any sign of movement, ready to let loose the hounds of death that would rip and shred their unfortunate victims with all the ghastly effectiveness of this new type of warfare.

The man lay still, knowing that a single movement would bring about his death and he prayed that the outline of his form would not be noticed amongst so many other bodies lying out here in no-man's-land.

Several minutes earlier he had levered himself out of the German trench on the edge of the wood and had begun his long, arduous crawl towards the British lines. Out here he was very much alone, exposed to the attentions of both sides.

He knew that the German sentries had been briefed to allow him safe passage but he was acutely aware of how fragile that protection was. A change of sentry, a man whose nerves were on edge from staring out into the gloom, a moment of panic – each factor could work to send a bullet flying in his direction.

The flare began to die away after a few seconds and he breathed again. Raising his head slowly from the mud of no-man's-land, he saw the outline of the British trenches some forty yards away and began to pick his spot. This would be tricky but it was a moment for which he had trained for some time and he knew exactly what he would do.

Staring ahead he looked for his next shell hole. Spotting one to his front he crawled slowly from the haven of the one he had occupied for the past few minutes across the shattered ground to its sanctuary. Passing yet another British corpse, he inhaled the sweet stench of decay already setting into the man's bloated body. The spirit had long gone and now it was time for the rats and the flies and the crows to feast.

A scuttling to his right indicated the presence of the creatures, gnawing on another corpse. He turned away in revulsion only for a large, fat rat to run across his path. It stopped, regarded him with disdain, as if contemplating him for later consumption, and then continued on its errand.

He began crawling forward again until his left hand disappeared into slimy ooze and he realised with disgust he was next to another dead British soldier. The man's face grinned at him in the dying embers of the flare and for a moment he thought the man was still alive but the empty eye sockets, picked clean by crows, stared vacantly into his own.

He swallowed hard to maintain his composure, drawing heavily on all his training in self-control, and was thankful when at last he slid into the relative safety of the shell hole some seconds later. He rested for a short while and recovered his senses. The increasingly dangerous nature of his position was not lost on him and he knew he had the most hazardous part of the enterprise still to come.

Out over the lip of the shell crater he went again, his heart beating furiously despite his best efforts to remain calm, as he made his way towards the parapet of the British trenches. One mistake now and a .303 bullet would end his mission at once. He would join the rest of the legion of the dead out here in the valley of death.

Fighting once again to control his breathing and praying that an inexperienced sniper from his own side would not shoot him in the back, he edged closer to the British line. When he could hear British voices he stopped and listened intently. Cigarette smoke rose in a wispy cloud, lifting gently in the air and he could pick out the different tones of men's voices. There was no mistaking the Welsh accents he could hear drifting out of the trench so, slowing his breathing, he began the much-practised charade.

"Hey, Tommy. *Kamerad. Kamerad.*"

The talking in the trench ceased and a flurry of movement ensued. Rifles came over the top of the parapet and this time he prayed an over keen Welshman would not shoot him first and ask questions later.

"Hey Fritz, you out there?" a voice riddled with suspicion asked.

"*Ja. Ja. Kamerad. Kamerad,*" he responded.

There was silence for a few seconds and all he could hear was the sound of Lee-Enfield rifle bolts being cocked. Then an English voice asked, "Do you want to surrender? Is that it?"

"*Ja. Kamerad,*" he replied and waited.

The voice said, "Then come forward slowly. No funny business or we'll shoot. Understand?"

"*Ja.* No funny business." And he crawled forward until the muzzle of a British rifle was only a yard from his head. He stopped and was quickly grabbed by several pairs of hands and yanked over the top of the parapet, falling with a crash headfirst onto the duckboards below.

Even through the pain of the fall, *Leutnant* Otto Ziegler of Department IIIb smiled inwardly with relief. He was still alive.

CHAPTER 23

5th July 1916

IT HAS BEEN said that we are never lonelier than when we travel abroad and so it was with Harold Bratton as he joined the mass of men who marched along the dusty road that hot July afternoon. On they marched, the long columns of men, footsore and fanciful, their songs betraying inherent nervousness at the thought of the coming conflict. Training and small-scale trench raids could prepare them only so much. They had been shot at and suffered artillery fire but this was to be on a far larger, far more devastating scale. And each man wondered how he would react, how it would feel to kill a man.

The long march had been exhausting, even to a fit man like Bratton. He had been in training for months but a long march over arid roads was something else. A break of five minutes in every hour was barely sufficient to keep him going. Looking around him he saw that he was not the only one who was suffering. Faces caked in sweat and dirt stared blankly ahead, mouths open. The stench of damp woollen uniforms made a pungent contrast with the sweet smell of the crops in the fields on either side of their route.

The roads they marched along seemed hundreds of miles away from war, but it was always in their thoughts. The dog-roses and the honeysuckle that sprang from the hedges were as familiar as those of home but the soldiers knew they were strangers here and they longed only to do their duty and go home.

All along the route he saw signs of the build-up for the next phase of the Great Push. Artillery guns hurtled past drawn by sweating horses. Lines of vehicles jerked their way towards the table of the great God of War. Aircraft circled overhead like vultures. And everywhere were columns of men, all making their way forward to the setting for the battles to come.

Like one small, insignificant part of an enormous machine he marched in unison with the lines of khaki-uniformed soldiers who flanked him. Penned in, like one giant millipede, the battalions marched on along the parched roads and lanes towards their appointment with destiny.

The omens had not been good. They had carried out several trench raids since April, with a mixed degree of success. A lot hinged on the wire being cut. Sometimes they had to depend on the artillery but at other times the opposing trenches were too close together and they had to use Bangalore torpedoes. *Bloody great invention*, he considered. He recalled one occasion when men had crawled out into no-man's-land, laid the long explosive-filled tube under the German wire and tried to set it off. Instead of exploding, the device had fizzled away, drawing attention to itself from the German trenches until a British officer and an NCO had to crawl out and retrieve it, as it was deemed a secret weapon, at great risk to their own lives.

Bratton recalled his sole experience of a night trench raid. In May he had been one of a party, led by a lieutenant, selected to take part in this most hazardous of enterprises. The wire had to be cut by hand this time, so an advance party was sent out into the quiet, black night to crawl slowly towards the German wire. Once they had arrived, they set to work with their heavy wire cutters and a few nervous minutes had passed while they tried as quietly as possible to make gaps in the terrible obstruction. On completing their work the main party was signalled forward and then it was his turn to crawl terrified across no-man's-land, knowing that a single inadvertent noise would bring machine gun fire down upon them. They passed through the gap and reached the enemy parapet unseen.

What followed had shocked him to the core. The trenches and their bays were full of German soldiers, some of whom quickly threw down their weapons and raised their arms in surrender. Such was the high pitch of nervous anxiety amongst the British soldiers that this sometimes made no difference and the Germans were bayoneted and shot where they stood in the act of submission. Others fought vigorously in their defence. He recalled seeing one man stabbed in the neck with a trench knife, the blood spurting all over the back of another man nearby.

Bombers had begun throwing bombs into the bays and a continuous roar of explosions soon provided accompaniment to the screams and yells of dozens of men fighting at close quarters.

Bratton had stabbed and shot at any figure he took to be clad in field grey and afterwards, when he reflected on the night's scenes, he could never be sure that he had always assaulted a *Boche*; in the darkness and confusion of a packed trench there was simply no way of always knowing who was friend and who was foe.

When he had heard Lieutenant Marsden's voice ordering the withdrawal after they had taken two prisoners, he had been one of the first out of the cauldron and he had run crouching back to his own lines as bullets flew past from both directions.

When he had reached the sanctuary of his trench he had trembled continuously for a long time afterwards. His hands had gripped his rifle until the blood stopped flowing and numbness had set in. Again and again he had replayed the horror of what he had just seen in his mind and it was some hours before sleep finally overcame his exhausted body.

He had barely slept in the days that had followed and just when he thought he had consigned the memory to a safe corner of his mind, there had been William Vincent's death and the memories had all reappeared like some horrible childhood nightmare that refused to end. It was not just the shocking manner of the corporal's death – though that had been bad enough. It was what had happened subsequently that had upset the even keel of his world and now troubled his sleep. The paper had been passed to him and with it the burden, the guilt and the responsibility to act on it. But how? He bit his lower lip as he tried to think what to do next.

Sergeant Williams's voice cut into his thoughts. "Bratton! Get your bloody pack off and sit down! If you want to stand there like a clown I'll make you do it for the next break as well!"

Bratton gratefully loosened the webbing straps that had been gnawing into his shoulders for the past hour and slumped to the ground. All along the lines of the endless companies of soldiers of the Welsh Regiment he saw men doing the same.

"Wake up, Harry. You look like you're away with the fairies." The speaker was David Denby, one of the men of his section. Denby brought out a packet of Woodbines and offered one to Bratton, who accepted the cigarette in silence. Denby was partially deaf and Bratton was not in the mood to shout conversation at him so he let him prattle on unanswered.

"God, mate, I know it was hard seeing Corporal Vincent die like that, but unless you buck up your ideas, you're going to be next on the list. We're going to see a lot more dead bodies over the next few days, you know."

Denby realised he had spoken the unspoken and his voice tailed away and both men looked around them at the faces of the groups of soldiers sitting by the side of the road, chatting, smoking, drinking from their canteens, and they both silently wondered who would be making the return journey to their billets when they were relieved after the attack and who would be lying dead in no-man's-land or at the bottom of a German trench.

Bratton flinched at the thought and a grim resolve replaced the indecisiveness of the past few days. Vincent had handed his map on to him. He had been chosen to benefit from it and he had to survive whatever was coming his way.

Keep your head down and volunteer for nothing, he recalled being advised. If that was what it took, that would be what he would do. Oh and pray of course that a bullet didn't seek him out.

On the previous day they had marched past the tented encampment of the cavalry, just west of Albert. The horses had stared at them with a complete lack of recognition or thought. The cavalry had been given priority on the roads and now they were waiting patiently for Harold Bratton and his pals to make the breakthrough that they would then exploit. Bratton had wished the horses luck as he had passed but resentment seared in him at the thought that the poor bloody infantrymen like him would be mown down in their hundreds to provide a gap for the polished men on shining steeds to race through and take all the glory.

Before long they were ordered to their feet once more and the long march resumed. The songs they had previously sung had faded now as the sound of gunfire became clearly audible in the distance. The great battle on the Somme was underway and each man knew that his hour of participation was approaching.

At last they stopped again and, after a short while, NCOs began to come down the line, barking orders at hot, tired men. Bratton and the others slumped to the ground and once more eased their packs from their shoulders. The break went on for longer than the usual five minutes so Bratton assumed they had reached somewhere important. An officer emerged from the chaos and began speaking sharply to a group some yards away. Bratton lit another cigarette and waited.

A long line of soldiers began coming down the road towards him. Their mud-stained uniforms and dirty faces spoke silently of days on the front line. Bratton realised that these were one of the units they were relieving and he watched them as they passed. They seemed to him to be very anxious to be gone and many words were exchanged between the two groups.

As they eventually disappeared into the distance, Bratton considered his surroundings. They were on a high piece of ground opposite a wood, whose trees stood still and green in the hot sun. The wood, however, conveyed a sense of menace, its dark interior hiding thousands of the enemy who even at this moment were probably eyeing him and his companions with evil intent.

Between the battalion and the wood was a small valley. *Open ground,* thought Bratton. *Clear open ground. Bloody hell!* Tomorrow they were going to be ordered to leave their trenches, walk down the hill and advance over the open ground of the valley floor, then up the slope to the edge of the wood. He could see nothing of the German defences but they were there, watching the British positions and waiting for the attack they knew was coming soon. From their front would come rifle and machine gun fire and from the right, from the adjoining main wood, which lay shaped like a hammer's head, would come enfilade fire, straight into their flank.

And all that would rip into human flesh, into men who had no cover, nothing to hide behind, no choice but to keep going and pray they were not shot. The bullets would zip and sing until they hit them like driving rain and the men who stood around him now would lie dying in this French farm field.

A wave of panic broke upon him and he forced himself to remain calm. He suddenly began to despair of remaining alive when the firing stopped at the end of the attack, and if he didn't, then his secret would die with him, unless his body was searched and the paper passed into another set of human hands.

He pondered once more the wood on the other side of the valley, its irregular patterns breaking up the skyline. What training had they had for this? They had practised assaulting trench systems cut into open ground, not attacking a wood the size of this one.

Bratton looked up to see a tall young officer of the relieved unit watching him and his colleagues settle into their new positions. The man stared as the troops noisily began to make themselves at home, his angular face and piercing eyes displaying an innate intelligence that impressed Bratton. He eyes fell on a white-and-purple striped ribbon sewn onto his left breast, the Military Cross, and Bratton knew at once that courage linked with intelligence meant danger for the Huns. The officer seemed particularly taken by the sight of one short officer struggling to assert his authority over the talkative rabble around him. Finally the tall officer shook his head and turned away to follow his men to the south.

Meanwhile the bodies of men killed by shellfire were thrown over the parapet and the soldiers set to work to deepen the trenches they now occupied. Bratton dug deep along with the rest, his mind focused now on his own survival and the prize that awaited him.

Sergeant Williams came along the line and called the men around him. With much hustle and bustle they eventually fell in and he began to read loudly from a piece of paper:

"Okay, boys. Order of the Day 5th July 1916: *'You have worked hard many months with an energy and zeal beyond praise to fit yourself for the task you have voluntarily undertaken. You have undergone the hardships of a winter campaign with fortitude. Eleven officers and forty-four NCOs and men have already received rewards from the King for gallant and distinguished conduct in the field. Your fellow countrymen at home are following your career with interest and admiration. I always believed that a really Welsh division would be second to none. You are today relieving the 7th Division, which has attacked and captured German trenches on a front of a little less than one mile and for a depth of about one-and-a-quarter miles. In this attack the village of Mametz was captured, the enemy have suffered heavy casualties, 1,500 German officers and men were taken prisoners, and six field guns were captured. I am confident that the young battalions of the famous Welsh regiments serving in the 38th Welsh Division will maintain the high standard of valour for which all three Welsh Regiments have been renowned throughout the war.'* That's it. Do your duty, boys. Now settle in and get some rest."

Bratton unconsciously pressed his hand to his tunic pocket where the map lay, determined that it would remain with him whatever happened. He looked suspiciously around him and subconsciously challenged any man to take it from him. But all he saw was men settling into the routine of trench life. Rifles were stowed and already tea was brewing and the noise of nervous conversations rang out. The British Army was preparing for battle and nothing would stop it now.

CHAPTER 24

5th July 1916

OSCENDALE ENTERED HIS office and endeavoured to pass North without anything more than a cursory 'good morning'. This was not about to occur, however. North was pleased to see his senior officer as he had a matter of the utmost urgency for him to attend to. Captain Oscendale did seem to be late to his desk this morning and North wondered whether the rumours of his sharing a bed with a pretty Irish nurse were true. Not without some resentment and jealousy, North got quickly to his feet as Oscendale entered the outer office, saluted crisply and proffered him a file. "Another Hun's done a bunk over to our side, sir. HQ are requesting that you interrogate him."

Oscendale stifled a sigh, looked at the file and then at North. *Was there a touch of mischief in those eyes?* He took the file with clenched teeth, his irritation at yet another distraction self-evident.

"Very good, North," he forced himself to say. "Get me a cup of tea first will you?"

North was delighted. The machinery of military bureaucracy had once more succeeded in allowing him temporary control over his officer. It was he, North, who now determined the actions of Captain Oscendale this day and he felt most satisfied with his exercise of power.

Closing his door behind him, Oscendale threw his cap onto his desk, knocking several neat piles of paper carefully assembled by North into a disorganised mess. *Good*, he thought, *that will give the man something to do while I am questioning another bloody Hun instead of investigating this case.* It appeared that, not for the first time, tension was rising between the MFP and the rest of the army. The army, it seemed, thought that it was time for more routine matters to interfere with Oscendale's investigation. Avate would allow him a free rein to bring the whole thing to a conclusion, he knew, but the army kept throwing obstacles in his path. He drew breath. Perhaps he was just being overly sensitive. The investigation would just have to wait for a short time whilst he undertook this chore.

Valère's words had shocked him. He knew of the delicacy of the moment, of the need to keep Anglo-French relations on an even keel, but even so, to hear the implications of such a desire so vehemently outlined by a provincial French policeman had been shocking. The veneer of justice was obviously very thin and his actions would now be hindered by factors beyond those of an ordinary murder investigation.

What also troubled him was what Valère would do next. Several times he had stated that he was looking for a local man as the murderer of Catherine Jaulard. So some poor local sod was to be tried for a murder he did not commit. And what was even more worrying was that if he were found guilty an innocent man would be executed. But was he innocent? Perhaps in some obtuse way Valère was right. Maybe Price did not kill Madame Jaulard. Maybe he was in the house just after the murder was committed. He could have come to the door as arranged, found it open, gone in and found her raped and murdered on the carpet of her living room. He could have panicked and hid, and then tried to bluff his way out of it. In which case the murderer was still at large. Valère would investigate it all very thoroughly, Oscendale had no doubt of that, and a man would be apprehended. If Valère did do his job properly then perhaps the right man would be caught. If not, well, the consequences were too terrible to contemplate.

There was a brief knock at the door and North entered with his mug of tea. "The prisoner is in a cell down on the ground floor corridor, sir. Will there be anything else?"

Yes, thought Oscendale, *solve this riddle of a case for me, you stupid man,* but said merely, "No thank you, North, that will be all." And North departed with an even crisper salute and Oscendale wondered momentarily who was ordering whom around today.

As Oscendale entered the room the German soldier stood to attention in an admirable display of Teutonic deference to a senior officer. Oscendale motioned the man to sit and opened the file on his side of the table. A guard stood stiffly to attention near the door and Oscendale wondered just how productive the next twenty minutes would be.

The man had been brought in from no-man's-land during the night, according to the hastily scribbled report. He had shown no resistance and was unable to speak English, so nothing of any value had been gleaned from him so far. He was a private in a Bavarian regiment and seemed delighted that he was off the front line and destined to see out the remainder of the war in a prisoner of war camp.

The German looked back at Oscendale with a blank, childlike countenance and seemed willing to help in any way he could. A small-town artisan perhaps, conscripted into the enormous German military machine, taken away from his wife and children and his routine of working life, thrown into military training and then the carnage of the Western Front. Now he was ready to throw in the towel, serve his time in the safety of a camp and be returned to his family, home and job when the war was over.

Oscendale studied his appearance. Dirty and unshaven, uniform covered with mud. Hadn't slept much recently. Probably his first time in the line. The terror of the artillery, the killing, it could all combine to break a man's resolve. Seemed fair enough to him. *Let's get it over with and back to the case.*

He began the series of standard questions he had used so often before and this time elicited only routine answers. The man had been in the German Army since 1915. Before the war he had been a carpenter. He had lost his enthusiasm as his friends began to die off and now he had had enough. He wanted to survive the war and return to his family as soon as the war was lost. No, he didn't know anything about any forthcoming attacks. No-one ever told men like him anything. They were just ordered to defend their positions to the last man and he was sick of it.

Congratulating himself on the accuracy of his suppositions, Oscendale closed his notepad. It seemed so routine that he decided to leave it there. The man had nothing to offer; it was a waste of his time and could have been conducted by any junior officer with a smattering of German.

He got up to go and the German stood stiffly to attention, a naïve look of gratitude across his face. *Nice end to the war in prospect for you, chum,* Oscendale thought, and Ziegler smiled back at him.

As the British officer left the room Ziegler sighed softly with relief. That had been the second hurdle overcome. The military policeman had not been difficult to fool and he was disappointed by the lack of challenge; he had thought the man would present a more worthy adversary. The steel grey hair and rugged face told of many months of active service and he had expected a more intense interrogation. It appeared not. It seemed the man was as stupid as other military policemen he had met on his own side of the line. No imagination. This might turn out to be easier than he had thought.

Lighting a cigarette, he began to ponder his next move.

CHAPTER 25

5th July 1916

THE PENCIL SCRATCHED on the paper and the form of an artillery gun emerged, its death-inducing barrel pointing defiance at the enemy. A short time later the figures of several attendant gunners had emerged from the clear white paper, their muscular torsos contrasting sharply with the cold steel of the gun they served.

Oscendale reflected on his drawing for a while. All this effort – the design and manufacture of the gun, its shipment to France, its testing and then its final alignment against the vulnerable human bodies who awaited death on the other side of no man's land. The sole purpose of the gunners – men from a variety of trades and backgrounds who now served – was to insert the shells that blew apart their fellow human beings who happened to speak a different language, or even in some cases the same.

Death came to everyone but it seemed indefensible to kill a man before his allotted time – but maybe this was their allotted time. Maybe this was the end of civilisation and they would all degenerate into a barbarous melee of killing until nothing of their former lives remained.

He sighed and opened the small wooden painting set that lay at his side. He deliberated then began the process of mixing his colours and applying them to the paper. The stark drawing took on a new life and substance at once, the greys, browns and greens lifting the image from the paper into something more lifelike and tinged with human emotion.

Moments like this were supposed to be his off-duty time, a break from the strains of his work, and this current case in particular. But the thoughts would not leave him alone and after some time he laid his pad to one side and retrieved a piece of bread from his pack.

The business of the war was all around him. NCOs barked orders at groups of men as gun teams rattled past. The smell of cooking pervaded the air and lines of chattering soldiers queued to eat while others unloaded endless piles of artillery shells from lorries that belched exhaust fumes into the air. He could have chosen any subject for his painting today but the gun crew, intent on their labour of siting their 18 pounder, had seemed to epitomise to him all that the war was and would be.

Price, or whoever he was, had rattled him. It was not just his tricky evasion of the questions he had put; he was well aware that with more time the man would slip up. It was the mention of Jack Parry that had disturbed him more than, hopefully, he had let on. He and Parry had been close, as close as any pair of officers working as an MFP team could be. When Parry had died it had affected Oscendale greatly but he thought he was over it. Apparently he was not.

He heard footsteps approaching and saw it was North. Sweating heavily, he climbed the mound on which Oscendale was sitting and arrived breathlessly at the top.

"Morning, sir. Thought you'd like to know. Lieutenant Price has gone."

"What do you mean 'gone'?" asked Oscendale in astonishment.

"Released half an hour ago, sir. Provost's orders."

Oscendale was confused. "What orders? Major Avate wouldn't order his release without consulting me."

"The orders were delivered by messenger, sir. All in order. I even phoned to check with the Provost's office."

Oscendale sprang to his feet. "This is ridiculous! Avate wouldn't order a suspected spy and murderer to be released."

"Nevertheless, sir, he's gone. Collected by two officers and driven away."

Frowning, Oscendale replied, "What regiment?"

"Sir?"

"What regiment were the men from?"

"Welsh Regiment, sir. Or at least they said they were. Had the badges, anyway."

Oscendale flung his paints and equipment into his pack and stormed away from the gun pit. The half-completed painting fluttered away on the breeze into the path of a soldier carrying a box of ammunition who trod it into the mud.

CHAPTER 26

5th July 1916

THE DOOR TO the office flew open and Avate looked up, startled, from the sheaves of paper he was reading at his desk. Oscendale burst in, red-faced and animated.

"Sir, why did you allow Lieutenant Price to be released?"

Avate looked at Oscendale with an almost fatherly patience.

"Because I have to obey orders, Captain Oscendale, the same as you have to."

"But Price is either a German spy or a murderer or even both. You and I know he's guilty and should be tried by a military court. Now he's wandering around behind our lines again ready to wreak more havoc."

"Have you considered the possibility that he's innocent?" Avate asked.

"Of course. But there's too much evidence in his behaviour to the contrary." Oscendale felt his anger ebbing as Avate's calm paternal manner began to have its desired effect. "How did his release come about anyway, sir?"

"A phone call this morning from HQ, followed by a written statement ordering his release an hour later."

"Who brought the order?"

"Two officers from his regiment. Took him this morning."

"And why wasn't I informed?"

"You were. I sent North to find out where you were. How was he to know you were off sketching again?"

Oscendale paused, his anger subsiding further. "It is supposed to be my day off, sir," he grumbled.

"Look. I was ordered to release him. For your information I think you're right. Price is a murderer, I agree, but someone, somewhere, wanted him released and I had to comply. He's gone and that's all there is to it. You'll have to start somewhere else. Was there anything in your interview with him that gave you any sort of a lead?"

Oscendale sat in a chair, the formality between the two of them now gone. "There was one thing. I'm pretty sure from something he said, a threat actually, that he's part of a bigger picture. Something much wider than just a sexually motivated murder. Someone didn't want him to talk to us and took him before anything leaked out. I realise there's no point in pursuing him. He's probably miles away by now. He certainly won't be sent back to his regiment, which would be far too obvious. I just wonder who he really was."

Avate nodded. "He's gone now. I don't think we'll see him again. This whole affair is growing and other people seem to be taking quite an interest in your murders. You believe they're connected and for what it's worth I think you're right. The question is, can you find a tenable link before someone cuts us out of it completely?"

Oscendale looked at Avate and said, "Someone is out to stop me solving this case but I'm damned if I'm going to let them. I still have other people to interview."

With that he rose and left the room, leaving Avate to his thoughts.

The French countryside sped past as the train made its way further south, past villages and fields. The door to the compartment opened and a railway official asked the collection of passengers spread around the seats for their tickets.

The British officer near the door reached into his pocket and removed his wallet. Extracting a small piece of coloured card he handed it to the ticket inspector.

"All the way to Marseilles, monsieur?" the man said. "A long journey, yes?"

The man smiled and retrieved his punched ticket. *A long journey? Yes, I'm on a long journey. But this is only the first leg.* His cover blown, it was time to move on.

A new assignment beckoned for him and he was grateful to be away from the variable weather of northern France. The sun of German East Africa was much more to his liking. He pulled his cap down over his face and began to doze.

CHAPTER 27

5th July 1916

PRIVATE JOHN EVANS was bored stiff. The prisoner he was meant to be guarding didn't speak any English and even if he had been allowed to converse with him he wouldn't have understood a bloody word.

He wasn't the slightest bit dangerous. Even he could see that. And it wasn't what he wanted to be doing anyway. His mates would be going into Albert tonight and here he was, standing in the corner of a stuffy room watching a cowardly German who'd given himself up playing with a matchbox and lighting endless cigarettes.

As a non-smoker himself he found the smell disgusting. His mind wandered off to the laughs he'd had with his new mates in the company. Great bunch of lads they were. He decided that he was enjoying the military life now that he was here in France. It wasn't half as bad as he'd been led to believe.

What was Fritz up to now? The German seemed to be having trouble lighting a match, breaking several of them in quick succession as he endeavoured to light yet another cigarette. God, wasn't the room full of enough smoke? Couldn't the man just suck that in instead? Even he felt a bit giddy with it all.

Evans decided the idiot needed assistance so he shouldered his rifle and walked over to the table. He was stunned by how quickly the man moved. So stunned in fact that he never saw the final blow to his throat that ended his young life.

Ziegler caught Evans's body as it fell and lowered it slowly to the ground. Pausing to ensure the young soldier's final gasp had not aroused the suspicion of anyone outside the door, he quickly began to unbutton his own tunic.

Within a few minutes the scene inside the interrogation room was restored to one of normality. A British soldier stood guard in a corner and a German prisoner sat slumped forward on the table, his head resting on his arms, to all intents and purposes asleep, with his face turned away from the door.

After about thirty minutes Evans's relief arrived and, passing a brief comment about the prisoner's apparent lack of stamina, Ziegler exchanged places with the new man and strolled out into the corridor.

He walked up the nearest flight of stairs and soon found the door he was looking for – marked 'MFP'. He drew the 1907 pattern Sanderson bayonet from its scabbard at his side and thrust it between the door frame and the door, twisting it until the wood splintered and the door swung free.

Darting inside, he used a typewriter to hold the door closed and began a search of the filing cabinets that stood along one wall. On the third one he found a drawer marked 'Deaths' and again used the bayonet to good effect to prise open the drawer. The lock snapped with a loud 'click' and he froze as voices could be heard coming along the corridor at the same time, but they passed without so much as a glance at the damaged door and he sighed with relief before continuing his task.

He pulled out the drawer and began thumbing along the line of tabs that marked each file. Alighting on 'V' he soon found the file belonging to William Vincent.

Scanning the pages within, he came across the name of the man he had been seeking – Captain Thomas Oscendale. Ziegler grimaced. So it had been the very man who had conducted such a perfunctory interview of him earlier that day. Life was full of strange coincidences. Good. The man had struck him as neither astute nor thorough. This mission should be one of the easiest he had yet undertaken.

He noticed another door leading off from the room and decided to see what lay inside. Ziegler pressed softly on the door handle and shook his head as it gave way. The lack of security of the English amazed him. It had been so simple to dispose of the guard and make his way out of the interrogation room. Still the alarm had not been raised and now he found that the door to Oscendale's office was unlocked.

He stepped inside and quickly closed the door behind him. Letting his eyes grow accustomed to the darkness inside the room, he saw the hunched figure of a sleeping man in a chair and swiftly skirted around him to the table at the far side of the room. Sifting silently through the objects on it he found nothing of interest.

To the side of the table was a wooden chair and on it hung Oscendale's uniform jacket. Checking the sleeper once more, he began to search the pockets and smiled with satisfaction as his fingers encountered a piece of paper in the inside pocket. He placed it in his own tunic pocket and began to step towards the door. He stopped as a thought struck him. To dispose of this inept policeman would give his masters a further advantage in the race to discover what was buried in Mametz Wood, but he thought of the man's laxness in questioning him and decided he was not a formidable enemy – and besides, Otto Ziegler did not kill sleeping men. No, this man would not present a threat to his mission.

Leaving Oscendale slumbering, he left the room as quietly as he had arrived.

CHAPTER 28

5th July 1916

THE GUARD BEGAN to grow suspicious after about an hour. Never the quickest of soldiers, it was this quality that had made Private Rhys Bibbey an ideal candidate for the monotonous duty of standing guard over a prisoner. However, even his lethargy was stirred when he noticed that the German prisoner had neither stirred nor made a sound in all the time he had been guarding him.

Still, he knew that Huns were cunning and dangerous animals so, taking his rifle from his shoulder, he fixed his bayonet and advanced carefully towards the sleeping figure. *Just let him try anything,* he thought, *and I'll run him through. That'll sound good to my mates. Killed an escaping Hun, I did. Probably get a medal and all.*

"Oi, Fritz, you all right?" he asked loudly. The figure remained immobile and silent. "Oi, wake up," Bibbey ordered, prodding the man with his bayonet. *Mmmmm, trying to play possum eh? Right!* And with that Bibbey poked the tip of his bayonet hard into the man's side.

He stood dumbfounded in horror as the body rolled off the chair onto the floor and Private Jack Evans stared up at him through glassy eyes.

"Sir! Sir! The bastard's legged it!"

The voice cut deeply into his dream and he struggled to fight his way to the surface of sleep while endeavouring to rise from the chair. Rubbing his eyes, he was conscious that his heart was thumping in his chest and the words that were being spoken to him were flowing in and out of his mind like darting fish.

"... gone, sir. Killed Evans, sir. Now he's on the loose."

The speaker was a wide-eyed private who looked to Oscendale for immediate orders on how to deal with this crisis. Oscendale was acutely aware that he had been in a deep sleep and tried to focus his mind and body on the catastrophe presented to him.

He stretched his legs, endeavouring to relieve the pins and needles he now felt from having fallen asleep in the chair instead of going back to his room. "Right," he said, coming to at last, "slow down, private, and tell me what happened."

He noticed it was still dark in the room and wondered how long he had been asleep.

The young soldier swallowed hard and said. "The prisoner, sir, the Hun, he's killed Private Evans and escaped. Don't know where he is, sir. Broke Evans's neck, waited for the relief and then was gone. He could be anywhere. And he's got Evans's rifle, sir."

Oscendale knew at once that he had made a serious mistake. Even the brief details of the escape, as gasped by the young private, alerted him to the fact that this man had fooled him. Damn! This was no war-shy conscript. This man was of a far more dangerous ilk. And now he was loose behind British lines armed with a rifle.

As his head cleared more thoughts entered it and he began speculating, not too wildly, he hoped, as to the man's motives. He could go on a killing spree before he was eventually cornered and shot. Unlikely. If he had wanted to randomly kill British soldiers he would have opened fire by now. The longer he spent behind British lines the more likely it was that he would be exposed and caught. A spy? More likely. In a British uniform he could blend in for several days, gathering information on the latest attack plans. But how would he send that information back? And what was he after? Soldiers' gossip? Documents? Maps? A map!

The thought struck him like a hammer and he reached for his tunic still hanging on the back of a chair where he had left it earlier. His fingers groped for the map and met nothing but the lining of the pocket. He searched the other pockets, hoping he had been wrong in remembering which one he had placed it in. Still nothing. *My God*, he thought, *he was here in my room. Armed with a rifle and a bayonet, too.* He exhaled a sigh of relief and a cold wave of dread swept over him as he realised how close he had come to being killed as well. Perhaps his inept performance in the interview room had saved his life. Another thick copper, not worth killing, especially in his sleep.

The map was gone but he had studied the map long and often enough to be able to recall most of the details and would have no real difficulty producing an approximate copy. He was less sure of the positions of all of the paths through the wood but was certain that, given the opportunity, he could find his way to the spot marked on the original map. Resisting the temptation to begin an immediate pursuit of the escaped prisoner, he told the panic-stricken soldier to tell Sergeant North to put together a guard detail to search the surrounding area and then went to his desk and began drawing the map from memory.

After he had finished he sat back and contemplated his error in not sensing that the captured German was anything but a frightened, war-weary conscript who wanted to see out the rest of the war in safety. The man had been an excellent actor, yes, and had duped several other men besides Oscendale, but as a trained policeman he should have conducted the interview with more rigour and thoroughness and should not have allowed the intricacies of this case to distract him from routine business. He made a half-hearted excuse to himself that he had been overtired and was still suffering pain from his arm wound and had therefore not focused on the job in hand. However, he knew that this was a lame response. Because of his sloppiness a man was dead, a trained killer was loose behind British lines and he was in danger of losing whatever was to be found at the location marked on the map. Perhaps the time for puzzle solving was now over. Perhaps what was required now was some more positive action.

Ziegler heard the commotion begin but by then he was well clear of the compound and was making his way along the road to the front line in the company of hundreds of other troops. His perfect English ensured that he fitted in well and was soon laughing at the soldiers' jokes, contributing several of his own and even joining in with the songs the Tommies sang.

CHAPTER 29

6th July 1916

THE LANE AT the rear of Number 14, Rue St Juliette was quiet. Its only inhabitant was a tabby cat that stared demonically at Oscendale as he crept past. He stopped outside a back gate with the number 14 on it and climbed swiftly over the wall before dropping down into the late Madame Jaulard's garden. His face blackened against the scrutiny of the half moon, he crept along the path until he reached the kitchen door. Cautiously he depressed the lever but found it held fast. It was as he expected. Inspector Valère didn't strike him as the sort of policeman to leave a murder scene open to all and sundry.

He turned his attention to the downstairs windows. Finding they too were all locked, he chose a window that looked more weather-beaten than the rest. Reaching into his pocket he brought out a thin steel blade. This he placed in the gap between the bottom of the window and the frame. Pushing downward, he felt the window give a satisfying jolt as the ancient, rusted lock snapped. He paused for a moment to ascertain that the slight click had not alerted any of the neighbours to his presence, then lifted the window until it was open sufficiently wide for him to climb into the house.

The room was cool and dark. He let his eyes adjust to the gloom and then made his way to the front door. He listened and could hear the occasional cough from the sole gendarme placed outside in the street. The man must have drawn the short straw, standing outside an empty house all night.

He moved back into the front parlour and began his search.

Fortunately the curtains were closed so he was able to risk a pencil beam from his military torch. He then worked his way through the other downstairs rooms but half an hour later had found nothing more than the minutiae of the dead woman's life – an assortment of keepsakes and bills.

Oscendale sighed. This might be more difficult than he had imagined. He thought for a while and then made his way quietly upstairs to Catherine Jaulard's bedroom.

A brass bed stood in the centre of the room, flanked by a tall wardrobe and a chest of drawers. He began with the drawers, sifting through their contents. Still nothing. He was not even sure what he was looking for, but he instinctively knew he would find something connecting her with William Vincent.

Finally, he lifted the mattress and heard a faint tap as an item dropped to the floor beneath the bed. He bent down and shone his torch on a brown envelope that had fallen there. He froze as he heard a noise downstairs. The front door was opening and a voice called out in French. *Damn*, thought Oscendale, the gendarme must have seen a beam of light. He was certain that he hadn't made any noises that could be heard outside.

He waited at the top of the stairs while the man searched the three rooms downstairs, then padded quietly down the stairs and into the front room as the man made his way into the kitchen.

After a short while the gendarme emerged from the kitchen and began a cautious climb of the stairs. When he turned into one of the bedrooms, Oscendale ducked into the parlour and out of the unlocked window, pausing only to check that the envelope was still safely tucked into his pocket.

Back in his billet, Oscendale sipped a cup of coffee as he read the letter he had found in the envelope under Catherine Jaulard's mattress.

My Darling,

I am writing this letter to put you straight on some things about me and my life.

Since I met you my life has changed. I see now what I've been missing all these years and I know you could feel the same about me.

When this lousy war is over I'll come back for you and we can spend the rest of our lives together. We can live anywhere you want. With what I'll have by then you won't need to worry about making ends meet ever again.

Say you'll be mine and I'll show you wealth beyond your wildest dreams.

All my love,

Bill.

X

Oscendale leaned back in his chair. So there was more going on between Catherine Jaulard and William Vincent than anyone suspected. Or was there? He read the crudely-composed letter again. *I know you could feel the same about me.* There was nothing in it that indicated that she had returned his affection. Perhaps his adoration was one-sided. Maybe she had just taken pity on a lonely British soldier far from home and her attentions had been misconstrued.

And then there was the mysterious reference to, 'wealth beyond your wildest dreams'. At the end of the war, whenever that was, Vincent would be no better off on a soldier's pay than when he enlisted. He had a wife and children at home to support as well. Was he envisaging abandoning them and bigamously marrying Catherine Jaulard? But then why had he hinted at wealth to come to his wife back in Swansea? A backup plan in case Madame Jaulard refused his attentions?

There was no doubt that Vincent had access to, or knew about anyway, a source of great wealth that he was keeping a close secret. Where was this huge sum of money he was promising his new love to come from? As a serviceman in France he had only limited access to travel. It was either at home in Swansea or here on the Somme.

The former was unlikely. If Mrs Vincent had access to any means of escape from the drudgery of her life she would no doubt have taken it. And he had seen the evidence of that. Yet Vincent's son's responses had hinted that the family was aware of some potential change in their circumstances. Perhaps Vincent could not contain his excitement and had written to tell them of his plans, hoping really to abandon his family and set up a new life with an attractive French widow.

And now Vincent was dead. If he had the money close to him it would have been disclosed by now. That led Oscendale to believe that it still lay undiscovered somewhere. But where? It had to be here on the Somme. But how could he have come by such knowledge? After all it was not the sort of thing a serving soldier would stumble across. He had also kept it secret from his fellow soldiers. Or was this the secret that Jackson and Howells had uncovered? If so they would have taken the money for themselves. If they were evil enough to blackmail and bully Vincent then they were no doubt capable of taking the money. But that hadn't happened.

And Catherine Jaulard was dead, probably killed by the mysterious Lieutenant Price, who in Oscendale's judgement was anything but a British subaltern. He had, it seems, discovered the relationship between Vincent and the owner of the local *boulangerie*, made an early morning appointment to visit her – how Oscendale was not sure – at a time when there would be no-one around to see him come and go, and had pressed her for any information regarding William Vincent. To her credit she had evidently refused to co-operate and had been murdered for failing to disclose the letter hidden under her mattress. The letter hidden by a flattered widow from the prying eyes of her house cleaner.

As she fell dying from a silent stab wound, no doubt with one of Price's evil hands clamped to her mouth to prevent her screaming in pain, she had torn one of his buttons from his overcoat. At the end of the day the letter told Oscendale, or Price, nothing more about the location of Vincent's mysterious potential wealth. And a decent, respectable young widow was dead.

CHAPTER 30

6th July 1916

THROUGHOUT THE DAY preparations continued for the attack planned for the 7th July. Opposing Harold Bratton and the rest of the 38th (Welsh) Division were units of the German 3rd Guards Division and the 28th Reserve Division. To evict these men from Mametz Wood a two-pronged attack was planned to begin at 8.00 a.m. on the morning of the seventh. The 17th (Northern Division) would attack from the west and the 38th Division would attack the eastern part of the wood now officially designated as the 'Hammerhead', owing to its shape. Once they were in the wood they were to advance to the central path or *ride* before proceeding northwards and southwards to clear the wood of the enemy.

As a preliminary, 17th Division was to attack trenches to the west of the wood under cover of darkness in the early hours of the 7th July. An intensive artillery bombardment would precede it.

Bratton slept little during the night. Neither did his companions. If this was to be his last night on earth he was not going to waste it by sleeping. There would be time for that either way in the future. All around him men passed the short hours of darkness in preparation for the attack. Sergeant Williams came down the trench and reminded the men to fill out their wills in the back of their soldier's 'small books' – a less than comforting thought.

The other men of the Welsh Regiment spent the night in the variety of ways that reflect the diversity of characters amongst human beings. Some found their solace in sleep –

and even within this category there were variations. Some men slept the sleep of the dead, some stirred fitfully and found themselves waking with cramp or a disturbance from nearby chatter or an item or a limb striking them in error. Some wrote letters home, some talked quietly over oily cups of tea, anything to spin out the hours or to shorten them, depending on a man's character and beliefs. Some prayed and some ruminated over their past lives. Either way, Bratton thought, there was no holding back the dawn and he chose to sit alone, detached from the others, both mentally and physically.

They commented on his aloofness, of course. He had to endure the jibes and the enquiries, but he knew it was meant to be this way. Besides, some of these men would die the next morning and he wasn't going to be one of them. After cleaning his rifle and bayonet, he checked his other equipment once more, and then rechecked it. When he was satisfied that all was as it should be, he smoked, inhaling deeply the calming fumes, and planned his future.

And all the time came the shriek and thudding, ground-shuddering explosions of shells bursting over and into the far side of Mametz Wood. The attack by 17th Division was underway. At times he briefly joined the others on the fire step, knowing he was safer than usual from enemy fire. The Germans would be cowering in their dugouts and trenches while all hell broke loose around them. He heard some men express sympathy for the plight of the Germans, knowing that each shell was bringing them death, but he felt differently. *Let the bastards suffer*; they were in his wood and he didn't care if every one of them became a bloody corpse by the morning.

CHAPTER 31

6th July 1916

"OH, I CAN get you into the wood okay, Oscendale. Your problem will be getting out again. When the Huns realise what we're up to they'll move more men to the edge of the wood and you'll have the devil's own job finding a big enough gap in their lines to get out again." Captain James Hill of the Welsh Regiment shook his head at the insanity of the plan he had just heard. Why anyone would want to enter Mametz Wood for reconnaissance purposes at this stage of the battle was beyond him. The flyboys had taken dozens of photographs and the German trench systems and blockhouses were well known. Knowing where they were of course didn't make them any easier to take.

"If you can get me into the wood I'll take my chances on getting back out again. I need to know what's in there." Even as he spoke the words Oscendale questioned his own sanity. Why didn't he just wait until the wood was taken? He could then explore the place in safety. But he knew that victory in this dreadful battle was by no means certain and he still harboured a vague feeling that he was in a race against an unseen enemy.

Eventually Hill sighed. "Righto. Then we'd better do it tonight. Any longer and we don't know what extra reinforcements Fritz will throw into the line. I'll contact the artillery boys to give us a gap in the bombardment. They won't like it but I'll tell them we have a special show going on for a while. We'll make it 1.30 a.m. Suit you?"

"Thank you, Hill," replied Oscendale and left to make his preparations.

The trench raiding party were a grim-looking lot and reminded him of the clientele in the Barry Dock Hotel on a Saturday night. 'The Chain Locker', as it was known the world over, was a docks pub *par excellence* and Oscendale smiled as he recalled the times he and his men had been called to break up fights between drunken sailors or dock workers, and once to take statements when an argument had gone too far and left a young Greek sailor dead on the pavement outside.

There were six of them. Each had a khaki balaclava over his head and his face smeared with oil and dirt. They wore dark grey woollen gloves and had discarded their tunics in favour of brown jumpers. They carried rifles and bags of Mills bombs and each had either a short knife or medieval-looking trench club with a studded end inserted into his belt.

The officer in charge introduced himself as Lieutenant James and the other men's names followed in quick succession, but Oscendale was too nervous to remember them all for more than a few seconds. Suddenly the devilish noise of the artillery bombardment ceased and an anxious minute passed in silence until at last James motioned that it was time to go. One by one the men scrambled up the wall of the trench and flopped over the parapet into the uncertainty of no-man's-land. Oscendale followed and noted that the men lay still at first while awaiting any response to their movements. Then began the terrifying belly crawl across to the German lines.

Moving from shell hole to shell hole across the floor of the valley to Mametz Wood, Oscendale marvelled at the qualities of these men. They seemed to know just when to move and when to freeze as if by instinct, but he knew that they were the veterans of several such raids and he cursed his selfishness in risking the lives of good men such as these for what could turn out to be a fool's errand.

After what seemed like forever the party halted, each man hugging the earth as he lay still. German voices floated on the night air and Oscendale wondered how close they were. Twenty yards? Fifty? With a shock he saw James dive forward and disappear, closely followed by his men. He realised that they were already upon the German trenches at the edge of the wood and he followed suit, falling rather than climbing into the enemy positions.

Immediately a German leapt on him, crushing him with his weight but Oscendale lashed out with his trench knife and the man screamed as the blade cut across his face. Without hesitation Oscendale plunged home the knife into the man's throat and saw his eyes roll backwards in a sea of blood.

All around him the fight was going on. He saw one of the men shoot two Germans with what looked like a sawn-off shotgun, whilst another began systematically hurling bombs along the trench to prevent other men reinforcing their comrades. James was rolling on the floor of the trench with a German, both men seeking a death grip, whilst another man calmly rolled bombs into the entrance of a dugout.

Oscendale was transfixed by the slaughter but knew his place was not here. He leapt out of the back of the trench and began a crouched run deeper into the wood. He had not gone fifty yards through the undergrowth before he ran into a German sentry on the end of a Mauser rifle, the wicked-looking bayonet inches from his chest. The man's eyes looked quizzically at him and then the expression became more distant as a red pool suddenly appeared in his left eye socket and he fell backwards onto the damp earth of the wood.

A figure appeared at Oscendale's side and he recognised one of the men from the raiding party. He felt foolish for not recalling the name of the man who had just saved his life but the man saw this and said, "Corporal Loram, sir. Captain Hill told me you might need some company and if a sniper is any use to you I'll tag along. Should be interesting." The man smiled grimly and Oscendale knew he was in the presence of a professional killer, a man who had probably silently dispatched many Germans.

"Thank you, corporal," he sighed with relief. He realised that he had been too optimistic in his capabilities and having this man alongside him was essential. But for Loram he would already be dead.

"Probably best not to hang around here for too long, sir," said Loram as they both heard the sound of approaching German voices. Oscendale nodded in agreement and without another word the two of them plunged deeper into the undergrowth.

The paths through the wood had all but disappeared as a result of artillery fire but Oscendale had his army compass and used the light of the moon to check his aerial photographs of the German positions. After some minutes they came to a clearing in the wood. Oscendale thought hard and he dared not use a light to consult his map again as they were now deep within the German defensive system. The moon had disappeared behind some clouds.

The blackness of the night exacerbated the evil aura of the wood. Shapes moved like spectres in the undergrowth. Taking advantage of the lull in the British bombardment, the Germans sought to reinforce their lines, adding to the arsenal of weapons already and in place for the coming attack. The wind blew and the old wood groaned in despair. Leaves rustled and fell and branches moved and creaked. Leaves hissed with venom as the intruders dug deeper into its heart and refused to leave.

The two men froze as they heard movement in the bushes close to their right. The heavy tread of military boots indicated the presence of several of the enemy. They dropped to the ground and lay still. Minutes passed. When he was certain that they had not been spotted, Oscendale gestured to Loram that he was moving forward. Loram nodded, his eyes sweeping left and right for any other danger.

Oscendale crawled gingerly towards the remnants of a clump of bushes and peered cautiously through them. A group of German pioneers were standing in and around a large hole in the ground. They were leaning on their shovels and picks, obviously taking a breather. One or two were smoking, while others discussed their work. Oscendale was surprised to find them here ahead of him. Were they excavating the foundations of yet another bunker or were they digging with a less militaristic purpose?

He and Loram watched the Germans for some time but it was obvious from the body language and the pieces of conversation that Oscendale managed to pick up that they had found nothing of interest so far.

At last a large piece of tree root was hurled from the site by a clearly frustrated pioneer and a squat German officer signalled that the dig was over. He folded his arms and turned away, clearly annoyed at the lack of progress. The pioneers began to pack away their equipment and within a few minutes all had left the scene apart from a solitary soldier who stood guard.

Oscendale chewed his lower lip until his companion whispered, "Is that it, sir? Is that why we came?" Loram was an experienced soldier but even he could see no point in continuing to watch a hole in the ground.

"Mmmm," murmured Oscendale. "It seems that someone

has been here before us. Time to go home, Corporal Loram, if you please, before the artillery starts up again."

"Delighted to obey that order, sir," said Loram, the relief audible in his voice.

CHAPTER 32

7th July 1916

THE NIGHT PASSED and at last streaks of yellow began to slash the sky behind the wood and the trees that had survived the carnage became more focused silhouettes against the dawn sky. Gradually the streaks opened like a huge demonic mouth and burned red and gold, setting the wood ablaze with colour. When the sun rose fully Bratton ventured a peep over the top of the trench, shocked at the view. The previous day's scene had changed. Where the valley had once been green grass lay a blasted wasteland. Where the trees had stood vibrant, there now stood hundreds of stumps of blackened wood. He wondered how anyone could survive a hell of such intensity and a wave of pity overcame him. He could only imagine the horror that would confront him and his pals when they walked across the valley and entered the wood.

The shellfire still continued but he was not willing to risk a sniper's bullet for much longer and dropped down into the trench to make his own final personal preparations for the attack. A few minutes later he stood in line and was issued with his rum ration. The fiery liquid burned his throat but washed through his veins with the feeling of hot bath water and he felt its immediate potent effect. He watched as the others stood nervously by, fiddling with straps and fidgeting with rifles, each man preparing himself mentally in his own way.

At 8.15 a.m. Major John Lee jabbed angrily at the cradle rest for the telephone which hung lifelessly in his hands. The barrage was going well and the wood was being torn to shreds, but there was still no sign of the smokescreen which would hide his men from the few Germans still alive in the wood.

At 8.30 a.m. the artillery barrage stopped and the order came to 'stand to'. Bratton and his fellow soldiers stood on the fire step of the trench. His heart beat furiously and his palms oozed sweat onto the stock of his rifle as they waited in silence for the order to go over the top. Someone cracked a joke further along the trench and was rewarded with a ripple of nervous laughter.

At 8.30 a.m. whistles blew and orders were yelled out. Bratton climbed the wooden ladder to the top of the parapet and levered himself out of the trench. To his left and right hundreds of men did the same and he was filled with a surge of euphoria as the intensity of the moment hit him. The great mass of khaki streamed forward. This was it, the end of the war. On to Berlin! The bloody *Boche* were all dead and he would soon be standing in the green fields beyond. A couple of weeks and he'd be back home in the pub telling stories of this great day to the accompaniment of beer and approval.

Then it started. An insect-like chatter began to his right and all around him men began to fall. A machine gun! *One of the sods was still alive.* He suddenly felt very alone and a wave of panic replaced the euphoria. What now? Was someone brave enough to advance towards it and kill the man?

He had no idea where the stream of death was coming from. He was about 300 yards from the edge of the wood and realised that he was unlikely to reach it safely. All around him soldiers who had not been hit were endeavouring to take cover.

Bratton threw himself to the ground, his heavy pack ensuring that his head hit the earth with a thump. He pulled his entrenching tool from his webbing, assembled it and began to dig. The field was full of furrows but the nearest shell hole was still some thirty yards away. The fire was coming from his right. *Okay, dig quickly and get behind a bank of earth.*

Suddenly a man hit the ground to his side and rolled near him. Bulbous eyes stared into his and blood began seeping from the man's lips. Bratton stared back in horror. Then the corpse jerked and twitched as more machine gun bullets ripped into the dead flesh. Quickly, Bratton turned the dead man onto his side and took cover up against him. The body's warmth comforted him and, bizarrely, he wondered who the man had been and if he had ever spoken with him. Then he spurred himself into action once more and continued to dig furiously.

Miraculously he had still not been hit and within a few minutes he had shovelled a mound of earth between him and the machine gun fire. He lay behind it and the corpse, made himself as small as possible and tried to think.

He looked back and saw some of the wounded trying to make their way back to the ridge. The German machine gunner refused to let them all escape and many were cut down until only the crawling ones remained, pathetically seeking the sanctuary of their own trenches, even as their lives ebbed away.

More machine gun fire had opened up in front of him and he saw the foolhardy or the brave who had kept advancing being cut down ahead of him. They died in a variety of ways, some fell lifeless, forwards or backwards, while others were torn apart as a series of bullets hit them, pieces of flesh flying off in all directions, their lives being scattered to the four winds.

Most desperate of all were the wounded, men who tumbled, half dead and half alive, to the earth. Their screams rang out above the havoc and the shrieks of men calling for their mothers assaulted his ears. He clasped his hands to his head and tried to shut out the noise. It was unendurable. Couldn't they have the good grace to die quietly? Then he pictured the faces, men who had been kind to him during his time in khaki. The word of advice during training, the cigarette offered to an anxious young man when he first saw the front line and the other voice in his head called out to him for compassion.

Again he tried to think. There would be no way into the wood today. He had to live, had to get out of here before he too was killed. This was supposed to be so easy, so straightforward. The barrage had cleared the way and he would enter the wood and retrieve the package. But it was all turning into a nightmare and fear started to take over his mind.

He slapped his face with his hand. *Right, if I lie here I'm going to die, so let's get the hell out of here,* he decided and lifted his head. To his left was a shell hole. If he could make it there he might have a chance. At least he'd be away from this machine gun fire. So he sprang to his feet and began to run.

CHAPTER 33

7th July 1916

THE MAN HE knew so well across the shell hole was shivering with fright, overcome by the terror of the events of the past few minutes. Bratton looked away, upset at seeing someone he cared about reduced to a state of near collapse. Overhead the woodpecker sound of machine gun bullets whizzed past on their way to their appointment with a human being. Another shell burst nearby and a piece of human flesh flew through the air and landed in the pool of water at his feet, sinking slowly into the ooze.

He turned away, revolted. Any second now and it would be his turn. A blinding flash, then oblivion. He wondered how many pieces his head would shatter into as the shrapnel flew into it. The other men around him were looking anxiously at the rim of the crater. Bratton couldn't imagine what difference it made. If a shell was on its way, how could they stop it?

But instead of a shell came figures. The Germans burst over the lip of the crater and leapt screaming into the hole. One of the British soldiers thrust his bayonet forwards but too late. Bratton saw the look of terror on the man's face as the German rammed his sawback bayonet into his chest. Blood gushed from his mouth and he fell backwards before beginning a slow slide into the water that filled the base of the hole.

Bratton lay paralysed with fright. None of the Germans had turned their attention on him yet; they were too busy bayoneting the other men around him, but it would happen soon, he knew.

A jet of fire burst across the crater and the man across the shell hole screamed. Bratton turned to see him ablaze. Flames licked his body yet still he moved, contorting in his agony. The fire came again, passing over his own head and another burning figure fell forwards into the hole.

Terror overcame him again and he covered his eyes with his hands like a child. Then a draft of hot air took his breath away. He gasped for breath and assumed that he too was now alight, his flesh roasting before his eyes. But he felt no pain. This was death then: painless and serene.

Then suddenly rifles began to crackle from behind him and the Germans started to fall.

"Come on, son. Let's get out of here!" shouted a voice and hands grabbed him and pulled him up the side of the crater to the rim, where he lay crying with fright, unable to move. Someone kicked him in the thigh.

"Get up! Bloody get up or you're going to die!" The gruffness of the man's voice forced him to open his eyes. Sergeant Williams was on one knee alongside him, firing his rifle in a desperate attempt to hold the Germans back.

All around him khaki-clad soldiers were falling back towards the British lines. The attack had failed, he realised. It was over. He looked up at the sergeant who had rescued him, delivered him from all this evil, just in time to see Williams's legs and torso being blown in different directions. The shell burst set Bratton's ears ringing: a prolonged monotonous scream.

He forced himself to his feet, his chest wracked by sobs. *It was madness, all bloody madness.* But in the madness a thought came to him as clear as day. Without a second thought he made it happen, then, appalled by what he'd done, he lurched forwards towards the trench from which he had emerged a lifetime ago. *Please, God, let me live,* he prayed. *Let me get into the trench.* More bullets flew past him and in front of him men continued to fall. Just a few more yards and he would be safe.

Then darkness and he knew no more.

Major Ronald Lee watched in horror as his men were cut down in front of his eyes. Calling the company runner to him, he scribbled a note, his hands shaking with a mix of excitement and terror.

"Here, take this quickly, Dawkins. Take it to the artillery observation officer at point 63. Tell him we need an artillery barrage now! Quickly! The men are getting cut to pieces out there!" His voice broke as he screamed the command in the man's ear, the deafening noise of machine gun fire making it difficult for him to be understood.

Dawkins nodded and was off like a shot, scampering out of the trench, over the parados and off into the distance. Lee watched him go and then turned his field glasses back to the unfolding carnage on the battlefield.

Men lay scattered all across the valley floor, but whether they were dead or alive was hard to tell. A wounded man would often lie still in no-man's-land so as not to attract any more enemy fire. Some men struggled gamely onwards until they too fell writhing or still on the ground. Lee's blood boiled within him. The artillery had evidently not done their job; the Germans were still encamped in the wood, very much alive, and now wreaking havoc on men he had trained for many months. He watched impotently until he heard the first welcome whine of an artillery shell, closely followed by dozens more.

His relief soon changed to despair as he tracked the fall of shot. Instead of bursting amongst the machine gun positions and tearing them apart, the shells began falling on and amongst his men, blowing pieces of them into the air. Limbs flew in all directions and showers of earth fell like the end of the world onto the soldiers cowering beneath.

Within minutes he had despatched another runner and some time later the firing stopped, too late to save over 400 casualties among the Welsh battalions. Lee's fury knew no bounds as he surveyed the remnants of his force, now crawling back across the valley.

Soon shell-shocked men began dropping into the trench all around him, their faces gaunt with the shock of battle. Some jumped in, some tumbled in clutching blood- soaked wounds. Lee ordered medical staff to attend to them but the order was redundant. They could see what had happened and reacted swiftly. Similarly, stretcher-bearers leapt out of the trench and began their hazardous task of retrieving the badly wounded from the battlefield, the German machine gunners making no allowance for their Red Cross armbands.

By evening heavy rain was falling, soaking the living and the dead. The soldiers in the trenches covered themselves as best they could and prepared to wait it out. To the wounded lying too close to the enemy lines to be rescued, the rain brought much-needed drinking water to slake their thirst. On the dead the rain fell unheeded, coursing off glassy eyes down marble cheeks to mingle with the blood and mud below.

CHAPTER 34

7th July 1916

OSCENDALE MUSED THAT life consisted not of holding good cards, but of playing well those one held. Something had driven Corporal Vincent to commit a most heinous crime – that of the cold-blooded murder of two of his fellow soldiers. It was also a cowardly crime. Shooting two men whilst they were unable to resist was the act of a coward under normal circumstances. But these were not normal times and from what he had heard of William Vincent he was no coward. That much he was sure of. But besides that what else did he have to go on?

Of previously unblemished character, Vincent had been up on a charge last month at the behest of Jackson and Howells and had been reduced to the rank of corporal. The charge had been neglect of duties and being under the influence of alcohol. Most soldiers drank, Oscendale knew. They always had, but why would Vincent risk his rank by drinking and being absent from duty? He had evidently been in a theatre of war before and had seen the horror that the actors perpetrated, so this must have been different.

Oscendale leant back in his chair and replayed the final moments of Vincent's life in his mind. He had spent some time carving the instrument of his own destruction, the piece of wood, and had done it publicly, as if he wanted to show others what he was planning. He had chosen a particular night to carry out the murder and knew he had no hope of escape. He had then deliberately run up to the sentry and killed himself in front of him. But why? To traumatise him? Revenge? If he had wanted to escape surely he would have shot the sentry and not carved the piece of wood in order to reach the trigger to shoot himself.

He needed to talk to the last man to have seen Vincent alive. They had known each other for some time so Vincent must have had a particular reason for not killing him and instead turning the rifle on himself. There must be more behind the bland statements arranged so neatly in the Court of Enquiry file. Lifting the telephone receiver, he spoke briefly to North and sat back to await the results of his enquiries. In the meantime he passed the minutes by checking over the latest plans for traffic control and the reports from the gathering posts behind the lines.

Thirty minutes later his door opened and his bumptious sergeant stood in front of his desk.

"Bad luck, sir," said North with a deadpan expression.

"Sorry?" said Oscendale. "What do you mean bad luck?"

"It's the witness to Vincent's suicide, sir. Private Bratton. He's been killed in the fighting at Mametz Wood."

Damn! Thought Oscendale, but said nothing at first. His leads were closing up around him. *Probably very conveniently for someone too,* he mused.

"How did it happen, do we know?"

"The first casualty reports have just come in, sir. Shell did for him, they think. No sign of him when the battalion returned to the trenches. Couple of his mates reported seeing a shell burst near him and he wasn't seen again. Like I say, bad luck, sir."

Oscendale looked at North and saw no sign of regret. It was understandable of course. No witness, no dispute, no investigation. Murder brought on by shell-shock, followed by the convenient suicide of the murderer. Case closed. Next please.

"All the same, I think I'll go up the line to talk to his mates to see if he said anything before he was killed. Get me a lift please, North."

Oscendale thought he detected a sigh as North turned and left the room.

So Bratton was dead. Another young man killed and certain not to be the last. Luck played its part, of course. A shell bursting near a soldier could kill everyone around him whilst leaving the man in the centre of the blast completely untouched. Oscendale had heard many examples of lucky escapes for himself. Over a few drinks, soldiers in *estaminets* would show each other lucky charms they carried and regale each other with tales of how they had saved their lives. The fortunate few would hold up pocket books, Bibles with bullet holes drilled deeply into them where a German bullet had penetrated so far and then been stopped by divine providence or British materialism. Dented Princess Mary tins that had been issued to all soldiers for the first Christmas of the war also made regular appearances. It really was a matter of fate. You would still hold your helmet tight to your head when enemy shells starting falling on your trench, though. And as someone once remarked, there weren't many atheists in a trench.

Still this did seem an unusually cruel trick of fate to deny him access to the very man he wanted to interview next. He would have to start by casting his net slightly wider and interview some of the other men in the company. He looked again at the report of the Court of Enquiry into Vincent's death and picked out two of the witnesses.

Acting Corporals Cooper and Chadwick were a good place to start.

CHAPTER 35

7th July 1916

"KEEP YOUR HEAD down, sir, and you should be all right. These trenches are pretty deep and the Hun doesn't have the high ground here. Watch out for the trench mortars though. If you hear one, fall in the shit. If you don't, well you're probably dead already."

The soldier grinned at him and showed lines on a face already old before its years. The Rhondda accent gave an irresistible charm to the warning and Oscendale found himself grinning back at the young man.

They set off along a maze of communication trenches, packed with all the paraphernalia of warfare. They routinely had to press themselves against the sides of the narrow trench to allow stretcher-bearers and men taking empty supply containers to pass.

After an hour they reached a T-junction. Without hesitation, the soldier turned left and the trench widened onto the main trench. The detritus of war was everywhere whilst sullen, exhausted men stared at him as he passed. Oscendale had been in front line trenches many times and had experienced the horror of seeing death and mutilation around him but he still felt keenly the glare of men who stared with hatred at his military police uniform and red cap cover.

All along the trench he saw the face of battle: tanned, pained faces that had experienced much during the past few days. These men had followed their officers over the top earlier today and would do so again tomorrow. Their thoughts on the purpose of the war they kept to themselves; what they displayed was a grim awareness of the proximity of death. They had seen their friends and their enemies die horribly. They had seen sights that they could never have imagined during their hardworking lives in south Wales before the war began. These were hard men drawn from the industrial areas of the valleys and beyond, and from a wide variety of backgrounds and trades, all now thrown together in this morass of killing.

Oscendale's role was to ensure good order behind the lines, but sometimes this meant making tough decisions regarding men scared and scarred by the horror they had seen. He had had to lock up men who had got drunk as a way of escaping from the sights and sounds of battle. He had seen men shot for alleged cowardice when he, and the men who sat in judgement, knew that it was not the solution to shell-shock but a means of deterring others from exhibiting similar behaviour.

War had meant work for the Military Foot Police from the outset. When the British Expeditionary Force had begun to assemble at the Channel ports prior to its departure for France, the MFP had been set to work on traffic control on a hitherto unseen scale. They had also been charged with keeping civilians out of the dock areas, ostensibly for security purposes, but also, as Oscendale knew, to prevent tearful farewells from affecting the morale of the troops – something he thought was rather harsh.

At first the MFP contingent had been small, but it had grown exponentially over the following two years and not simply as a consequence of increased indiscipline. Oscendale knew that the Corps of Military Police, comprising the Military Foot Police and the Military Mounted Police, was now a large and complex organisation, which brought its own particular problems.

Trenches and roads required policing in order to ensure the smooth flow of traffic required by the commanders. But the *estaminets*, billets and even the brothels that grew as a consequence of the war meant that other duties arose from time to time. He had also been on duty at 'straggler posts', set up to prevent men from leaving the front line areas. Most of the time he had dealt with soldiers who had become separated from their units as the genuine result of the confusion of battle. Such men were collected together, fed, re-equipped and returned whence they came.

But most distressing of all were the terror-stricken men who were picked up by the MFP and brought to him for assessment. Sometimes they sat on a chair, hugging themselves and rocking back and forth, refusing, or unable, to answer his questions. At such times he saw the true psychological effects of modern warfare and the fragility of the human spirit in the face of such destructive power, and it disturbed him.

However, as a result of the brutality of some of his more zealous colleagues, he knew the MFP were loathed and even hated by the troops. This made his job even more difficult as he often met with sullen resentment or downright obstinate silence when investigating cases. But he still felt the sense of morality he did as a pre-war policeman. The law was there to be enforced for the good of all. He had always believed that and saw no reason for that basic belief to change now he was part of the military. Having seen how routine death could be over the past two years, he was even more determined to ensure that the war was not used as an excuse to mask criminal behaviour.

Laudable aims but he knew that such subtleties were lost on most of the men he passed now. They saw him and his ilk as the bullyboys, the men who shirked front line service, who were there only to pounce on their mistakes when they inevitably made them. He had seen it in the faces of soldiers before and he saw it now in the reactions of the men he passed.

Their resentment took many forms: an occasional muttered oath, a stare of defiance, or sometimes a man would spit with undisguised venom, not directly at him naturally, but those watching knew what it meant.

And yet had they known it, or allowed it to sink in, they would have realised that basically he was on their side. More than that even, Oscendale had nothing but admiration for the fighting men of the British Army, and also of their enemies. His experiences in the war had taught him that the propaganda image of the 'Hun' or 'Johnny Turk' was just that – a picture designed to portray the enemy as an inhuman beast so that men had no compunction about killing him.

In fact, his experiences at Gallipoli had left him with high regard for the fighting qualities of the Turkish soldier. Their bravery had been without question, as had that of the British and ANZAC soldiers he had served with, and, on more than one instance, fought alongside.

The trenches in the front line were not unknown to Oscendale. He had been on the Western Front since being evacuated from Gallipoli during the previous summer and had been part of the general retreat in 1914, so he knew how dangerous they were. It still amazed him when he read reports of the deaths of soldiers new to the front line who had poked their heads over the top in broad daylight to catch a sight of the Hun and had slumped to the foot of the trench with a sniper's bullet hole in their faces. It also surprised him how men failed to keep their heads down whilst moving along trench systems and, passing through a shallower section of trench, were killed because they failed to duck.

But he also retained steadfast admiration for the men who fought here, who, when on sentry duty at night, would stand with their torsos clearly exposed to the enemy snipers on the basis that if you were going to be shot you stood more chance of surviving if the bullet entered your body rather than your head.

And here they were again, the men who were prepared to risk their lives for a cause that had become blurred. The wood had to be taken because someone had decided it was necessary. In the best traditions of the British Army, they did not question the judgement of their superiors, but attempted to do their bit and stay alive until it was all over.

Their chances looked slim he had decided when he arrived at Cliff Trench and looked out across the battlefield that was being fought over. The ground was bereft of any natural cover and the Germans had the advantage of an unseen presence in the wood. From there they could sweep the ground with machine gun fire and artillery shells while Welsh soldiers scrabbled in the earth for anything to protect them. He wondered whether he himself would be willing to go over the top in the morning and decided with no little satisfaction that he would because it was his duty. Bravery didn't come into it. If you refused to climb the ladders out of the trench you would face heavy consequences, as well as the scorn and derision of your mates. You did it because you had to. It was expected of you and it was what you had trained for. It was as if your whole existence had been for this moment. You were here to serve your King and Country and if death was required then that was what would happen.

On and on they went, Oscendale following the stooping soldier as he skilfully negotiated all the obstructions that attempted to impede their progress – men and their equipment all being readied for the next attack. Bayonets were being cleaned, rifles oiled and Mills bombs primed. He watched the vignettes of trench life as he passed but felt detached, an intruder into the world of the fighting soldier. He was there for a purpose, as they were, but he would not be risking his life over the next few days and felt their silent condemnation as he passed. This was their world, the scene of their Golgotha and they were telling him to leave before they made their sacrifice.

Some were writing their last letters home, some would be writing again tomorrow evening, but no one knew which was which. Wills were being witnessed and scant possessions left to loved ones '*in the event of my death*'. An air of sadness and gloom hung over the trench and Oscendale felt as if he were party to another rite of passage, one that held such uncertainty for all present.

At last they stopped in a nondescript area of the trench where two soldiers were sitting drinking cups of tea.

"Here you are, sir. Corporals Cooper and Chadwick. I think they knew Harold Bratton as well as anyone. Seemed to spend some time together anyway. Give me a shout when you're finished. I'll be at the top of the communication trench."

Two pairs of deep-shadowed eyes were staring at him in

bitter resentment. *The eyes said it all*, thought Oscendale. *We are here fighting for our lives and yours – and your mates back in their cushy offices miles away from the Front.*

"Caught any deserters yet, sir?" said Cooper. "You won't find any here, I'm afraid. Just the dead and the soon-to-be dead."

The man's face was filthy and scornful, marked by the experience of the past few hours. Oscendale knew this would be hard work.

"I want to talk to you about Harold Bratton. He was a witness to a death I'm investigating."

"A death you're investigating? Well we've got plenty more here when you've finished with that one," said Cooper, and both men chuckled sardonically. Cooper then raised a finger in front of his mouth and blew out a long puff of air, waving his index finger in front of his mouth as he did so. The noise was uncannily like that of a machine gun, so much so that it brought Oscendale out in a cold sweat as his mind flashed back to the Dardanelles.

He took a deep breath, recovered his senses, and said, "Did Bratton say anything strange about the man William Vincent who shot himself while he was on sentry duty last month? Anything at all?" he persisted.

"Look, sir. Harry was shaken up by what he saw but the bastard killed two of our men and whatever he did afterwards was too good for him. But killing himself like that in front of Harry was terrible. He had nightmares about it every night." The man paused, reflecting. "Anyway he's gone now, poor sod, and there's no more bad dreams for Harry boy."

"How did he die?" Oscendale asked quietly.

"Shell burst, I suppose," replied Chadwick, speaking for the first time. "We went over the top this morning, got about thirty yards before the machine guns and artillery opened up. Harry was on my right, about ten yards away. A shell came over, burst, bang, and Harry fell. Piece of it hit me here, see?"

Chadwick showed Oscendale his helmet. An oval-shaped dent pitted the right-hand side of his helmet. With his helmet off, Oscendale observed the dark-haired youth with the furrowed brow and for the second time that day he felt troubled.

"So you didn't see him again?"

Cooper laughed bitterly. "Put it this way. When we came back with our tails between our legs two hours later he didn't exactly wave us a cheery hello, *sir*." The stress on the last word was meant to provoke him but Oscendale dismissed it.

"But you saw the body, yes?"

"Yes, sir. What there was of poor Harry. No face mind. All burnt it was. Probably the heat of the shrapnel piece. But he was still there where he'd fallen. Took his identity tag for the sergeant." Cooper stared gloomily at the bottom of the trench.

"Did he ever say much about Vincent? About his dispute with Sergeant Jackson and Corporal Howells?"

Cooper fell silent. Chadwick thought for a while and, after glancing at Cooper, said, "Only that he felt sorry for the bloke. Said he'd been a decent sort of sergeant to him before the drinking took over. When he got busted he became all quiet like. Moody."

"Why did he start drinking?"

Chadwick snorted. "Why do any of us start drinking? Because we like it."

"And it helps. You know what I mean, sir?" added Cooper.

Oscendale knew exactly what he meant. And not just during a war. He had dealt with too many drink-related crimes to know that it both helped and hindered people's lives.

"When did it start getting out of hand, affecting his duties as a sergeant?" he asked.

Cooper answered, "Oh, about six months ago. We all turned a blind eye to it at first, as he'd been such a good bloke – for a sergeant anyway. Then he started slipping, like. Missing duties because he couldn't get out of his bunk. Mind, Jackson and Howells had it in for him as well. They seemed to be always chipping away at him, giving him a hard time."

"How long had that been going on?" asked Oscendale.

"Months," replied Chadwick. "Got a bit embarrassing, you know, in front of the men. Vincent never seemed to have the guts to stand up to them. It got so that we were telling him to do something about it."

"And how did he respond?"

Chadwick shook his head. "No good. Told us we didn't understand and they were just larking about."

Oscendale thought for a moment. "What did you think of Sergeant Jackson and Corporal Howells? How did you get on with them?"

A silence fell over the group. Chadwick spoke first.

"Bastards, sir, the pair of 'em. Not saying they deserved to die like that, but they had something coming. Thick as thieves they were and always on the make. That's what made it worse to see Vincent being bullied like that. They just laughed about it all."

Oscendale pondered for a moment. There had to be some reason behind Vincent's erratic behaviour. What hold did the two dead men have over him?

"Have you any idea why he let them get away with it?" he asked.

Chadwick spat into the gap in the duckboards at the bottom of the trench before replying. "Nope. Whatever it was, it was something secret between the three of them. Maybe it was something Vincent had done in the past. Maybe one of them found out about it and confronted him with it. We never knew what it was, anyway. And now it's gone to their graves with the three of them."

Oscendale paused before he asked the next question. "The two of you were in the hut when Jackson and Howells were shot. Cooper, why did you say in your evidence to the Court of Enquiry that you only heard one shot?"

The two men looked at him quizzically. Cooper spoke for the two of them. "Because that's what I heard, sir. There was only one shot. I know both men were shot but me and John only heard one shot. I'm sure of that and you are as well, aren't you John?"

Chadwick scratched his shoulder and said, "Yes. I only heard one shot. Weird that mind, seeing as how the two of them were shot."

Oscendale pounced. "Chadwick, you are probably unaware that I've read the transcript of the Court of Enquiry and your evidence to it. Do you want to reconsider what you just said?"

Chadwick sat rigid and his gaze switched to Cooper. "How do you mean, sir?"

"Listen, son. You told the court that you heard two shots. I am aware that bullet wounds were found in both Jackson and Howells. Unless Vincent had lined them up one behind the other, another shot must have been fired. You heard it. How come?"

The man squirmed uneasily. Cooper spoke. "Tell 'im, John. It can't hurt now."

Chadwick nodded. "Right. The thing is, sir. I was supposed to be relieving Harry on guard duty but me and Coops had had a right skinful and I slept through the change. If I told the court that I'd have been up on a charge myself. Harry didn't say nothing and I was grateful to him for that. Always will be."

"So did you hear two shots?" pressed Oscendale.

"Yes, sir. I know I heard them both but I can't remember whether they were close together or not but I definitely heard Harry come in to check on Jackson and Howells."

Oscendale's mind started racing. "You heard Bratton come into the hut?"

"Yes. He must have come in to check on them while everyone else was outside. I never got up 'cos... well, I couldn't if you know what I mean, sir."

Oscendale replayed that event in his mind and came to a conclusion that appalled him. He decided that he had extracted everything he could from the two men and thanked them and left. As he turned the corner of the traverse he couldn't be sure but he thought he saw Cooper's fingers make a crude gesture in his direction. *The lot of the military police officer was never easy,* he mused and left the men to their forthcoming ordeal.

The soldier who had been his guide reappeared. "All done, sir?" Oscendale nodded and they began the journey back. The soldier spoke over his shoulder as they went. "Actually, sir, I didn't think you'd get anywhere with those two. Not really the forthcoming type. However, there's a Private Johnston you might get more out of."

"Thank you. Where might I find him?" said Oscendale,

reflecting that he had indeed made much progress and now had an infinitely clearer idea of what had happened in the hut.

"Bit of a trek, I'm afraid, sir. He was evacuated to the Base Hospital at Etaples after an accident a couple of days ago."

Oscendale groaned inside. *Bloody Etaples.* Where the stock of the MFP was worse than low.

He and his guide made their way back along the communication trench but his way was suddenly barred by a heavily built soldier holding a magazine in front of him. The man half turned towards Oscendale, spotted his insignia and said, "See this?" indicating the magazine he was reading. "See what it says?"

Oscendale regarded the magazine. Entitled 'Blighty', it showed a grinning Tommy on the front cover, a pipe gripped firmly between his teeth. Beneath him was the wording '*Pictures and humour from our men at the Front*'.

"My mam sent it out for me," explained the man. "Said she bought it at Cardiff Station last week."

He pointed at the last line on the cover. *Every copy sold sends three more to the trenches.* "Now I wonder what that means, sir. Three what? Three more bullets, three more men or three more bits of lavatory paper like this."

He laughed at the crudity of the joke and Oscendale decided he had had enough of this particular brand of humour. He pushed past the man and headed back along the communication trench, deep in thought, while his cheery guide led the way.

CHAPTER 36

7th July 1916

THE *ESTAMINET* WAS full tonight. *Plenty of khaki getting filled up before going back to the hell of the front line*, thought Oscendale. After his experience that day he felt like doing the same. His interview with Chadwick and Cooper had just hinted he was on the right track. But where it was leading he had no idea.

The report of Bratton's death had troubled him. Bratton dying was inconvenient and regrettable but he had never met the lad and therefore should have felt only the general, impersonal sorrow he had experienced for all the other deaths of the past few years, yet he did not. The open ground between the trenches and Mametz Wood had been ripe for killing and all the soldiers who had left the trenches that morning were subject to the vagaries of fate. A rifle bullet, a machine gun round, a shrapnel burst, a high explosive shell, all could kill or maim a man before the lottery of hand-to-hand fighting with bayonets, knives and fists that awaited anyone lucky enough to reach the German trenches.

And now, somewhere out in no-man's-land lay the body of young Harold Bratton, unreachable and unburied until the ground was taken. Oscendale knew there was no guarantee of ever being able to see the body. A fallen man could be churned into a thousand pieces by the carnage wrought by artillery shells. He had known of the corpses of men simply disappearing, atomised or sinking out of sight into the mud of a shell hole, entering the earth itself.

"Mind if I join you, Oscendale?" A clipped voice cut into

his musing. He looked up from his beer to see the balding head of a major of the Welsh Regiment smiling down at him. Oscendale did not recognise the face.

"Gruar. James Gruar. Welsh Regiment," the officer prompted, obviously seeing the lack of recognition on Oscendale's face as he sat himself in the chair opposite. "Understand you're on the Vincent case. Bad business but the beggar got what he deserved before you lot could catch up with him. Bit frustrating for you though, eh? Would have been good to have seen him shot. Can't have that sort of thing going on behind the lines. Far too many Huns to kill without killing our own chaps."

The man paused to take a drink from his glass and that gave Oscendale the chance to study the face. Fiftyish. Career soldier. Boer War ribbons on his tunic. A man brought up in all the military doctrine of his antecedents. Probably one of a line of soldiers, all as dull and unimaginative as each other.

The next comment proved Oscendale wrong.

"Best leave it there don't you think? Don't want to be raking up too many glowing embers eh? Bad for morale."

And then Oscendale twigged. This was no nincompoop officer. He was being warned off by a clever imitation. This figure was no front line officer but had all the aura of Military Intelligence. It was in the voice. *Good try, mate, but no prize this time.*

The man fell silent and awaited Oscendale's response. The buffoonery was gone and he knew the man was not used to taking no for an answer.

Oscendale sipped his beer once more before replying. "A suspicious death is a suspicious death. My job is to investigate it. Anything less would be a dereliction of duty."

"Suspicious? How? Surely a suicide isn't suspicious?" The

man was giving up ground. Oscendale knew he had won already. *But what was the prize and did he want it?*

"Two men die. Another man dies shortly afterwards and to top it all my main witness to it all has been killed. What would you call it?"

"Oh come on. This is a war, you know. People die in all sorts of ways. The man had cracked. Lost it. End of story." The blue eyes now began to stare at Oscendale and he knew the conversation was reaching a crucial point.

"My job is to investigate," Oscendale persisted, "and I shall continue to do so until I am happy there are no outstanding facts."

The major sighed, downed his drink and stood up. He donned his cap and touched the peak with one finger before turning to go. After one step he twisted back and leaned forward so that no one else could hear his words.

"Too many deaths already, Oscendale. Don't want any more do we? I'd forget it if I were you," he hissed.

He smiled briefly before walking slowly out of the room, glancing around him as he went.

So he was not the only one interested in William Vincent's death and those of Jackson and Howells. But why would Military Intelligence be warning him off? A murder and a suicide were not the things that usually interested men of Gruar's ilk. Not much espionage involved in this case – or so it had seemed up to this point. Then either he was reading this case completely wrongly and there was more to this than met the eye, or Military Intelligence were somehow way out of kilter with their usual cloak-and-dagger operations.

Whichever way he looked at this it seemed the case was becoming more of a challenge with each passing hour, but he could not say he was disappointed at the prospect of pitting his wits against those of Military Intelligence, as well as the more mysterious elements of the cause of the murders themselves. And then there was the link with Catherine Jaulard.

The night was cold and dark when he emerged several beers later from the estaminet. He had drunk more than he should have but at times like this he always thought *why the hell not?* It never did him any harm and he could always get up for work in the morning.

The street was empty apart from two soldiers who stood chatting near a lamppost about thirty yards away. He walked towards them, his mind turning over the evening's events and it was a surprise when one of the soldiers suddenly stepped into his path.

"Bloody redcap," the man grunted and threw a fist towards his face. Oscendale may have been drunk but his instincts were honed from his time as a young policeman. He blocked the punch and kneed the man in the crotch. The soldier fell groaning to the floor and writhed around with his hands clasped to his groin.

Oscendale turned to the other man who hesitated.

"Look, son, it may not be obvious in this light but I'm an officer and if you follow your pal there you'll be up on a charge. Your choice." He hoped his little speech would deter the man but he saw the right hand move quickly and the glint of a knife blade sliced past his chin as he reeled backwards.

The man came forward again, forcing Oscendale to retreat towards a wall. His fallen companion was endeavouring to rise to his feet.

Then a voice rang out in the darkness. "Move away boys and go and play somewhere else, eh?" A metallic rasp sounded and Oscendale knew it could only be the sound of a bayonet being drawn. His attackers knew it too and they turned and ran, or at least one of them did; the other stumbled like a great ape towards the end of the street.

A corporal Oscendale recognised came forward into the streetlight. "Sorry about that, sir. Some of the boys don't have any manners."

"Thank you, Loram. It was starting to get a little awkward there," replied Oscendale in gratitude. "Rather fortunate you came along."

"That's okay, sir," replied Loram. "Two to one ain't fair odds anyway." Sensing Oscendale's puzzlement at the coincidence he said, "Oh. Captain Hill thought I should keep an eye on you, sir. I'll wish you good night then." And he was gone, walking confidently down the cobbled French street.

CHAPTER 37

8th July 1916

MAJOR DAVID VEDMORE of the Army Intelligence Branch cursed as he nicked himself with his razor. *Damn the man! Things had been progressing so smoothly until he stuck his interfering nose into what should have been viewed as a routine suicide.*

Routine? he mused. *In a war like this one, men were frequently going off their rockers and choosing the easy way out.* Vedmore had no time for such behaviour or the malingerers who imitated shell-shock in the hope of a quick passage home. It was his job to check that the spineless doctors sent only the worst cases back to England on the troopships.

Yes, things had been running smoothly until that Assistant Provost decided to get too big for his boots. The Military Foot Police was anathema to Vedmore. Too bloody independent for his liking. He had heard stories that staff officers had used MFP men as typists and orderlies, even servants, just to keep them from poking their noses into too many regimental affairs. *Good job too*, he thought.

Having finished shaving, he washed and dressed before going through to his sitting room for breakfast. Having comfortable quarters in a French château on the outskirts of Albert was a decided perk, he decided, but really represented a just reward for the fine work he was doing in keeping the Hun at bay.

His batman Kemp had placed the morning's communiqués alongside his breakfast. As he munched his toast and marmalade he sifted through a collection of buff envelopes and typewritten sheets. The morning's post also lay in a neat pile on his desk.

He shuffled through the letters and stopped as he held the lilac-coloured envelope with his name inscribed on the front in jerky handwriting. He inhaled deeply as he contemplated whether or not to tear open the top.

He had been married for twenty-three years and had two sons serving in the army, one here in France, the other in training at Preston. He was proud of them and, although he naturally hoped that they would not be required to make the ultimate sacrifice, he was keen for them to acquit themselves well in their new roles. After the war was done, careers perhaps in banking or something similar could follow until they retired early to comfortable houses in the country.

His wife, however, was another matter. They had met at a school event when he was a young teacher, making his way in the world. She had been the older sister of one of his pupils and there was an immediate mutual attraction. Marriage had soon followed and then the boys, but, as with some marriages – though seemingly not those of his friends, he mused – they had followed different interests.

Vedmore had been ambitious and when the opportunity to go for the deputy head's job at the grammar school had arisen he had actively sought it and was rewarded. It was a job he enjoyed and thought he was good at, and Eileen had supported him at first.

However, her absent-mindedness had begun to escalate. Missed fragments of conversations had turned to mute withdrawal and then the paranoia had begun.

When he had sought to do his bit and asked the headteacher's permission to enlist in 1914, the man had looked at him with envy and questioned why a man of his age would be willing to risk his life when there were plenty of young men in British society who were available instead. The comment had stung

Vedmore and he had nevertheless presented himself at the High Wycombe recruiting office only to be told he was too old and unfit.

He had considered his paunch and slight asthma, and then returned later to ask whether, as there was no place for him in the infantry, he could contribute by serving behind a desk. The irony was not lost on him.

He had eventually been given a desk job at Military Intelligence, presumably based on his academic background, and had enjoyed the task of sifting, summarising and organising the multitude of reports, memos and scraps of information that came his way. He had mixed well with his superiors – his career in teaching grammar school boys left him at ease with men from affluent backgrounds – and was recommended for promotion last year. He now found himself in France with a comfortable billet and a task that was not dissimilar to his previous role, but which brought him in closer contact with the real action of front line warfare.

The move took him further away from Eileen and her neurosis. She could now run the house in High Wycombe and while away her days while he was serving at the Front. The enforced separation did not trouble him. In fact he felt liberated and free. He no longer had to account for her actions with embarrassed guests and friends, and the change would do them both good.

His foray into the world of cloak-and-dagger had been foolish, he decided. That damned policeman had seen through his attempted disguise. Whether it was his over confidence or his over estimation of his bit parts in local repertory performances, he had assumed that he would be able to carry off the role of one of the regimental officers he came across on a daily basis with some measure of success. It was disappointing therefore to have been humiliated in such a way, and it stung him deeply.

However, he had watched with some satisfaction as the two goons he had detailed for the second part of his plan had assaulted Oscendale. And then the accursed figure with the bayonet had appeared. It had been frustrating of course, but there was always another chance and he really had to make sure that this tiresome man was out of the way before the main part of the project came to fruition.

With his best agent now heading for another assignment in East Africa, his cover blown, he absent-mindedly began gnawing at the skin around his finger nails as he wondered how to accomplish this.

He set aside Eileen's letter and its no doubt disturbing contents, and examined the other letters he had received, their sheer volume further reinforcing his self-importance. One in particular intrigued him and he set aside his toast to give the item his full attention.

It was the report of a meeting that had taken place on 3rd July at a château near Koblenz – a meeting of the German general staff for the area. Vedmore's telephone surveillance team had intercepted a phone call from Koblenz to Berlin and had also obtained a verbatim report of what had been discussed from the spy that British Intelligence had placed in the château.

Vedmore read through the report and noted the information on the planning for the offensive that had taken place the following morning. It was a shame they had not obtained the information in time.

He scanned the list of those present and two names leapt out at him. *Hauptmanns* Bernhofer and Stoltz were well known to him as two of the rising stars of German Military Intelligence and their attendance at such a meeting was unusual to say the least. What the spy had also noted was that the two men and several other officers had left the meeting much later than the main body. They had obviously stayed behind to discuss something of note. Vedmore's curiosity was aroused. If Department IIIb was active in the area of the Somme then there was certainly something afoot.

Reaching for his inkstand he began to pen a memorandum.

CHAPTER 38

8th July 1916

ETAPLES WAS A sprawling place – a factory for producing front line soldiers, men who were capable of killing a stranger at a moment's notice. Not for the first time Oscendale pondered the fact that part of his job in wartime and in peacetime was to investigate a killing of another human being and to bring the perpetrator to justice. But who would bring the perpetrators for the killings of millions of men to justice after this lot was over? No-one of course, because this was legitimate killing. The government demanded it, the King demanded it, and the country had been persuaded to demand it. It insisted that young men be recruited and trained to participate in this great conflict. But this was now killing on a scale too vast to be imagined when they all signed up for the great adventure in 1914.

Its breeding ground was in Etaples. Here, in this ever expanding military camp, men were put through their paces, trained through endless repetition to act as one body, one mass of men who obeyed their orders unquestioningly.

As he disembarked from the train he looked up and saw the mass of the camp spread out before him: one neatly edged rectangle of white on the side of a hill, looking well scrubbed and sterile in the sunlight.

The camp was comprised of tents, endless rows of tents, testifying to the ever optimistic view of the General Staff that this was to be a war of mobility and that even here in Etaples, on the northern coast of France, miles from the front line, the men should be ready to pack up and go the moment the

German line was breached. Inevitable collapse would follow and the infantry and the cavalry would sweep through the gap and the war would be over shortly thereafter.

There were just a few wooden buildings scattered amongst the canvas lines, he noted, their cheerful YMCA signs offering some solace and some reminders of home to the men located here.

There were also the hospitals adjacent to the camp and these contained several wards, each ward being covered by three marquees. Here the wounded were brought every day, their numbers currently escalating as the result of the great offensive on the Somme. Oscendale wondered at the capacity of these medical services to cope with such an unprecedented demand. He had heard rumours and read several reports of enormous casualties, especially on the first day of the battle, the 1st July, which swept away the early optimism. He had read accounts of men cut down in waves all along the Front as they advanced across no man's land into a hail of machine gun and artillery fire. Men lay in terrible pain for hours on end before they were rescued and brought here to Etaples – if they were fortunate to survive the complex system of regimental aid posts, dressing stations and field hospitals.

He passed through the main gate and asked for directions to 38th IBD, the area of the camp he knew was allocated to the Welsh Regiment. In the distance he could see the parade ground, known to all and sundry as the 'Bull Ring', where sergeant instructors with yellow bands on their sleeves ordered several columns of soldiers back and forth, accompanied by shrill cries and blasphemous oaths.

Oscendale watched for a while as the various groups practised rapid loading, for which he could definitely see a point, and marching drill, which he knew served only to relieve a soldier of whatever initiative and imagination he had left after basic training back in England. One group was throwing Mills bombs at imaginary Germans, while another charged straw–filled sacks suspended from wooden frames which they were encouraged to spear with fixed bayonets. Passive, mock Germans. Oscendale knew it would be a lot more difficult when the enemy soldier was similarly armed and prepared to fight back with some vigour.

In the distance he could hear the sound of crackling rifle fire coming from the Sandhills Range just outside the camp and also wondered how accurate the rifle fire would become when the Kitchener soldiers were confronted by veteran German soldiers who had a similar intent in mind.

Oscendale entered the 38th IBD area and met the familiar bristling a military policeman encountered when confronted by 'proper' soldiers. The two men sitting back to back outside a tent cleaning their rifles stopped what they were doing and resisted the temptation to level the weapons at him. Men lying on the ground sat up and the men on fatigues ceased finding their tasks interesting and stared at him, resentment filling their eyes.

Not going to be easy this, he thought once more.

"Private Johnson, come 'ere!" barked the sergeant at Oscendale's shoulder to a callow youth sitting some yards away on a box. The young man responded and moved quickly to stand stiffly in front of his NCO, his right hand wrapped in a clean, white bandage. He took a quick glance at Oscendale then reverted to staring right through the sergeant with all the practised ease of an experienced soldier.

"This officer would like a word with you, Johnson, so I'll leave him in your capable hands. Oh and make sure your bloody rifle is clean by this afternoon's parade."

"Yes, sergeant!" the young man bellowed and the NCO turned on his heel and was gone.

Oscendale told the soldier to stand easy and, deeming the area, with its multitude of interested eyes and ears and recently descended oppressive silence, an inappropriate venue for a confidential discussion, he gestured towards a cleared area at the end of the row of tents. Johnson nodded and moments later they were sitting on two battered boxes smoking Oscendale's cigarettes.

"How's the hand wound, Johnson?" Oscendale opened.

The soldier looked down at the dressing. "Oh, it's alright, thank you, sir. The knife went through the fleshy part. Aches a bit but it'll be okay. Just a stupid accident really."

"Glad to hear it. Look, I want to talk to you about William Vincent."

No anxiety in the soldier's eyes. Good, thought Oscendale, *maybe I can get somewhere this time.*

"Righto, sir," the young soldier replied. "What do you want to know?"

"What was he like as a sergeant?" Oscendale asked.

Johnson drew heavily on his cigarette then replied, "A good bloke. Plenty of time for us lot, like. Wasn't keen on all the bull. We did some, of course. Had to. But he didn't dish it out just for the sake of it."

"What about Jackson and Howells? How did he get on with them?"

"Oh they were as thick as thieves for a while. Then like kids in a playground Jackson and Howells turned on him. Started to niggle him, you know. Almost provoking him to see how far they could push him, like. Course he tried to get them back in line but never tried hard enough if you know what I mean. They always seemed to have the upper hand. And when Jackson was made up to sergeant that's when it really started. Vincent kind of drifted off into himself after that. Never saw much of him. Mind you, it was still a terrible shock when he did it. Blew his head right off. Blood everywhere." He paused at the memory and took another long pull on his cigarette.

"You were one of the men who gave statements to the Court of Enquiry, weren't you?"

Johnson nodded. "Yes I was, sir."

"If I remember rightly you said you only heard one shot being fired."

"That's right, that's what I told them. One shot."

"So how come Howells was shot as well as Jackson?"

"Well I reckon I must have slept through the first one – the shot that killed Sergeant Jackson, I mean. It must have been the second shot that killed Corporal Howells that woke me."

Oscendale thought about the logic of such a remark and then decided to press on.

"So what did you do after you woke up?"

"I got out of my bunk, all startled like, and saw Vincent running out of the hut. The other lads woke up and we all asked each other what was going on. We thought the Germans were here so we got dressed quickly and all ran out of the hut as well."

"What did you see outside? Describe it for me."

"I saw Bill Vincent lying dead on the ground with a pool of blood around his head. Some of the lads were bending over him and some were running off to get help. Some of the more squeamish ones stood in a group a few yards away, talking. After a while the MO came and examined him and we had to carry him inside."

"Where was Private Bratton while all this was going on?"

"Harry? I dunno. It was dark like and everyone was sort of milling about. I guess he was in one of the groups somewhere."

Oscendale pictured the confusion of the scene in his mind and an idea began to form.

"You said you helped to carry the body back to the hut?" he asked.

"Yes, sir. Me and a couple of the lads were told by the sergeant to pick him up and carry him inside on a blanket." Johnson shuddered at the recollection.

Oscendale had a thought. "Who was the last person to leave the hut?"

"How do you mean, sir?" asked Johnson, his face reddening and clearly perturbed at the direction this was taking.

Oscendale breathed deeply. "What I said. Who was the last person to leave William Vincent's body that night?"

Johnson's guilt was showing and he lowered his eyes to escape Oscendale's stare.

"Come on, Johnson, I know there's something."

"Okay, it was me, sir. I was the last one out anyway."

"And you took something from his body?" Oscendale persisted.

Johnson fidgeted and said nothing at first, then seeming to have weighed up the options of telling the policeman the truth, he decided at last. He reached inside his trouser pocket and withdrew something that he held out to Oscendale.

"I was going to hand it in, sir, honest. Just haven't got around to doing it yet."

Oscendale took the envelope and withdrew the letter from inside. Scanning its contents he replaced it in the envelope and put it inside his tunic pocket.

"You realise that removing evidence from the scene of a crime is a serious matter?"

Johnson reddened again. "I know that, sir, but Vincent was always going on about the fact that he knew something we'd all like to know and I suppose my curiosity got the better of me and I wanted to know what it was. He didn't need whatever it was any more. I just wanted to know what it was that he used to tease us with. As it turns out it weren't nothing. Just a letter from some bloke called Karl. I couldn't make head nor tail of it. I never had the chance to put it back so I kept it."

"Look, Johnson," said Oscendale. "It was none of your bloody business and you should have kept your thieving fingers to yourself. You should have left this where it was. You've interfered with my investigation and if I hadn't tracked you down this may never have come to light. You'll be hearing more of this."

Johnson lapsed into a sulk and resumed his smoking. Oscendale unfolded the letter and began to read:

My Dear William,

I am writing this letter not knowing whether you are dead or alive. It is a strange sentiment and I hope that God has protected you from this terrible catastrophe.

Seeing you again two years ago was a shock. I thought at that moment that my time had come but thankfully I was spared.

You may remember the document I gave you. I wonder if you still have it. You may have suspected that it is of high importance and you are right. It came into my hands in the first weeks of the war and if you look at it carefully it gives you the location of an item that could change a man's life forever. As your old friend, I ask that you keep it safe until this war has finally finished. After the war we should arrange to meet up and I can tell you what it all means.

No good will come of this war but I must admit to quite enjoying some of the experience. The food is good and the men are in high spirits. With luck it will all be over soon and I will be able to buy you a drink in the Three Arches in the Hafod. You can toast your regiment and I'll toast mine – the Bavarians. Here's to the good times we had before all this mess started.

Your friend, Karl.

So this was the letter that Vincent's wife had forwarded to him recently from Swansea!

But before he could ask Johnson any more questions he became aware of a loud conversation starting behind him and he turned to see a major and a pair of lieutenants approaching. The major strode purposefully up to him, his swagger stick beating a rhythm on his thigh. Oscendale rose to meet him as the lieutenants struggled to keep pace with the major's swift gait.

The man stopped in front of Oscendale and his moustache twitched as he spat out the words. "What the hell do you think you're doing, captain, grilling one of my men without so much as a by-your-leave from me?"

Oscendale forced himself to check his rising anger. Officious officers were the bane of his life. "Captain Oscendale, sir. Military Foot Police. I am investigating the death of…"

But the major interrupted him. "I don't care if you're investigating the death of the bloody Kaiser himself! You do not stroll in here and start quizzing one of my men. Got it?"

As the man reached a crescendo of rage, Oscendale felt a piece of saliva land on his cheek. Slowly raising his hand to wipe it off, much to the major's embarrassment, he countered, "I am at liberty to interview any of your men, sir, and I think you will find that I do not need your permission to do so."

The man's face turned puce and Oscendale prepared

himself for another tongue-lashing. Instead the man abruptly seemed to run out of words. He turned on his heel and began his journey back to whatever office he had emerged from. Oscendale saw Johnson grinning and decided it was time to go.

CHAPTER 39

8th July 1916

THE MAN BEHIND the desk nodded as Oscendale walked in.

"Assistant Provost Marshall Oscendale, sir!" the NCO stated as Oscendale and Avate fixed eyes on each other.

"Thank you, sergeant," Avate responded in a quiet voice which belied his strength of will, a fact that Oscendale could pay testament to as the result of several previous awkward encounters. He knew he was there for another grilling and thought he knew why.

When the sergeant had departed, Avate leaned back in his chair but made no motion that Oscendale was to sit as well. The seconds passed and Avate's eyes never left his assistant's.

At last he spoke. "When a major of the Welsh Regiment rings me and tells me that one of my men," he paused as he searched for the right words, "a 'bloody boyo from the valleys' unquote, has been interviewing his men without any proper authority and quote 'sticking his nose into the regiment's affairs' I have to listen."

Oscendale smiled to himself. So he was right; it was the pompous little major he'd encountered at Etaples.

"I should be bemused at what you're up to. I should be annoyed that what the army deems as a convenient suicide, which saved them the trouble of a court martial and a bloody firing squad by the way, should take up every minute of your time for the past week or more, particularly when the French police are also on my back to keep you away from the Catherine Jaulard murder."

He paused to clasp his fingers together and Oscendale

wondered which way Avate would go next. He sighed quietly with relief at the words that followed.

"But I know you, Tom Oscendale, and I know you're the best policeman I've got. If you think there's something in this, and God knows what it is, then I'm happy there is. So go and find out what the blighter was up to before he shot himself and I'll deal with Major Griffiths. Consider yourself bollocked and keep me informed."

Avate smiled thinly and Oscendale knew that the man's pre-war experience at Scotland Yard was the defining factor in how his work was perceived. An inexperienced man would have caved in under the pressure from the regular army. But Avate was a detective first and a soldier second. Besides which he usually trusted Oscendale's judgement. Not always, but usually. And obviously on this occasion he was granting him some leeway.

"Thank you, sir. There is something behind all this and I have some leads but not the whole picture as yet. It's more complicated than a German defence system but I'm getting closer to the truth every day. Give me the time and I'll give you the answers."

Avate looked at him closely. The frown disappeared and he spoke. "Then don't waste time talking to a desk Johnny like me. Get out there and do some proper police work." Avate's head lowered once more to the pile of paperwork he had been studying some minutes previously.

CHAPTER 40

9th July 1916

OSCENDALE WATCHED KATHLEEN'S face as she slept.

There had been other women in his life and they seemed to enter it as quickly as the paperwork landed on his desk. The trouble was that they left it just as quickly whilst the caseload lingered and grew. But he always held something back now. Having loved and lost once before he had vowed never to be hurt like that again. The pain had been too great. He had been younger then of course, but he still felt the sense of betrayal keenly. No, he would never give as much of himself again, nor as freely. He would never expose himself so totally and so fully just to have his hopes and dreams crushed by another woman. And it had worked so far. Amidst all this horror and death, women had given him brief companionship and a reminder of all that was good about being a man. *Islands of tenderness.*

Was Kathleen any different? Yes and no. In the short time they had been together she had moved into his life and fitted in well with his lifestyle and routines. She was never demanding, always understood the calls of his work. Accommodating and yet independent, she lifted his spirits immeasurably when they were together.

They had met when he had visited a military policeman who had been injured whilst on duty near Amiens. When he arrived at the VAD hospital and asked for the man she had smiled and asked if he was coming to arrest her for not healing him quickly enough. He had liked her black humour and made an excuse to visit the injured policeman the following day. He had selfishly wished away visiting time and upon leaving had plucked up the courage to ask the red-haired matron her name.

Their affair had blossomed since then and she spent every night with him now, apart from when the demands of the ever increasing influx of sick and wounded soldiers meant she had to work nights as well.

And after the war was over? Was there a future for them then? Propped on his elbow, watching her sleep, he doubted it. Nothing as good as this would last and nothing good, it seemed to him, would come out of this war. It would be back to arresting drunks in the streets of Barry for him, with perhaps the excitement of an occasional murder which would probably turn out to be just another natural death.

With a start he suddenly realised that he didn't know what Kathleen was going back to. This damn case and their live for today philosophy meant that he hadn't paid her much attention of late. He really had no inkling what her hopes and dreams were once this lot was over.

Irritated with himself, he rose and began his preparations for another working day.

"Phone call for you sir," North informed him as he arrived in his office thirty minutes later. "Captain Evans."

Doctor Idris Evans had been a friend of Oscendale's for many years. His father ran a chemist's shop in Barry and he and Oscendale had worked together on several cases of suspicious death requiring medical expertise. Idris, bespectacled and academic-looking, possessed a keen medical mind, one that Oscendale had been grateful to on several occasions since he had joined the MFP. Now a doctor with the Royal Army Medical Corps, he had enlisted at the same time as Oscendale, both using their backgrounds to good effect.

"Good morning, Idris, and how is the world of medicine today?" Oscendale prepared himself for what he knew would be a cynical reply.

"Well, if the fools stopped sending me so many dismembered young men and didn't expect me to patch them up and send them back to the Front again it would be fine. As it is, the fighting here on the Somme has given me quite enough death to last me the rest of my life. However, my lack of sleep for the last three nights has made me irritable and morose so I'm not really very good company, Tom." *He was softening*, thought Oscendale, who could only imagine the gruesome sights that Evans witnessed each day in the Casualty Clearing Station.

"Still, I have managed to find time amidst all this mess to have a look at that body you wanted me to examine. William Vincent, yes?"

"That's the one, Id. Did you find anything interesting for me?" Oscendale began gnawing his lip as he finished asking the question.

"As a matter of fact I did. You were right; the man wouldn't have died immediately. He used the carved piece of wood to reach the trigger but instead of placing the rifle barrel under his chin and doing the thing properly, he put it to his left cheek and fired the bullet at an angle into his face."

"So how long afterwards would he have died?" Oscendale asked, his brow now furrowed.

"Difficult to say, Tom. Could have been a few seconds or a few minutes," Evans replied.

"And did he mean it?"

"What? To die more slowly? Ghoulish I know but I'd say yes. He didn't want to die straightaway and for some ghastly reason he chose to die a lingering death. Macabre if you ask me. Was he all right, I mean was he of sound mind?"

"I'm not sure. He had a few things going on but to choose to die that way? I don't know." Oscendale tried to imagine the dreadful suffering of Vincent's last few moments of life.

"Well, that's it then, Tom. That's all I could say about him."

"Thanks, Id." Oscendale was about to hang up when a thought struck him and he decided to make one more demand of his old friend. "Look, I know you're up to your eyes in it but could you take a look at two more bodies for me?"

"The men he killed? I wondered if you were going to ask me that. Streets ahead of you, old boy, as usual. Sergeant Jackson, nothing unusual. Unless you call being shot in the head at close range unusual. But Corporal Howells, now that's another matter."

Oscendale felt his pulse quicken.

"Go on. What do you mean?"

"Well, my initial reading of it was that Howells hears the first shot – the one that kills Sergeant Jackson. He sits up and Vincent shoots him in the chest, yes? That's what I understand the Court of Enquiry determined."

"That would seem to have been the likely scenario, yes," said Oscendale wondering where his friend was leading him.

"Well, when I looked at the wound in Howells's chest I found he had been bayoneted first and then shot afterwards. And by the nature of the wound he was shot some minutes after being bayoneted."

"So somebody finished him off?" queried Oscendale.

"Exactly," announced Evans triumphantly. "Your original MO who conducted the postmortems wants striking off for not checking the wound, or should I say wounds, properly."

Oscendale thanked his friend profusely and immediately pulled out the report of the Court of Enquiry. There it was. Several witnesses who were present in the hut mentioned hearing only one shot. He had put that down to the fact that they were sleeping off a night's drinking and the first shot hadn't registered in their alcohol-soaked brains but Idris's findings now placed the scenario in a totally new light. Someone had entered the hut, presumably after the alarm was raised, found Howells was still alive and had shot him at close range, muffling the sound of the retort, in order to silence him. So Chadwick was right; there had been two shots and the second one he had heard had been that fired into Howells's chest by Harold Bratton when he entered the hut. So Bratton had killed Howells, but why? What secret had Howells, and indeed Jackson, taken to their graves with them? And why had Vincent been determined to botch his own suicide in order to stay alive in agonising pain for a few minutes longer?

Oscendale thought he knew or rather who would know.

"North!" he bellowed. "Get me a lift up to Mametz Wood."

CHAPTER 41

9th July 1916

CORPORALS COOPER AND Chadwick sighed with exasperation as they saw the MFP officer making his way along the trench towards them. Hadn't he had enough? They certainly had. It had been a bloody awful day. The attack planned for today had been postponed and the Huns were still sitting there in the wood, malevolently grinning at them across the valley. *Why couldn't this bastard copper leave them alone?*

"Cooper and Chadwick, on your feet," ordered Sergeant Parkinson. "This officer of the Military Foot Police would like the benefit of your company once again, though God knows what he sees in you two miscreants."

Oscendale gestured to the men to resume sitting on the firestep and pondered his first question.

"Look, I know you've been through the mill today but I need to ask you a few more questions. You probably think I'm wasting your time but it's important to check one or two details with you, alright?"

Chadwick looked at Cooper and the two men shrugged.

"Think back to those days before Harold Bratton was killed. Did he seem different in any way?"

"How do you mean, different?" Cooper was as sullen in his responses as he had been previously.

"Just different to how he had been."

"Scared like? We were all bloody scared. Still are."

Oscendale knew it was the wrong approach and tried something else.

"Did he receive any letters, any news, anything that seemed to cheer him up at all?"

Both men shook their heads.

Oscendale stood up to leave when Cooper said, "Course, you could ask Josiah, his brother. They were quite close."

Oscendale stiffened. "His brother? I didn't know he had a brother."

"Yes, pretty close too."

"Which regiment is he with?"

"Ours," said Chadwick. "He's in the next battalion along. That's if he's still alive. Haven't seen him for a few days."

Harold Bratton's brother was sitting on a water container cleaning his rifle. Oscendale studied him as he approached. The man wrapped a piece of cloth around a length of string, dropped a brass weight into the breech, caught it as it emerged at the end of the barrel and pulled the cloth through. He did this several times before he noticed Oscendale's shadow fall across his legs.

"Josiah Bratton?" Oscendale broached, noting the usual look of suspicion when Bratton's eyes alighted on his MFP cap.

"Yes, sir," he answered, standing as he did so. Oscendale noted that he still held the rifle fast.

"Your brother was Harold Bratton who was killed in the recent attack?"

"Yes, sir. That's right."

"I'm sorry to hear that." Oscendale studied the young man. He seemed worn out, distant, focused on something far away.

"Thank you, sir. I was quite close to him when he fell. Had to write to our mam about it. Dunno if she's even got the letter yet." The man's eyes fell to the floor and Oscendale could feel his grief.

"Must have been hard. You two being so close."

Bratton returned his gaze to Oscendale's face, sensing that this officer had been enquiring about him before this conversation began. He became more guarded.

"What's this all about, sir? Obviously not just about Harold's death, is it? Had he been in some sort of trouble before he died?"

"Could be. Did you speak much to him in the days before the attack?"

"Yes, we saw a bit of each other, us being in the same part of the line and all. Didn't mention any trouble though. Why?"

"Did he mention a William Vincent?"

Oscendale saw a flash of understanding dart quickly across the man's eyes but in a second it was gone.

"No, sir. Wasn't he the bloke who killed two of our own men?"

"Yes. Did Harold mention anything about him?"

"No, sir. Didn't mention anything. I heard all about what happened from some of the other lads."

Oscendale knew the man was lying but couldn't work out why so he tried another tack.

"What happened to your brother's things?"

"After he died you mean? Well, they were just packed up ready to be sent home to our mam and dad. Dunno if they've gone yet, though."

Oscendale left the man to resume his rifle cleaning and was intrigued to see that he didn't look up once as he walked back along the trench. There was something not quite right in what he had said. Plausible, but certainly not entirely accurate.

CHAPTER 42

9th July 1916

"AH, OSCENDALE. SORRY to have kept you waiting." The remark was made without the slightest hint of sincerity and Oscendale knew that the officer behind the desk thought so little of military policemen that he could have stayed outside and rotted in the anteroom as far as he was concerned. He was the sort of nondescript, paper-shuffling officer who kept the machinery of the war moving smoothly. A pale brown moustache hung neatly trimmed on his upper lip – his badge of office. Time had little meaning. The war was not to be finished soon so one might as well take some time and care to ensure that all allotted tasks were fulfilled with punctilious attention to detail.

In fact Oscendale had been sitting outside kicking his heels for nearly an hour whilst a collection of other ranks came and went through the château doors with all the look of an army preparing for yet another great offensive.

"Sit down, please," the man said and gestured towards a chair. "How can I help you?"

"Corporal William Vincent."

"Ah yes," the man interrupted. "A sad case. Drank himself into a state of paranoia and shot two of his fellow NCOs, yes?"

Oscendale ignored the erroneous summation. "I'd like to know what his duties were in the days leading up to his death."

"Fairly routine I expect. The battalion was withdrawn from the line and was refreshing and re-equipping ready for the assault on Mametz Wood. Nothing important, I shouldn't think." The officer had not moved a muscle to consult any documentation.

Oscendale was not to be dissuaded by this officious little man. "Nevertheless, I'd like to see a copy of the battalion's war diary for May."

The officer shrugged and lifted a telephone. "Smith, bring in the war diary for the month of May, there's a good man."

A few seconds later a young clerk arrived with the document. Oscendale scanned the pages. Nothing unusual until the night of 14th May.

The account read:

At 00.35 a trench raiding party led by Lieutenant Marsden and comprising of six other ranks and Sergeants Jackson and Vincent left our trenches. Their objective was to glean information as to the enemy's strength in sector 4.13A near Mametz Wood, cut the wire and to take prisoners if possible. The party managed to reach the enemy's front line trench unnoticed. They entered the trenches and took two of the enemy prisoner. On their return they came under heavy machine gun fire and two men were killed. One man was wounded but was able to make his way back to our lines. The prisoners were searched and questioned and then passed back to headquarters for further interrogation.

Oscendale raised his eyes to meet the officer's. "Was Lieutenant Marsden present during the questioning of the two Germans?" he asked.

"Of course. Not sure we learnt much though, if my memory serves me correctly. Anyway, we soon passed them on to your Johnnies for a proper grilling."

"And is Marsden here now?"

"Yes, should be with his section on the range."

"I'd like to speak with him."

The adjutant shrugged again and lifted the receiver. *A man clearly in love with his work*, thought Oscendale.

Lieutenant Stephen Marsden was a tall, thickly set young man with jet-black hair. He stared suspiciously at Oscendale but an obligatory cigarette and a few remarks about the recent fighting at Mametz soon put him at his ease.

"You were present when the two Germans you brought in on the night of the 14th of May were interrogated?" he began.

"Well, not really an interrogation, sir, just a few routine questions. It was the information on their shoulder tabs, their regiment, plus the bits and pieces we found on them that told us most. They were bloody terrified when we grabbed them. They'd been just about to brew up when we arrived. Killed a few, the others ran off and these two just shoved their hands in the air. Wasn't so easy getting back but we made it. Of course the chaps were a bit rough with them when we reached our own lines but I seem to remember Sergeant Vincent putting a stop to that. Took a bit of a shine to one of them, made him a cup of tea and gave him some cigarettes. Can't think why. Blighter's mates had just killed two of our men."

Oscendale pondered the lieutenant's words. "Who conducted the questioning? You?"

"Yes. I did. Oh and Vincent of course. Insisted on staying. Said he'd write down what they said for me. Most accommodating."

A germ of an idea flashed though Oscendale's mind.

"Did you ever leave them alone, Marsden?"

"Leave them alone? What, the Huns? No. Oh, only when I went to telephone for your lot to come and get them, and to make my report to the CO Apart from that, no. And they weren't alone anyway. Vincent was with them."

Oscendale could barely bring himself to ask the next question.

"And the Germans. What regiment were they from?"

"Bavarians. Cocky pair too once they'd got over their fright."

"Do you remember their names?"

"Of course. Not likely to forget something as exciting as that night in a while. One was Friedrich Bruntz and the other was Erich Reizenberger."

"And what happened to the two of them after you'd finished your interrogation?"

Marsden took a long pull at his cigarette and leaned forward. "They were both escorted to the rear, as procedure states. Sergeant Vincent volunteered to take them."

I'll bet he did, thought Oscendale.

CHAPTER 43

9th July 1916

THE SENTRY STOOD smartly to attention and waved him through after he produced his identity card. The gravelled road opened onto an airfield with aircraft parked in neat rows at the side of a huge open field. He was driven to the airfield's only building, a temporary-looking wooden construction.

"Lieutenant Payne, please," he asked of a mechanic attending to an aircraft's engine, and was directed towards a blonde-haired man who stood talking to another mechanic next to an aircraft.

"Lieutenant Payne? Captain Oscendale."

"Ah yes," replied the man with a grin. "Good morning, sir. I received your message and volunteered to be the one to help you out. I hope you don't suffer from air sickness as it could be an interesting flight."

Oscendale warmed to the man's easy-going manner, so different to the many encounters he had had since the beginning of the case.

"To tell you the truth, Payne, this will be my first time in an aircraft, so I'm not sure quite what to expect."

Payne smiled again. "First time up, eh? Just remember not to jump out until we land and you'll be all right."

Oscendale smiled nervously. This was not something he was looking forward to doing but yesterday evening a thought had struck him and the only way of quietening the nagging voice in his head was to check the ground out from the air. Of course it could be another mad idea and, worse, could be the death of him, but he had to know.

"Right then, sir," interrupted Payne. "Let's get you kitted out and into the old kite."

'Old' was not a word that Oscendale needed to hear at that moment and he looked nervously once more at the collection of wire, fabric and wood that would support his life for the next hour and began to wonder once again if there weren't an easier way to check out his theory.

Ten minutes later he was clad in a borrowed flying suit and was perched in the front seat of a BE2c of the Royal Flying Corps. Payne was sitting behind him which was rather disconcerting as it gave Oscendale the feeling that *he* was in fact flying the plane, and that worried him.

The mechanic stood ready at the propeller for Payne's instructions, which came far too soon for Oscendale's liking. The blast of air as the propeller span furiously took his breath away and the noise from the engine battered his eardrums as the aircraft began to gather speed.

The ground rushed past and Oscendale decided he had better obey the old adage and not look down. It made no difference and as the aircraft left the ground his stomach sank towards the base of his spine, or even somewhere beyond it, and a feeling of terror overcame him as the ground fell further and further away below him.

Payne banked the aircraft towards the east, a manoeuvre that further alarmed Oscendale, and it was not for some minutes that his pulse slowed and his breathing approached something nearing normality.

Spoken communication was impossible owing to the roar of the engine and the rush of air so he sat still until Payne tapped him on the shoulder and pointed to the right. Risking a look over the side of the cockpit, Oscendale saw the brown scar of the front line and the shattered remains of Mametz

Wood. He was amazed at the regularity of the trenches, their zigzag patterns cut into the landscape, and further struck by the contrasting greenness and apparent normality of the land on either side of the battle-scarred area of conflict.

Oscendale took the map from a pocket inside his flying coat and attempted to orientate himself against the lie of the land below. The damage done to the wood by the fighting of the last week had ironically made his job easier. Instead of an umbrella of trees, the features at ground level were now clear. He could pick out the paths and streams through the wood, as well as the more sinister shapes of trench lines, pillboxes and other defensive fortifications. The outline of the wood was much changed from the map he attempted to hold steady in his hands, buffeted as he was by the air stream, but he soon managed to find the section of the wood he was looking for. He looked for the path where he and Loram had seen the German pioneers digging but found the distance between heaven and earth too great.

He turned around and motioned to Payne to fly lower. The pilot grinned and thrust his joystick forward. The nose of the BE2c tipped towards the ground and Oscendale's stomach lurched again as the ground rose towards him. Payne levelled off and began another circuit over the wood. Oscendale spotted the hole the Germans had made and attempted to cross-reference it on his map. He frowned and switched his vision several times between map and landscape. The path at the side of which the Germans had been digging, the one he had assumed was correct, seemed slightly too far away from a nearby stream. Could the stream have altered its course over the past few years? With artillery fire churning up the landscape, natural features like streams could change direction as the ground around them shifted.

Then he noticed a faint, light grey streak running parallel with the path. At that moment the BE2c lurched slightly and the streak disappeared. Oscendale indicated to Payne that he'd like another pass and Payne obliged.

As the aircraft began its second run over the area three jagged holes suddenly appeared in the fabric of the aircraft's nose right in front of Oscendale. A second later Payne threw the BE2c into a dive and the feature that he had wished to see again became all too apparent and all too close. Oscendale's mind raced with the possibility of what he had just witnessed and the fear that the aircraft was about to crash.

He attempted to turn around but Payne pulled hard on the joystick and the aircraft tore to the right, gaining height. Oscendale felt he was being sucked out of the cockpit and wedged himself even more firmly against the narrow sides of the enclosed space. Looking to his left he saw a blue German Albatross fighter shoot past, its black gothic cross sinister-looking in the morning sunlight. He knew that he was completely in the hands of the pilot seated behind him. The G-forces the BE2c was currently experiencing made it impossible for him to turn around so he hoped and prayed that Payne had not been hit. If he had then he was about to watch his own death approach completely unable to do anything about it.

The aircraft made another manoeuvre and Oscendale sighed with relief. Payne seemed to know what he was doing but he felt totally impotent, unable to assist the man in any way. He watched in fascination as the German Albatross suddenly appeared in front of him again and jumped as a Lewis gun mounted on the wing above his head rattled and spat lines of red bullets towards the German aircraft. Black smoke began to emerge from the engine and fire erupted.

Oscendale looked in horror as the German pilot stood up in his cockpit and scrambled out. He knew that British pilots had no parachutes but the Germans did and he watched with appalled fascination as the man, whose clothing and parachute were on fire, plummeted to his death.

There was no time to dwell on this macabre event. The BE2c shuddered as once more bullet holes appeared in its fabric. Payne pushed the nose of the aircraft towards the ground and, just when it seemed as though they were both to die in an appalling crash, he levelled out and began hedgehopping back towards the airfield. The pursuing German fighters – how many there were Oscendale had no idea – evidently thought Payne had lost his mind and deemed it unwise to follow.

A bumpy landing later and the BE2c was once more parked up on the airfield.

Payne removed his flying helmet and, with the ubiquitous grin, said to Oscendale, "Same time tomorrow, sir?"

Oscendale's response was unprintable.

CHAPTER 44

9th July 1916

AFTER A STIFF whisky, Oscendale was able to consider the outcome of his brush with death over the wood. Flying was not something he would call attractive but it had confirmed his suspicions. The path he and the Germans had assumed was marked correctly on the map was not the right one. The real path was some metres away from it to the east. But how could a path be lost in just a few years? And was it done deliberately? Oscendale had no idea at present but he now knew that the Germans had been digging in the wrong place.

The German spy who had stolen Muller's original copy of the map had not been seen since his escape from his cell but neither had there been any reports of suspicious events behind British lines that Oscendale could link to him. He therefore felt it was safe to assume that the spy had somehow returned the map to the German side of the lines. But as the map was now clearly incorrect, it would make no difference – the German pioneers would always be digging in the wrong spot. The actual location lay somewhere else entirely and his spirits rose as he felt sure that he was the only one who knew this.

"There's a Corporal Loram outside, sir. Said you wanted to see him." North's stentorian tones cut into Oscendale's thoughts.

"Ah yes, North. Send him in please."

"Looks a rum type to me, sir, to be honest," said North in a lowered tone.

"Yes, North, and that's why I want to see him," responded

Oscendale irritably. He really must find himself a better assistant, he vowed.

North saluted and ushered Loram into the room. *Bloody officers,* he thought, *who the hell did they think they were?*

Loram saluted and stood to attention. "Sir!" he said.

"No need for any bull, Loram. I need your advice on something. Come over to this table and tell me what you think. And give me your honest opinion."

He and Loram hunched over a large-scale map of Mametz Wood on which were marked all the latest British and German positions. Oscendale had added the grey path he had seen from the BE2c and the other features he remembered from Muller's map. He explained to Loram what he had seen from the air and Loram whistled as the truth dawned on him too.

"So the Huns were looking in the wrong place? You're saying that the path has been deliberately moved over the past few years in order to mislead anyone who finds the map?"

"Well it's certainly possible. Which means that whatever is buried at that spot is valuable and someone wants it to remain there until after the war is over."

"Which could be years, sir," Loram said with a frown.

"Exactly. Now if someone was to come along and dig in the right place, goodness knows what they might find." Oscendale looked at Loram with his head slightly cocked.

"Someone like you and me, sir."

Oscendale smiled. Not only was the man an excellent sniper, he was quick-witted as well. No wonder he was still alive.

Loram stood up from the table. "So what time do you want to go, sir?"

Oscendale thought for a moment. "So you think it's possible for the two of us to cross no-man's-land again, get past the German front line, get into Mametz Wood, find this spot, dig up whatever's there and get back safely to our own lines?" The sheer scale of what he was asking suddenly hit him.

Loram shrugged. "Put it this way, sir. If we don't try we'll spend the rest of our lives wondering and that'd be a shame, wouldn't it?"

Oscendale nodded. It was worth the risk.

CHAPTER 45

9th July 1916

"SO WHAT ARE conditions like inside the wood, sir? Do we know?" Lieutenant Burford asked the man sitting opposite him in the dugout.

Captain Hobson looked up. There was a nervous excitement in the man's voice; his words had been tinged with fear and Hobson contemplated the best response to make. *No good setting the youngster off now. Best keep him calm.* "HQ is not sure," he replied, realising at once that this would probably worry Burford more, but it was the truth. "It's obviously not been tended to at all since 1914 and any piece of wood, large or small, that is not maintained is inclined to be, how shall I say, overgrown and therefore difficult to pass through. If you add to that the damage caused by the recent shell fire, I think we'll probably find conditions, once we get inside, rather a challenge." He saw from the young man's face that this was not the reassuring answer he had been seeking but Hobson was a realist. *God, at a time like this,* he thought, *the last thing we need are lies,* and he wondered what effect his words would have on the lieutenant.

"But I understand there are paths through the wood. They would make our progress easier. Won't they be passable?" Burford persisted.

"I suspect that these paths, or rides, you refer to that existed long before the war have been blown to hell and back since then. I would also surmise that fallen trees will block them in places. They're also bound to be overgrown after nearly two years of neglect. Not sure they'll help us at all, actually."

Burford looked crestfallen as the enormity of the task became clearer and a melancholy settled on him. "All in all, a pretty sombre picture you're painting, sir," he said gloomily.

Hobson did not reply. Instead he lowered his eyes once more to the trench map in front of him, its crisscross patterns of German trenches cutting across the outline of the wood. *All we're talking about at the moment are the difficulties once we get into the bloody wood,* he thought. *What worries me more is the damn open ground we have to cross first.*

Burford sensed his mood and let silence fall between them for a while.

"The men are in good spirits, sir. They'll see us through," he said at last, unable to bear the awkward silence any longer.

"Oh, I don't doubt their spirit, Burford. It's whether they get close enough to the Germans to show it that worries me." He returned his thoughts to the map once more and Burford decided it was time to attend to his routine duties elsewhere. He stood up, saluted and made his way out of the dugout.

The plan was unsophisticated and blunt, Hobson mused, when he was left alone in the damp and the dark of the dugout. The attack on the 7th of July had been a costly, ill-planned failure and he was determined not to waste the lives of hundreds of men of the battalion he had trained for so long in preparation for this moment. But what realistic chance would these men have of succeeding in a headlong rush across open ground towards the edge of the wood where the Germans lay in wait? If the artillery did their job and kept the Germans' heads down for long enough then perhaps the casualties would not be as high as he feared. But if the bombardment lifted too soon to the next target and the Hun machine gunners were able to return to their positions to begin firing on the exposed men, then the carnage could be terrible.

Outside the dugout Burford walked through groups of men who were preparing to spend the hours of darkness that remained in a myriad of ways. From further along the trench he could hear the hymns rising up on the still night air and he realised that the men were not unaware of the desperate nature of the attack on the morrow and were attempting to ensure that their souls would be saved if they were to fall.

Hobson looked again at the order sheet he had received:

38th (Welsh) Division Order Number 39

9th July 1916

1. The Division will attack MAMETZ WOOD tomorrow with a view to capturing the whole of it. The hour of the infantry assault on the edge of the wood will be 4.15 a.m., but all troops will be in position by 3 a.m.

2. From 3.30 a.m. to 4.15 a.m. the Artillery will bombard the southern portion of MAMETZ WOOD.

3. From 3.55 a.m. a smoke barrage will be formed in the neighbourhood of STRIP TRENCH and will continue for 30 minutes.

4. At 4.15 a.m. the Artillery will lift gradually to a barrage north and west, maintaining a barrage on WOOD SUPPORT.

5. At 6.15 a.m. the Artillery barrage will lift and the Infantry will capture and consolidate the line.

6. At 7.15 a.m. the Artillery barrage will be lifted to the north edge of the wood and the Infantry will advance and consolidate themselves inside the north edge of the wood, making strongpoints.

There it was then. It all looked so logical, typed out on paper. All planned out with perfectly timed precision. Except that Hobson knew that human beings did not run to timetables. A man's fear could overcome him at any time and he could fail. The name of the wood leapt out of the page, typed there in capital letters by a clerk miles from the reality of the front line. And here he was, about to lead his men into action for the first time. The reality, he suspected, would be to watch his men die all around him and he wondered how he would react when confronted by it all. He hoped he would do his duty and lead the men to a glorious victory, but deep down he, like every other man that night, wondered whether he would be the one to crack, and, worse, do a bunk in front of the other men, to his everlasting shame. The enormity of the moment came over him and he laid the order paper back on the rough table, embarrassed by his uneasy thoughts.

CHAPTER 46

10th July 1916

THE MEN OF the 38th Welsh Division preparing for the next assault on Mametz Wood understood little of the great scheme of which they were a part. Their world was closing in, its borders defined by the comradeship of men alongside them – the welcome routines of cleaning and checking equipment, and of meal times and inspections and sentry duty.

And in the distance, ahead of them, the black mass of the wood stood watching in silence on the hill. Like some giant, formidable mythical beast it stared motionless at the insignificant individuals who sought to fight over its corpse. Dew fell from the blasted branches of its trees like the blood of the dead. Its bone-like tree stumps pointed starkly at the heavens as if accusing them of the agony it was enduring. Nature was dying amidst a frenzy of killing.

The southern edge had been blasted so thoroughly by shell fire that the trees were no longer the verdant vegetation of just days earlier. The landscape had been battered and the ground churned up so badly by the ploughshares of war that in place of the tightly packed trees that had stood there at the start of the attack, only a barren wilderness remained.

The trees were almost gone. In their stead stood rows of broken trunks like the rows of temporary grave markers. They mocked the men who were to advance over the bottom of the valley, calling them to their doom, reminding them of their mortality. *We will mark your passing for a while,* they seemed to say, *and then we, like you, will fade and be gone.* Ready-made markers of the dead. Brown and black, burnt and fractured reminders of the past, they marked the passage of time and the absence of civilisation.

Amidst this desolate landscape the Germans waited, huddled in their defensive positions, keenly awaiting the next attack of infantry from the British lines.

They had tried once and failed, and out there lay the bodies of their pals, turning crimson and blue in the summer sun, swelling like ripe fruit. The soft, warm rain of the past days had left the bases and walls of the trenches a clinging, cloying mass of wet mud that pulled at a man as he trudged through to his starting position. It was his turn now. Others had been before and had failed. Now it was up to him and his world encompassed only this and the minutes, or if he were lucky, hours to come.

The thought of death was too horrible to dwell on so a man looked around at the other faces near him. Who would it be? Him? Or him? Who would be alive when the sun set on this day? Surely himself. Surely all his experiences of life to this point, his childhood, his growing up, had not led just to here and now? Was this to be the end of everything? Just darkness? And all alone.

Welsh hymns were being sung softly. Voices murmured in the morning air. Melodic sounds gave vent to fear and fatalism:

Guide me O thou great Jehovah
Lead me through this barren land.

And barren it was. The artillery had continued to do its work and the ground was torn and twisted and rent asunder by the force of man's ingenuity. Nature had no answer to it. Cowed and timid, it lay there like a frightened woman, awaiting the next blow of a husband's hand.

The call came at last to make ready, and final adjustments

were made to webbing and packs and pouches, as if doing so would make any difference. Comfort. How did one die comfortably? Still it helped to reassure a man, to take his mind off his own death for a moment or two.

The soldiers of the Welsh Regiment stood nervously on the fire steps, their rifles clutched to their chests. This was the fourth day of the battle for the wood and they knew the odds on them being killed or wounded were shortening each time.

And fate might have determined that today was the day to die. Could one do anything about it? Could you alter the fact? Change the future or the lack of it?

Many tried. Bibles and photographs were kissed, lucky charms patted and secured. Prayers were said.

"Don't worry, lads. Jerry's bound to run out of ammunition sometime!" quipped one wag as each man pondered his own mortality and they counted down the minutes to the start of the attack. The artillery shells still screamed overhead and the explosions shook the ground as the German positions took yet another pounding. But it was never enough. Each man knew that, whether from experience or the tales they had been told as they huddled in the trenches or dugouts.

At last the time came. The whistles blew and the orders were shouted. The men poured out of the relative safety of the trenches into the hail of machine gun fire and artillery shells which burst around and amongst them.

Bodies began falling immediately. The zip of the machine gun bullets turned to a dull thud as they found their victims and men pitched forward in the prayer of death. Limbs cartwheeled through the air, providing danger in themselves, as artillery shells from German guns far away burst shrapnel overhead which ripped into bodies at lightning speed.

Nature had its own peculiar shrapnel. The flint pieces that lay scattered on the surface of the cool, brown earth flew through the air as explosions gouged holes in the ground. The pieces of cream and steel-grey flint punctured bodies, tearing off pieces like the teeth of invisible beasts of prey.

A man threw up his hands and pitched into a shell hole. Who would be next? The next to be entrapped in this web of bullets and metal shards?

Still they went on, their jaws firmly clamped, rifles clutched in pale hands devoid of blood. *Any second now and it will be me. How will it feel? Will I feel anything? God, just a 'Blighty' one, please. Enough to send me home, that's all.*

Ziegler made it to the first shell hole and threw himself into it, feigning death.

An hour later the firing had stopped. Bodies littered the valley and the cries of the wounded punctuated the silence of the air. The survivors were back in their trenches and Ziegler made himself as comfortable as he could and waited for nightfall.

CHAPTER 47

10th July 1916

THE LIGHT IN the dugout blurred and flickered an evil yellow as Bernhofer entered. Two pairs of dark-rimmed eyes met him as he ducked beneath the low doorframe and entered the subterranean world. This was no timber-lined, comfortable, deeply dug shelter with its own electricity supply as he had experienced in other parts of the German line. This hastily constructed cave was a throwback to a prehistoric existence and he wondered once more at how far civilisation had fallen that men were reduced to living like this. But he also knew the expediency of the construction – its purpose was to keep officers alive so that they were ready to lead their men when the next attack came.

The invidious musty smell of damp earth and damper men greeted his arrival. The two infantry officers had the unforgettable experience of battle carved deep into their faces. They were young men but their youth was gone forever. What remained were grey uniforms blending into greyer faces, and a sense of despair at the certainty of death; but he was struck by an absolute resolve in their being that impressed him.

"Good morning, gentlemen. *Hauptmann* Bernhofer. I believe you were expecting me?"

The two men remained seated and, as he was senior in rank, he could have pushed the point – as, no doubt, some of his erstwhile colleagues would have done – but Bernhofer was a reasonable man who had been a infantry officer himself once and he knew the strain these two men had been under, not just during the past days, but over the last two years.

The dark-haired *Leutnant* spoke first, his lips dry and cracked. "Yes, *Hauptmann* Bernhofer, we were told that someone would be paying us a visit."

Bernhofer studied the speaker for a moment. Like all infantry officers he met in the front line, the man was of indeterminate age. He hadn't shaved for some days and dark stubble framed a weather-beaten face. His uniform was mud-splattered and spoke silently of days of battles. His responsibility was undoubtedly a heavy one and the physical signs manifested themselves in a slight shuddering of his hand as he reached for his grey coffee mug. Bernhofer noted that as an officer from Military Intelligence he was not offered refreshment; these men felt he had no business being here and would be delighted when he departed.

His companion had resumed writing his report on the events of the past few hours and saw no reason to take part in the conversation. His blonde hair tumbled down across his forehead as he immersed himself in his task. Military Intelligence this far from the safety of headquarters meant only trouble for someone and he saw no purpose in becoming involved in something so dangerous. There was enough danger for any man all around them.

Bernhofer decided it was time to press on with his own task. "I have read your recent reports and see that you experienced a penetration into our lines by a British raiding party on the night of the sixth and seventh?"

"Yes," said the *Leutnant*. "It seemed like a routine trench raid but, given the work the pioneers were conducting on one of the rides nearby, it seemed appropriate to let headquarters know of it."

Bernhofer knew that Sollner had ordered groups of pioneers to dig at various locations in the wood, but without either copy of the map to hand they had been digging blind. Sollner knew roughly the area in which it, whatever it was, lay, but he was growing increasingly frustrated by the lack of results. The latest dig that Sollner had ordered next to the ride he thought had been indicated on the map had proved fruitless but he was still convinced that something lay hidden nearby. It seemed absurd to him that the map would have been drawn and the spot marked if there was nothing of any consequence there. He was convinced that the spot had not been examined by anyone else previously – the pioneer officer had reported that the latest patch of ground seemed undisturbed before they began their task. However, the fact remained that there was nothing there so the only conclusion he could draw was that the map was incorrect. The spot could not be far away but the question was where. He could hardly order the pioneers to dig holes everywhere close to the spot, especially during the course of a major battle. He had to be certain where the correct location was before he lost any remaining credibility he had with his superiors. And now he had handed the task to Bernhofer who had decided to try a different approach as there was still no word from his own agent behind the British lines.

"Was it a large party?" he asked.

"Not large but enough to penetrate our lines. Strangely, they took none of our men prisoner, although they had the opportunity, but we managed to kill two of the Tommies."

"Did the British retrieve their dead?" Bernhofer enquired.

"No, they were driven out of our trench before they were able to do so."

Bernhofer asked to be shown the bodies and was led out of the dugout and along the trench until they reached the latrine area.

"Best place for them," said a large soldier as he passed Bernhofer. "Keeps all the flies in one place."

The bodies of the two dead soldiers lay on their backs, eyes staring vacantly at the early dawn sky. One had been shot in the head and a piece of his skull was missing, the remainder consisting of a mass of dark red congealed blood and creamy-coloured brain matter. Flies were busy breakfasting on the soft tissue and Bernhofer looked away, revolted.

The second man had been bayoneted in the side and his face still carried the signs of his death agony. Bernhofer bent down to examine his clothing. No insignia, naturally. A trench raiding party would strip all signs of their regiment from their clothing before going into no man's land so that the enemy had no means of identifying who was in the trenches opposite them.

He patted the man's uniform and felt for any items beneath the cloth. He then searched his pockets and found nothing so with a deep breath he turned his attention to the man's companion in death.

Trying not to look at the mass of flies that refused to be disturbed from their gorging, he conducted a similar routine on the man's clothing and was rewarded when his fingers encountered a piece of metal in the dead soldier's trouser pocket. He reached further inside and removed a cap badge, the three Prince of Wales feathers above the motto 'Ich Dien' and the words 'The Welsh' leaving him in no doubt as to which regiment the owner had belonged. This act was strictly against British regulations, he knew, but the man had probably considered it a good luck charm which he had refused to leave behind. The veteran perhaps of several other close quarter encounters with the enemy, it had previously served him well so he had seen no reason to leave it behind. On this occasion he had been wrong on two counts. He had broken a cardinal rule of a trench raiding party and the badge had failed to give him any good luck. His previous survival had been due to his training and the hand of fate, not the piece of metal that Bernhofer now held in the palm of his hand.

He slipped the badge into his own pocket and rose. Checking his watch, he was just about to bid goodbye to the sullen officer when the world seemed to stop.

For a fraction of a second he thought he had suddenly lost his hearing. Then his eyes saw the right arm of the *Leutnant* fly off. A huge hand hit him in the small of his back and he was propelled forward. Great geysers of earth began to erupt all about him. He could still hear nothing but could see the officer writhing around on the ground, desperately trying to stem the flow of blood from his empty shoulder. His mouth was open and he was screaming with pain but Bernhofer could hear nothing. He felt his back but could detect no injury so he assumed that it had been a shockwave that had flung him to the floor.

He crawled back along the trench towards the safety of the dugout. Shells were falling everywhere, in front of the trench, behind it and occasionally in it as well. He passed several remnants of men, torsos, limbs and heads scattered along the length of the trench. The structure of the defensive system was collapsing, walls were caving in under the intensity of the bombardment and several times he had to scramble over mounds of earth in order to make progress.

Bernhofer rounded a traverse and saw that the sanctuary of the dugout had gone. A shell had fallen directly on the roof and whoever had been inside when the barrage commenced was now entombed there. He looked around wildly for an escape from the carnage that was unfolding all around him.

The ground beneath his feet moved again and he lost his balance and fell onto a soldier who was staring in horrified fascination at the slurry of steaming pink entrails emerging from his stomach. Bernhofer rolled off the dying man and stumbled further along the trench.

He reached another cavity in the trench wall and crawled into a small empty dugout. He had chosen his end, his last place on earth. If he was to die it was to be here, in a damp earthy chamber, rather than being blown apart or watching his body die out in the open. Here he would stay until the opening was sealed. Then he would breathe the stagnant air until he slipped into unconsciousness.

Above him the hammer blows of the gods still fell. He flinched and covered his head with his arms, as one shell seemed to explode directly above him. He prayed for the shelling to stop and pressed his hands to his ears in the hope of preserving his hearing should he survive, then he closed his eyes and waited for the final explosion.

After three quarters of an hour the bombardment ceased, as if someone had turned off a machine and the silence returned. Then it recommenced, but the shells were now falling further away to the north. Bernhofer opened his eyes and saw that the light and dust were still coming through the doorway. He crawled forward, pawing at the earth that had begun to pile up outside it. A few minutes later there was enough room for him to crawl through and he emerged blinking into the sunlight.

The trench line had vanished. A chaos of mounds of earth and broken pieces of wood were all that remained. Items of equipment lay all around, as did the remains of men. A few shocked survivors began to emerge from their burrows and each stared about him with stunned disbelief.

Bernhofer's training cut through the haze in his mind and he began to order the men to retrieve their machine guns from dugouts and to mount them behind any mound of earth they could find. Within a few minutes he had produced deadly order out of chaos and the machine guns stood ready to do their work. The guns had been assembled and lay like a line of fingers poised and ready to strike.

He could not yet see the Tommies for the tangle of uprooted trees and blackened stumps all around them but he could hear the sounds of fighting as the enemy approached the first line of trenches at the edge of the wood. Then he saw the first khaki figure moving cautiously through the trees and braced himself for the impending fight.

The artillery fire had churned up the ground in front of them. Some of the younger trees had been beaten down and fallen trees and branches had formed themselves into barricades behind which Bernhofer and his newly acquired command lay.

The men fidgeted nervously and waited for his order to fire. He raised his right arm and allowed the Tommies to get closer until it seemed certain that they would be overrun. When he was sure that they could not miss he dropped his hand.

In unison the machine guns and rifles opened fire. The staccato shriek ripped through the wood and bullets tore through human flesh. The British fell everywhere and the cries of the wounded went unnoticed against the metallic chatter of the killing machines that rent the air.

In a few minutes it was all over and Bernhofer ordered

the guns to cease firing. Then the screams of the wounded rose like a demonic choir and Bernhofer became human once more, troubled by the death and suffering he had just ordered. He turned and looked at the men alongside him, panting and wild-eyed. They had survived.

CHAPTER 48

10th July 1916

THE BRITISH BARRAGE had begun at 3.30 a.m. The shriek
and whine of the shells began in the far distance and hurtled
overhead to explode with fearsome force on the southern
part of the wood. The Welsh soldiers peered over the
parapets of their trenches and watched with a growing
sense of exultation at this display of the enormous power of
Man over Nature. Trees were uprooted and branches and
trunks blown into the air. Great volcanoes of earth burst
upwards and soil and debris and pieces of human beings fell
in a deafening manifestation of the devastating effect of the
efficiency of modern warfare.

Private Stanley Morgan watched in awestruck fascination
as the bombardment rained down on the German positions.
He looked briefly along the trench at the soldiers waiting
quietly with fixed bayonets. He loaded ten .303 cartridges
into the magazine of his rifle and put another in the breech,
ready to fire when needed. He patted the canvas bag on his
chest nervously, where two Mills bombs sat waiting to do
their terrible work, and he wondered whether there would
be any need to use them after the artillery had finished with
this section of the wood.

At 4.15 a.m. Colonel Edwards, who had lain fifty yards
ahead of the trenches out in no-man's-land watching the
bombardment, stood up, took off his steel helmet and, as the
shelling moved on to the next target further into the wood,
motioned with it for the first line to advance.

Without a moment's hesitation, Private Morgan and the

rest of the first wave climbed out of the trench and moved off in perfect order across no-man's-land. Colonel Edwards repeated his motion with his helmet when the line had advanced 100 yards, and the waves of infantry came on towards the wood, which sat battered in the near distance, almost invisible now owing to the smoke of the exploding shells.

As the Welshmen started their advance the German artillery opened fire, shells bursting amongst the advancing waves, hammering holes in the lines. Men began to fall in heaps on the ground and the living murmured prayers and shouted defiance in equal numbers.

At last they reached the edge of the wood. A grey soldier sprang up in front of Morgan who, conditioned to react without hesitation after months of training, stabbed his bayonet into the man's stomach. He watched as the man fell gurgling to the floor, his hands clasped to the red hole in his uniform. Morgan watched the man dying without compassion and felt a surge of strength and determination course through his veins.

A bullet hit the soldier on his right who fell yelling to the floor, clutching his thigh. Morgan looked up and saw a German sniper strapped to the upper branches of a tree some thirty yards away. The bombardment's shock waves had blown leaves from the branches and the man sat partially exposed. Morgan lifted his rifle and, taking careful aim, a new-found coldness steadying his arms, opened fire. Immediately, the sniper's G98 telescoped rifle fell from his arms and clattered through the branches to the earth below. The man lolled backwards in his fixed position, his face pointed towards the heavens.

Elsewhere, soldiers worked feverishly with their bayonets and rifle butts to break down the undergrowth barring entry to the wood. Years of neglect had left parts of the edges of the wood impassable, and they tore and hacked in their frustration to join their comrades who were already fighting within.

Morgan forced his way in eventually and stumbled on bodies from both sides lying on the ground where they had fallen. Some lay still and dead, others reached out to him as he passed, imploring him for solace or water or both.

Like corpses, the broken boughs stretched across the ground. Ready for burial themselves, they mocked the passing men who planned to live on. Skeletons of nature, this was no passing of the seasons but an unnatural wiping away of life itself.

Amongst the splintered branches lay the dead. Contorted unnatural shapes, they lay next to, across and, in some cases, impaled on the broken wood – Man and Nature locked together in death.

He pressed on as the cacophony of noise grew louder all around him. Men fought hand to hand in clearings and around the trunks of the trees. His heart hammered as he envisaged a German infantryman appearing from behind every tree he passed, bayonet aimed at his torso. He watched in fascination as two soldiers who had evidently bayoneted each other simultaneously watched the other die. It was as if the world had gone mad, he decided, as men fought to kill and survive.

Morgan joined up with a group of men and they made steady progress as the Germans began to fall back in front of them. Suddenly their progress was halted by a platoon of Germans who refused to retreat; he called on them to surrender as they were surrounded but no reply came, so the Welshmen dropped to their knees and began firing until each German fell in turn.

After the slaughter was over, Morgan cautiously advanced towards the bodies, his rifle extended and a round in the breech. The Germans had fallen in grotesque poses, legs twisted under bodies, arms flung back behind heads. Their dark grey uniforms were now stained red in parts and ever expanding pools soaked through the cloth onto the floor of the wood. He poked a few with his bayonet to ensure they were dead but felt only pity now for the wounded ones who groaned in agony as they watched their attackers advance. Out of respect for their courage the soldiers let them live and moved further on into the undergrowth, Morgan's blood lust dissipating rapidly.

CHAPTER 49

10th July 1916

BRATTON LAY WITH his face pressed to the dead leaves on the floor of the wood as the bullets wreaked their havoc all around him. They whistled over his head and splintered the wood of the trees above him. Several times large chunks fell on his back but he resisted the temptation to check himself for injuries. To do so would have attracted another burst of machine gun fire from the German positions up ahead.

After a time the firing stopped and he listened to the sounds of men dying to his left and right. He wondered who they were, if any of his mates were amongst them or whether they were part of the group he had seen retreating out of the wood as the attack petered out in failure. He knew he could have attempted to join them but that was not in his plan. His destiny was about to come to fruition. This was his time. He had waited all his life for an opportunity like this and he would seize it or die in the attempt.

By the time that darkness fell he was stiff with cramp; his muscles and joints grumbled as he attempted to rise without being seen and targeted.

He had studied the map several times during the day and had chosen his route carefully. Looking cautiously about him and listening intently before he set off, he moved deeper into the undergrowth.

"I congratulate you, *Hauptmann* Stoltz," said Michael Bernhofer with the stiffness of a loser. "Your man Ziegler certainly delivered on this occasion."

Stoltz smirked with the glow of the victor and nodded in return.

"He is my best agent and I was confident he could retrieve the map," replied Stoltz. It is always best to trust a professional, I find."

Silence fell between the two momentarily as both men's eyes remained fixed on the other. It was a warm evening and the windows were open but the warmth of the room lent an edginess to the sparring of the two adversaries.

"It is good that we now have the map and can proceed to the next stage of the plan," interjected *Oberst* Sollner, sensing the growing hostility between the two men. "Now let us plan the recovery operation before the wood falls and it is lost to the English."

The other officers in the room were relieved by Sollner's words and gathered at the table to view the map that Ziegler had taken from Oscendale's tunic pocket. Bernhofer and Stoltz nodded at each other to declare a temporary truce in their battle for supremacy and joined Sollner at the map laid out on his table.

But Bernhofer held back slightly, curious though he was to view the contents of the document. Inwardly he fumed. His own agent had been close to retrieving the map for him, he knew, but Stoltz had stolen a march on him and the speed at which the man Ziegler had recovered it had surprised him greatly. The game was now over and he had lost. Stoltz would now enjoy the favouritism of this group of officers. His would be the name suggested for promotion and his would be the subsequent rewards. For Bernhofer there remained only second place in a field of two.

He suddenly flinched as Sollner's voice shouted, "But this is just the map that Muller drew from memory! It's not the original map from 1914! It's the copy – flawed and useless! We have dug at the spot indicated on it. It's wrong. The stupid man couldn't remember the right spot!" He jabbed angrily at the piece of paper. "It's not here!"

Sollner whirled round to face Stoltz. "Your man has brought back the map that Muller had on him when he was killed by the British after he had been captured. The map he took back from my possession! But it is not the original map I wanted, Stoltz!"

Stoltz twitched as all eyes in the room focused on his. The silence at the end of Sollner's rant hung in the air and he knew he must respond somehow. "I am sorry, *Herr Oberst*. I assumed that the British officer had the original in his possession already, not just this copy. My agent found only this one in his jacket. The original, as we suspected, was passed to a British soldier by Muller in 1914. We have the soldier's name – William Vincent – and we know that he committed suicide after murdering two of his fellow soldiers. My agent found all this in the British files. What we still don't know is where the map went next. It was not found on Vincent's body and there is no reference to it in his file. I assumed that this was the original." He paused and swallowed hard, hoping he had been able to save some face.

Sollner lowered his voice to a whisper. "Never assume, Stoltz. Particularly twice." He turned to Bernhofer and smiled without humour. "It appears Bernhofer that the gods have given you a second chance. Find me the original map."

Bernhofer looked at Stoltz. His head was lowered, heavy with the shame of public failure. Bernhofer felt a rekindled surge of excitement.

The game was not yet over then.

Later that evening Bernhofer sank deep into his hot bath and turned the cap badge he had found on the dead soldier over in his fingers. As he attempted to soak away the tension of the day he thought about the direction this hunt was going in. It was too much of a coincidence that the British had sent a trench raiding party into that sector of the wood. He wondered what they could possibly hope to achieve by doing so. Their intelligence sources would have told them which German regiments were stationed in the wood well in advance of the first attack on the seventh, and if they had wanted to disrupt the defence system they would have sent in a far larger group of soldiers.

That left him with the inescapable conclusion that someone on the British side was seeking the exact same thing that he was: whatever was buried near that ride in Mametz Wood.

A female voice called to him from the adjoining doorway. He placed the badge on the side of the bath and turned his attention to other, more pleasurable matters.

At the same moment Bratton was making his way cautiously through the dense vegetation of the wood. He knew that one false step now would bring rifle or machine gun fire upon him and his quest would suddenly cease. But tonight he felt almost invisible, immortal, as if God had chosen him for this express purpose. And if it wasn't God then why should he care? All his life he had known poverty and hard work, and the misery of drudgery. His time in the army had been a welcome escape from all that and he could not say that he hadn't enjoyed it – even the killing. The Huns were the enemy and deserved to die. Now he had the chance to change his life forever.

He froze as he heard voices talking nearby in a language he did not understand. He peered warily through the leaves of a bush and saw two German soldiers standing outside a concrete machine gun emplacement. They were smoking and sharing some topic of discussion which seemed to be getting one of them quite animated. Bratton skirted carefully around the area until he came across the path he was seeking.

The ride ran straight between lines of broken trees and was pockmarked with shell holes and covered with fallen trunks. He looked up and down its length before crawling across it and disappearing into the undergrowth on the far side. The shelling had blown away much of the vegetation and to his surprise he saw the outlines of not one but two rides running through the wood.

He kept very still and recovered his breath until he was absolutely certain that he had not been observed. He took out the map once more, checked his position and gauged twenty yards before dropping to his knees. With breathless excitement he began to dig. The moist earth came away easily beneath his entrenching tool. The metal blade suddenly hit a stone and he cursed himself for his own impatience as the sound rang out amongst the silent, watching trees. He had come so far and it would be terrible to ruin it all now through too much haste.

He put the tool carefully to one side and began to dig with his hands. At last his fingers closed around a wooden box some twelve inches square with a smooth surface. He dug quickly now, all rational thoughts gone from his mind. Could this be it? Within seconds the box was free of the grip of the ground and, struggling with the unexpected weight, he lifted it up from its tomb. He tried to open it. Locked. *Of course*. Any box that contained something of the value Bill Vincent had told him about would be locked. He drew his bayonet and inserted the tip into the lock. With a click the lock was broken and the lid flew back. Bratton reached inside and his hand met a score of cloth bags which held hard objects that squirmed and wriggled as he dug deeper. He removed a velvet bag with a drawstring, pulled it open and reached inside. Dozens of small hard bevelled objects met his grasp and, with hands trembling, he drew one out. He knew straight away what it was and quickly brushed the soil from his hands before holding it up to the moonlight.

The light flashed and danced from the surface as the jewel reflected the pale light of the moon. His heart beat faster as he realised that this was the culmination of all his hopes and dreams. It was more than he had anticipated. Vincent's dying word rang again in his head. *Diamonds.*

Suddenly he froze. Someone was moving through the trees behind him. Stowing one of the small jewel bags inside his tunic, he replaced the box and quickly covered it. If he was captured now he did not want to lose everything. He grabbed his rifle and began to back away into the bushes, peering hard into the gloom as he went.

Into the clearing came a German soldier holding a Mauser rifle. He looked around until his eyes alighted on the entrenching tool. Bratton held his breath as the German examined the object. Raising his Lee Enfield to his shoulder, Bratton rested the foresight on the German's face. He was just about to risk everything by pulling the trigger when the man called out and several other soldiers quickly joined him.

A patrol. Bratton knew now that there was no chance of retrieving anything more from the spot. Thankful that he had quickly swept some earth and leaves into the hole, he turned away. What he had in his pocket would have to be enough – for the present anyway. He would have preferred the lot, he mused, but could not complain. He would come back for the rest soon, he promised. But even so there was enough in his possession now to change everything forever. Smiling to himself, he began the dangerous journey back to his own lines, planning what he would buy first with his new-found wealth.

If he made it back, that was.

CHAPTER 50

10th July 1916

THE NIGHT WAS dark and the wind keen as Oscendale and Loram crawled slowly across no-man's-land. The star shells burst overhead and the chatter of machine gun fire could be heard sporadically in the distance.

I must be mad, thought Oscendale. *The 38th Division is struggling to take this wood and for the second time in a few days I'm trying to get into it almost single-handed to wander around in the dark looking for God knows what. At least I now know where to look.*

The 38th Division's latest attack earlier in the day had, however, made his job somewhat easier. The British now had a toehold in the wood and it was this that he and Loram had designated as their jumping-off point. The lines of trenches were less regular here and the German defensive positions consisted of a series of strongpoints, with support trenches further back. They had consulted one of the most up-to-date British maps of the German defences before setting off, but even the officer it belonged to had admitted that they were not sure what the *Boche* would throw up that night in an attempt to impede their further progress.

Suddenly, Loram motioned to him to lie still and Oscendale froze with his cheek pressed to the slimy mud. Hunched figures were moving around just ahead of them. A German wiring party, he assumed. The men moved slowly and cautiously, twisting the great corkscrew spikes into the earth before stringing lines of barbed wire between them. He and Loram were forced to watch them for fully twenty minutes before they completed their task and moved away to the west.

They crawled cautiously forward again until they were up against the newly laid belt of wire. It was not the thick, heavy, spiked wire that Oscendale had seen in carefully prepared defensive positions. This was hurriedly done by men who were afraid of being discovered and machine-gunned, and they crawled beneath it before continuing their journey.

After some minutes the hulk of a strongpoint appeared before them, slowing their pace still further; they both knew that one metallic click of rifle striking belt buckle would bring a rain of fire from the embrasure above. But they had stripped their equipment right down in readiness for this moment and made safe progress deeper into the stumps of trees that now formed the wood.

They found a shell hole and drew breath. Producing a light to consult the map was impossible so Oscendale had memorised its features earlier that evening. Obsessed with the map as he was, this had not taken long.

He indicated to Loram that they were now close to the spot where they had seen the German pioneers fruitlessly digging, and crawling out of the shell hole they soon reached the path. Glancing up and down its shattered line, they crossed it and began searching for the grey scar that Oscendale had seen briefly from Payne's BE2c.

It took them only a few moments as, sweeping the ground with his hand, Oscendale scattered a thick layer of earth and wood debris to uncover a gravelled surface. So he had been right! This path had been constructed, used before the war, then abandoned, or perhaps deliberately covered, in recent times.

He moved to the spot he was seeking and, with Loram

crouching, rifle at the ready and eyes scanning in all directions, he began to dig.

He realised he was in the right spot as the ground yielded suspiciously easily to his entrenching tool. After digging for a few seconds he hit a hard object with a sound like a pistol shot, but the wind still blew and the noise faded quickly into the darkness. He puzzled momentarily at the softness of the ground but knew it was unsafe to delay.

Risking no further sound, Oscendale put the tool to one side and began digging with his hands. His fingers felt a large shape in the soil and he clawed feverishly to prise it free. He easily broke it loose from its hold in the earth and as he held it in his hands suspicion became conviction as he realised that someone else had mirrored his actions – and recently too judging from the state of the ground and the broken lock on the box. There was no time to attempt to open it or to dwell too long on this new development so he quickly placed it inside the empty haversack he had brought expressly for the purpose and turned to signal to Loram that he was done and that it was time to set off for home.

Except that Loram wasn't there.

A brief surge of panic overcame him but he realised that the darkness and the fear and the excitement of the event were throwing his emotions into a higher gear and he forced himself to remain calm.

"Good evening." A voice spoke behind him. He turned to see a German officer holding a Luger pistol pointed at his head. "Please pass to me the object I have just watched you retrieve from the ground. I am so pleased that I have not wasted my time on such a filthy night."

The officer was flanked by several soldiers who stood motionless, rifles at the ready. Oscendale noticed that one of them also held a British entrenching tool in his hand. Realising that his situation was hopeless, he reluctantly removed his haversack from his shoulder and was about to take out the box when a rifle shot cracked and the German officer slumped forward onto the ground.

The German soldiers stood frozen in shock. Four more shots rang out and four of the men fell to the ground. The remaining two panicked and ran off in the direction from which they had come.

Feeding fresh cartridges into his rifle, Loram emerged from the blackness behind Oscendale.

"That was a close call, sir. Just as well he didn't bring a whole company. However, I think those Huns will be back with their pals in a few minutes so I suggest we get out of here."

Oscendale nodded in agreement and the two men disappeared once more into the cover of the night.

CHAPTER 51

10th July 1916

THE CRAMP IN his left thigh began to burn as if a glowing piece of shrapnel had entered it. He took a chance and slowly moved it back and forth a little to get the blood circulating again. It was always the same muscle that protested, he thought ruefully. But then being held in the same position for hours at a time was bound to irritate parts of the body.

He blinked and looked again through the telescopic sight fitted to the top of his G98 sniper's rifle. Still nothing moved out there in no-man's-land. The moon provided perfect visibility for him and he knew that the conditions were unfavourable for the British to stage a trench raid so he was not hopeful of anything happening before dawn. But he had the patience of a man who had been trained well and who had spent many fruitless hours staring through a glass optic at the enemy lines. He knew that he could not be seen – his camouflage suit made sure of that – but he might have just one chance all night and he had to make the most of it.

He moved the foresight of his rifle towards the enemy parapet and silently asked just one Tommy to raise his head inquisitively over the top. Just one target – it was all he usually needed. A quick settling on the shape, a gentle squeeze of the trigger and the man would be dead, like dozens of others before him. How many exactly he could not recall. He knew that some of his colleagues kept a score, but that had never been his way. Reviled by the men on his own side, who knew that a sniper in action usually brought enemy artillery fire raining down upon them, and loathed by the enemy for his unseen killing of their comrades, he was a lonely killer and a lonelier man.

Brushing the black mood from his thoughts, he concentrated once more upon his task, moving his sight back to the craters that punctuated no-man's-land. The minutes passed and his thigh began to ache once more. Just as he was about to withdraw from his position and try somewhere further up the line, he detected a slight movement near a shell hole. He adjusted his sight for the shorter distance between the deadly rifle and his intended target and waited for the movement to repeat itself. Within seconds he saw it again, or rather saw him again, for it was an enemy soldier crawling slowly back towards his own trenches.

He wondered where he had come from. There had been no reports of attacks upon their lines that night so what was a British soldier doing making his way back towards his own parapet? He could have been wounded during the day's fighting – it was the custom of the wounded to wait until dark before attempting to return to their own lines. It was a risky business in daylight but at night one risked being shot by either side.

He watched again as the man halted his progress. He did not look wounded. Perhaps he was a Forward Observation Officer who had spied out targets for the next day's artillery fire, or a member of a listening post endeavouring to glean information from the men's chatter in the trenches opposite. Whatever his task had been, it was over now, he decided, and focused on the back of the man's head. He prided himself on his accuracy of shot and would pick the smallest target he could, confident of his own skill. He began to squeeze the trigger, conscious once more of the ache in his thigh. His grip tightened and a sharp crack indicated that the bullet was on its way.

Bratton saw and felt the mini-explosion of dirt in front of his face. Small pieces of dirt flew into his face and eyes, temporarily blinding him. *Sniper! Bloody hell!* He knew that he had to get into his own trenches quickly so he stood up and, wiping the dirt out of his eyes, began a zigzagging run towards his own lines. A rifle fired ahead of him, its muzzle flash clearly visible in the darkness. *Don't shoot at me, you silly sod,* he thought, and flung himself prone on the ground.

"Hey! Hey! Don't shoot! It's me, Bratton!" he cried, tears of fear running down his cheeks. "Stop firing, for God's sake!"

"Get in here, Bratton, before the bastard has another shot at your arse!" said a voice he recognised as belonging to Sergeant Parkinson.

Another voice he didn't recognise said, "He won't be firing again, sarge. I got him."

Oscendale and Loram had found no difficulty returning to their own lines, quickly retracing their steps back to the newly established British front line in the southern part of the wood. Oscendale had gone off to report to his superiors on their find but Loram had found it difficult to sleep after the excitement of the evening so had decided to make himself useful fulfilling a task he had recently been allocated.

Loram had waited as patiently as the German for the man to make a mistake. There had been reports of a sniper being active in the sector for some days and he had been ordered to find and eliminate him. As soon as the German had fired at Bratton, he had marked the spot and focused his optical sight on a sandbag that was a slightly different shape to the others around it. Scanning the area to the left and right he spotted a slight gap between the sandbag and its neighbours. He focused and squeezed the trigger. A rifle barrel emerged out of the gap and then was still.

The sentry walking along the length of German trench noticed the sniper clad in his camouflage smock. He watched him for a while, impressed by the man's concentration on his task. How these men kept still for so long was beyond him. He knew that he didn't have the patience. After a while he decided to initiate a conversation to relieve the boredom of his duty.

"Seen anything out there?" he asked pleasantly.

There was no reply from the sniper. *Hmmm, surely he can talk*, thought the man, so he repeated the question. Still no reply. *This was just rude,* he thought, *who does he think he is?* So he shook the man's shoulder.

The sniper's head flopped backwards to reveal a hole in his face where his nose had been.

CHAPTER 52

11th July 1916

THE FOLLOWING DAY saw the Germans still occupying the north and western parts of the battleground. The 14th Battalion of the Welsh Regiment, including Private Morgan, Lieutenant Burford and their fellow soldiers, were relieved and withdrawn from Mametz Wood.

As they walked back through the shattered, twisted remains of the wood, the survivors saw men in khaki and grey lying dead on the ground everywhere they looked. The fighting had been fierce and the bodies paid silent testimony to that fact. Worse were the sections of body parts that lay scattered around the abandoned equipment, ammunition boxes, coils of barbed wire, food containers, gas helmets and rifles. Red pools of blood stained the leaves on the floor of the wood and as the men passed they gave silent thanks for their continued survival. How long it would last, none of them knew.

It was raining. *It was always bloody well raining,* thought Sergeant Albert Millbourne of the Labour Corps. At least it always seemed to be raining when they had to do this job. And what a job it was. Moving bodies from one hole to another. 'Concentration' was the official term for it. Millbourne and his lads had a few other names for it. It boiled down to the same thing anyway. Digging up a dead bloke, or what was left of him, seeing if he had any identification and then loading him onto a cart and reburying him somewhere else, all nice like.

That was if they could find anything. Shell bursts did terrible things to human beings, Millbourne knew. You got rolled into a hole, covered up and then the Hun bastards let loose again and churned the whole ruddy lot up. Blew corpses into the air until they were just bits. Unrecognisable bits. And he was supposed to make sense of this mess and label them up all neat and proper. Sometimes you could, sometimes you couldn't.

And now it was all to be done in a hurry. Someone was getting sensitive about all these bodies being blown out of the ground and sprayed all over the battlefield. Bad for morale. *You bet.* So he and his squad had to dig up the men they'd buried just a few days ago, and cart them off to an undisturbed area. *Rest in peace. My arse,* he thought, and threw away the butt of the cigarette he'd been smoking as he heard his name being called.

"Sarge! Hey sarge! Here's a queer thing. What do you make of it?" The voice belonged to Corporal Garland. Good man, Garland, but a bit too wary of strong drink for Millbourne's liking.

"What's the matter now, corporal? Another one without his head?"

"No, sarge, stranger than that. Look, there's two in one hole."

"So what? Maybe one of your lazy sods decided to double up. Probably nearly time to knock off and he didn't fancy digging another hole."

"Sorry, sarge, but I know we buried them all proper. We never put two in this grave, I'm sure of it."

Millbourne shrugged and said, "Okay, let's have them out anyway. See who they were."

The burial party stood up to their calves in thick, clinging mud and looked up at Millbourne as he stood over the grave. The look of disgust was plain to see but Garland got them moving and before long two bodies, each in a mud-plastered groundsheet, lay alongside the empty grave.

"Who's supposed to be in there?" asked Millbourne.

"Just 69387 Private David Denby, sarge," Garland responded.

"Then who's the other bloke? Any ID?"

"No, his face is burnt to hell and back, no identity discs, but he's Welsh Regiment according to his badges."

"Search through his pockets. See if he's got any letters or cards on him," ordered Millbourne, becoming irritated by this interruption to his well-organised routine.

The men looked at each other and hesitated. Going through a dead man's pockets was bad enough, but one who had lain underground for several days was enough to daunt even the bravest of them. Eventually Garland barked at a thin-faced soldier and he began the ghoulish task. Nobody spoke as the man dug deep into the corpse's pockets.

"Nothing. Nothing at all," he said, after what to Millbourne seemed a very brief examination. Still he couldn't blame the lad. Horrible job really.

"What's that?" Millbourne's keen eye had caught sight of something lying half-buried in the bottom of the trench.

One of the men lowered himself into the grave and pulled at a piece of cloth, jumping back in disgust as part of a blackened arm emerged.

"It's his ruddy arm," he said in disgust and threw it out of the hole.

"But look what's on it, you idiot," said Millbourne, and he held up the arm and began to remove a silver object from the wrist. "And, if you look on the back of this wristwatch, my friend, you'll see that it's a gift from his mother to one Josiah Bratton. So you'll see that's our man. Gawd, it's a good job I'm here to help you idiots through life."

CHAPTER 53

11th July 1916

THE MEN GATHERED round the large Louis XIV table displayed a range of human emotions. There was scepticism from several of the 'brass hats', incredulity from some others, boredom from one or two, and excitement from the more enlightened. This latter category mostly comprised the members of British Intelligence, who had entered as a separate group to much whispering and a few pointed comments from the other members of the assembled group.

"I think we are all here now, Oscendale, so we can begin." The speaker was a solid-looking man whose demeanour and colonel's uniform suggested he was used to a position of command.

Oscendale stepped forward from the side of the room. From a bag hung on his shoulder he brought out a large object wrapped in a piece of cloth. He placed it on the polished table and began to unwrap it. His sense of drama could not be hidden and he found he was rather enjoying the rapt attention of so many men of power.

The object that emerged was the wooden box, now restored to its former lustre by some careful attention after so long in the earth of Mametz Wood. It was a walnut colour with small gold bands adding strength to its structure. Oscendale lifted the lid slowly and all eyes in the room focused on his hands as he drew out a well-filled green velvet bag from amongst many. Knowing what was about to occur, he enjoyed one more look at the surrounding faces before he poured the contents onto the table.

Several men gasped as objects the colours of the rainbow tinkled onto the polished wood, their brilliance dancing as the light above caught their myriad hues.

"Good grief!" a lone voice said and Oscendale knew it was his cue.

"Gentlemen, may I present the diamonds of the Comte de Mametz. I'm told you are looking at objects worth several million pounds on today's jewel market."

His act of drama over, Oscendale became the focus of attention as the assembled men sought to satisfy their curiosity. He was happy to oblige.

"The Comte de Mametz was one of the wealthiest men in France and when the war began two years ago he began making plans to prevent his wealth falling into German hands – even if he couldn't save his property and lands. However, his plans collapsed due to the speed of the German advance in this area in the first weeks of the war. He himself was not in the best of health anyway."

"Where is he now?" a major of the South Wales Borderers asked.

"No-one is sure. We believe he was able to make his escape from the Germans in August 1914, though he cut it fine. He made a fortune dealing in diamonds and lived, as you can imagine, a more than comfortable existence, but he decided that it would be too dangerous to take these diamonds with him. Remember there were German spies in the area at the time and an old man, accompanied by servants – however small a retinue – would arouse attention, so he thought it best to bury the diamonds on his land and return for them as soon as possible. You may recall that few high profile figures were admitting to the possibility of the war extending beyond

Christmas, so the Comte thought he would be returning to dig up his property in just a few months."

Oscendale then related the events of the past few days.

"But wasn't it rather risky, drawing a map? Anyone could get hold of it. And besides, he must have been able to remember where he'd buried it? It was, after all, on his land," queried the colonel.

"If anything were to happen to him during his escape he wanted the information to be passed on to a relative. Somehow the German soldier Karl Muller got hold of the map and this was where nature may have conspired against the Germans," replied Oscendale. "The original ride had become overgrown, or disguised perhaps, and a new one had been produced by their own troops. They were digging in the wrong place."

Oscendale deliberately refrained from telling the group the rest of the story as he was still uncertain of the final links of the chain.

"Clever," piped up one of the junior officers. "Except that we outsmarted them, what?"

Yes, I outsmarted them, thought Oscendale, *but I don't feel too clever about it.*

"So that's it then, Oscendale. I suppose you're feeling rather pleased with yourself." Major Vedmore had appeared at his shoulder as the room broke up into a welter of group conversations, and he smiled without a hint of humour. "Now you can return to your traffic duties and investigating thefts of baguettes."

Oscendale turned to face the man who had acted out such a poor charade in the *estaminet* several days ago. He knew that Military Intelligence would be peeved to have lost out to a humble military copper and that Vedmore would not forget his loss of face.

"Not really, Major Vedmore. Can I remind you that several men have died whilst searching for those diamonds, some of them British soldiers."

Vedmore edged closer and spoke so that none of the other men in the room could hear him. "Now listen here, Oscendale. I warned you once to keep your bloody big copper's feet out of my business and you chose to disregard my advice. You've had your moment of glory and now it's time for you to go back to your little office and contemplate a return to civvy street."

Oscendale felt his anger rise. "Somehow I don't think so. The jewels are here but I intend to find out what else has been happening. I suggest you go back to your Boy's Own cloak-and-dagger stuff."

"You've been warned, Oscendale. Keep to what you know best and leave the big boys' stuff to me," Vedmore hissed before turning to another group of officers, a smile immediately returning to his face.

CHAPTER 54

11th July 1916

"OH, AND I'VE done a bit of digging for you as well, sir. Seems the Comte had one particular employee he was a bit thick with. Gardener-cum-oddjob-man. He might be able to tell you a bit more about him. And the good bit is that he still lives nearby."

"Now how did you glean that particular piece of information, Loram?" asked Oscendale.

"Well, a man has to have his vices, sir. Turns out he and I drink in the same *estaminet* in town. Seen him around before. Surly sort of bloke, mind."

"What's his name?" said Oscendale, mulling over the fact that Loram was proving to be a man of many talents, and not just a damn fine shot.

"Laurent, Etienne Laurent. Still works locally, I'm told."

The café was quiet. *A bit early for the khaki brigade just yet,* thought Oscendale.

Laurent sat at a table, one of several sipping at their beers, but Oscendale identified him at once. He had watched Oscendale as he entered and Oscendale wondered for a minute if the man already knew his purpose.

He sat at the bar and ordered a beer. He noticed that Laurent did not seem as voluble as the others and waited patiently for his opportunity. It came when Laurent rose and approached the bar to order another drink.

"Good evening, Monsieur Laurent," he said when the

man had received his drink and was just turning to rejoin his comrades.

The man stopped and fixed Oscendale with his dark eyes.

"Captain Oscendale, we meet again," Laurent replied. He glanced across at his companions and lowered his voice, "We can speak outside, not in here. When I leave, follow me some minutes later."

Laurent did not rush his drink and it was not until some twenty minutes later that Oscendale saw him bid goodbye to his companions and leave the café. Oscendale waited an appropriate length of time and, after finishing his drink, followed him through the door.

It had begun to rain again and Oscendale looked up and down the now darkened street but could see no sign of the Frenchman. He chose to turn right for no reason other than the rain was no longer being swept into his face and had gone no more than thirty yards when a figure stepped out of a doorway in front of him.

"So you have found the Comte's jewels then?" Laurent's voice murmured.

Oscendale frowned. His opinion of the man had been right. This was no mere baker.

"How do you know?"

"This is a small town, Captain Oscendale. People talk and news like that doesn't stay secret for long. Some of your officers should be taught to hold their drink and their tongues in those fine military colleges of yours."

"Did you help the Comte bury that box?"

"Of course. The Comte was in no physical state to dig holes in the ground."

"And then you covered the path and made the new one to mislead anyone who found the map?"

Laurent snorted. "We knew that someone in the château was light-fingered. Objects were going missing in those first few weeks of the war and it seemed that they might have their eyes on the big prize – the Comte's diamonds. If he left Mametz with them he could be set upon and robbed, even with my protection. He decided to leave them where no-one could find them. We covered the path so that anyone who acquired the map would waste his time digging alongside the wrong one."

"Did you discover who the thief was?"

Laurent smiled. "Of course. But only after he had passed the map to the *Boche*. He had dug himself, found nothing and then traded it to them for some favour or other."

"And what happened to him?"

"What should happen to all thieves and traitors," Laurent spat. "His throat was cut."

"By you?" Oscendale enquired.

"Captain Oscendale, you are a policeman. Put it in your file and investigate it when the war is over."

If we all live that long, thought Oscendale.

"And the Comte will now be reunited with the family diamonds, yes?" said Laurent.

Oscendale hesitated. He knew that once the jewels were in the hands of the British authorities they would be reluctant to let them go. After all, millions of pounds were needed each day to fuel the furnace of the war. But would they be willing to risk a diplomatic spat with the French?

"I'd certainly like to think so," he replied, but he could tell from Laurent's face that the man was as sceptical as he was. Laurent threw his cigarette on the ground and with a sniff of disdain walked away.

CHAPTER 55

12th July 1916

THE PILE OF paperwork on his desk grew taller each day. The British Army loved its paperwork all right. '*Grave Reburials.*' Why on earth this should land on his desk, Oscendale didn't know. So he sipped his cup of tea and began the long, monotonous task of scanning yet another pile of official documents.

He froze as he read a name on the third sheet:

Report from Burial Team 237 – Sgt Millbourne Labour Corps.

On 11th July 1916 I was instructed to form up a working party to exhume several dozen bodies of buried soldiers who had been killed during the recent attacks on Mametz Wood.

During the afternoon my attention was drawn to the fact that two bodies had been found in a grave marked for one man. The temporary cross indicated that the man's name was 69387 Private David Denby. The burial team noticed that another body had also been placed in the grave.

The second body's identity tags were missing, as was his left arm. I found the arm lying in the bottom of the grave and a wristwatch was attached.

Oscendale noted that Sergeant Millbourne's prose was perfectly suited to the dry, emotionless requirements of military documents:

I removed the wristwatch as I was aware that soldiers with private wristwatches often have them engraved on the rear and I thought this might provide a clue to the man's identity. This it did. On the reverse of the face were inscribed the words 'Josiah Bratton'. I deduced that this was the identity of the man. There was no insignia of rank and

there were Welsh Regiment badges on his tunic. I therefore decided
that the second body was that of Private Josiah Bratton of the Welsh
Regiment, killed on the 7th July.

I reported the matter to Lieutenant Adams who ordered me to
make this report which is what I have done.

The report was signed 'Sergeant A. Millbourne'.

Oscendale was stunned. Finding two bodies in one grave
was not unheard of and the practice of finding dismembered
corpses on battlefields and hurriedly pushing them into shell
holes was widespread, particularly if the men involved were
still under enemy fire. But for it to be carried out behind the
lines was unusual. He wondered for a moment whether he
was letting the intricacies of this case get the better of him,
allowing his mind to run off at ridiculous tangents.

But it all came back to the name on the wristwatch. He
had spoken to Josiah Bratton on the 9th of July, two days
after he was supposed to have been killed, according to
Millbourne's report, so what was his wristwatch doing on
a dead soldier's arm? There could, of course, be a perfectly
reasonable explanation. He could have become involved in a
card school and have lost it during a gambling bout.

As for the double burial, the unknown man could have
been laid to rest first, the burial party interrupted and Denby
laid on top later.

Oscendale decided he would like to see the wristwatch,
so grabbing his cap he strode out of his office, brusquely
informing the comatose North of his destination, and walked
out into the rain of another summer's day on the Somme.

CHAPTER 56

12th July 1916

MILLBOURNE WAS AN oaf of a man. A regular soldier before the war, he had found himself a cushy, if unpleasant, role as head of a reburial section. He saluted Oscendale smartly but the paunch which strained at his tunic and particularly his belt indicated that his active soldiering days were over.

"Good morning, Sergeant Millbourne. Tell me about this unusual burial you came across yesterday," opened Oscendale and was treated to an almost verbatim retelling of the report he had read earlier.

When Millbourne had finished his moribund account, Oscendale asked him about the present location of the wristwatch. Millbourne's already red face reddened further and he meekly responded that it was not too far away and that he could lay his hands on it if the officer wished. Oscendale wished and a few minutes later Millbourne returned with said object in a small waterproof pouch.

Oscendale removed the watch from the bag and studied it. English made, not expensive, of a type that was becoming increasingly popular amongst ordinary soldiers, as if to count down their remaining hours, or in some cases minutes, on earth. Morbid but entirely understandable. Oscendale could empathise with a man wanting to know how long it would be before he was ordered out once more into the hell of no-man's-land and was determined to ensure that those moments, which could be his last, were not frittered away. You were rarely ready for death but at least it was of some comfort to know how long was left until the die was thrown – live or die. *How ironic*, he mused.

He turned it over and read the inscription which was just as Millbourne had reported. The watch had stopped but whether as the result of the man being hit or the water which now clouded its face was impossible to tell. Still, it could now be returned to its rightful owner in whatever condition it was in.

Oscendale thanked Millbourne and noted the look of first disappointment and then puzzlement on the man's face when he informed him of his intention to return the watch to Josiah Bratton – though whether this was because he had lost an object of minor value from his probably extensive collection of 'souvenirs' or because he had now lost the proof of the name of the second man in the grave was unclear.

Private Josiah Bratton's face did not bear the look of a man delighted to be reunited with his property.

Oscendale had made his way to the support trench where the soldiers of the Welsh Regiment were now refitting ready to be poured forward in relief and had found Bratton cleaning his Lee-Enfield once more. Did the man ever do anything else, apart from gambling perhaps?

He greeted Oscendale with some suspicion but then Oscendale received that sort of greeting from most men and was, in fact, more suspicious when a soldier greeted a policeman such as himself with any kind of warmth. Everyone had secrets to hide, even him. But when he removed the wristwatch from his pocket and held it out to Bratton the man did not react in the way he had expected. In fact he almost seemed to shrink from taking it, so Oscendale drew it back once more.

"It is your wristwatch, isn't it?"

A moment's hesitation. Enough to put Oscendale on his guard.

"Yes, sir. I lost it a few weeks ago," replied Bratton.

"How?" Oscendale asked simply.

"In a trench, or out there, I dunno." He nodded over his shoulder towards the front line and no-man's-land in the distance.

"Not gambling then?"

Oscendale sensed that the man knew that this would have been a better lie. More witnesses for him to try and track down. Some of them already dead or evacuated to hospitals miles away or even back in Blighty by now.

"No."

He paused to let the man think for a while and then tried a long shot.

"When did you argue with your brother?"

Bratton looked up, uncertainty in his eyes.

"Argue? Me and Harold? Well no more than brothers usually do, you know. Nothing in particular; I mean nothing major at all."

"Then why was he wearing your wristwatch?"

Bratton looked up in surprise. "What? Wearing my wristwatch? What do you mean?"

"This wristwatch was found on the arm of a man buried after the attack on the seventh, the day your brother was reported killed. His body hasn't been identified yet and I'm betting that this man was your brother, wearing your watch."

Bratton hung his head and his body was soon wracked with sobs. That was one of the most distressing parts of this war. Men who back in England would behave like men, keeping their emotions in check, were reduced amongst all the carnage of the battlefield to ordinary souls, capable of showing widely varying emotions. Out here it was acceptable to show your grief. At home, on leave, you reverted to being a stiff, emotionless man, whose self-control was everything.

Oscendale said nothing. A few men further along the trench looked across but resumed their routine chores and paid little further attention when Oscendale caught their eyes. They didn't want to know why their mate was crying. There was enough sorrow to go around for everyone.

"I lent it to him to bring him good luck. That didn't bloody work did it?" He paused as he struggled to contain his memories of his dead brother. "I'm glad he's been found at last, sir," said Bratton when he had recovered his composure.

Oscendale handed him the wristwatch, placed his hand on his shoulder and left Josiah Bratton to his own silent contemplation.

CHAPTER 57

12th July 1916

OSCENDALE BEGAN HIS latest report for Avate. The diamonds had been recovered and the British Government had extra resources to plough into the war effort. Most likely the Comte de Mametz, wherever he was, would die before the war was over; as he was childless and his wife had predeceased him, the jewels would anyway have gone to relatives. They would contest the matter in the French courts for years, by which time the war would be history, the personnel in government would have changed, and the matter could be dealt with quietly. Case closed.

But if that was all this case was ever about, why had Vedmore tried so hard to warn him off? An officer in British Intelligence had a caseload every bit as large as his own and yet he had focused his efforts on trying to intimidate Oscendale almost from the start. There was something hidden here that someone wanted to stay that way. But what was it?

He reached again for the file on William Vincent and began to go through it. Idris Evans had told him that there were at least two suspicious elements to that morning's events: the fact that Howells had been bayoneted and then shot, and that Vincent had, it appeared, deliberately chosen to die a slower death than would normally be the case when a man pointed a loaded rifle to his head.

And the only man who had been present when Vincent had died was dead and buried.

Or reburied.

He sat back with a start.

"North!" he shouted and the overweight policeman lumbered into the room.

"Yes, sir!" Whatever he thought about North, Oscendale could never fault the man's strict adherence to the regulations of the British Army.

"North, find out who conducted the original burials on the battlefield at Mametz of the men killed during the attack of 7th July. In particular, who was present at the double burials of David Denby and Harold Bratton."

"That would have been the men of the Welsh, sir. Burying their own, as it were."

Oscendale thought he detected a glimmer of compassion in North's voice, but if so it was soon gone.

"Good. Find out who exactly. And when."

North, for all his personal shortcomings, was thorough and quick at finding out information. Within an hour Oscendale had the names of the men who had comprised the burial party for Private Denby, and, as it had turned out, Private Harold Bratton. Two familiar names leapt out at him and by mid-afternoon the two men were waiting outside his door.

North ushered the first man in and Oscendale studied the man as he stood to attention a yard from his desk.

"Corporal Chadwick," he began, "the first time I met you a few days ago, you told me you had been near Harold Bratton when he was killed."

"S'right, sir. Not ten yards away."

"And you didn't see him again during the attack but saw him again when you returned to your own trenches."

"Yes, sir."

"You also told me that when you saw Bratton's body in no-man's-land his face was burnt but you took his identity tag."

"Yes, sir."

"And you are aware by now I'm sure that Bratton's body was found underneath another dead soldier's body in a single grave."

"Somebody did mention it, sir."

"I bet they did."

He paused as he watched Chadwick chewing his lip.

"I don't know how it happened like that, sir. We always put one body in a single grave when we can. It's different if we don't have time or there's too many bodies and not enough of us. Then we uses the shell holes. I can't understand it, sir."

"Neither can I, private." Oscendale rose to his feet. "I think you're telling me a load of rubbish. So don't take me for an idiot and tell me the truth! Who else was with you besides your oppo Cooper? There's no mention of Harold Bratton on the burial sheet you and Cooper are listed as having carried out."

A moment's calm fell on the room as the fury of Oscendale's words receded. Chadwick continued to chew his lip and then said, "Well, I might've been wrong, sir. I... I took a few identity tags from bodies that day and I might have mixed 'em up, you know."

"Go on."

"So it might not have been Harry what I took the tag from. I just never saw a corpse with his face and I just assumed the burnt one was him."

"But when you buried him with Denby, didn't you realise it was Bratton?"

"That's the thing about it, sir. And I swear on my life, we only put one body in that grave. I know I've lied to you, sir, but this is straight, honest. Just one body. How the other one got there I dunno."

Oscendale lifted his telephone and ordered North to bring in Corporal Cooper. Within a few minutes he had established the veracity of Chadwick's story.

Then he tried something else. "Cooper, did Josiah Bratton stay throughout the burials?"

"Yes, sir. Well, come to think of it, that is until the last one. Might have been Denby, I don't know. He said he'd finish the last one. Pretty good of 'im really. First time we'd worked with him and all." Cooper's discomfort was now as apparent as Chadwick's had been.

"Have you seen him lately?"

"No, sir," said Cooper. "Not since the burial party. Must be involved in other duties or something. Not in our part of the line, anyway."

"Bit strange, don't you think? The dead man's brother not coming to see you to find out more about how he died?"

"Perhaps he just wants to keep his distance, sir."

Yes, thought Oscendale, *and I think I know why.*

CHAPTER 58

12th July 1916

MAMETZ WOOD WAS silent. There were no leaves left to rustle in the wind. No birds flew overhead before landing on the branches to sing. The wood had been taken at last. The killing had moved on to new parts of the French countryside and more land tilled for the growing of crops for centuries would now be fed by the bodies of dead British and German soldiers.

Intruding on the scene were the piles of military equipment. The material manufactured and brought to this place to assist men in their task of slaughtering each other now lay abandoned and decaying. Rifles, ammunition, helmets, packs and coils of barbed wire were all strewn over the ground.

And everywhere the dead.

The clouds had greyed and the rain began to fall on the wood. In the trenches men reached for their oilskin ponchos and attempted to keep dry. Rain teemed off helmets as the intensity increased. The duckboards turned slippery and men cursed as they tried to move about.

And deep in the wood the rain fell, running off the branches and those leaves that still remained to the floor beneath, tapping like machine gun fire. It cleansed nothing; the evil of Man still remained. The rain washed the dead, turning their flesh to marble, lending a sculptural quality to the scene.

'Wood' was a misnomer now after the pounding of the last few days. Mametz Wood was really a collection of tree stumps, shattered trunks, broken military equipment and bodies.

Lots of them.

He walked quietly through the scene of the carnage. The burial teams had not yet been through. *Too much work in other areas of the Somme,* he mused.

The ground was no longer green, just a filthy morass of mud and blood. The killing that had gone on here over several days defied human imagination. Many of the bodies – of men who had once sung at parties and drunk with friends – were now gone, buried with temporary grave markers where their names were known, in unmarked holes where they were not. The pieces of the unnamed were thrown into pits and covered with mud. And there were those who had died unnoticed in the madness of battle, who had sunk into the ooze, been consumed by it and were doomed to lie there until later excavations found their remains by chance.

The debris lay all around his feet: pieces of equipment, shell fragments, rusting bayonets and unexploded ordnance. He wandered dazed through it all until he heard the voice.

"Josiah Bratton – or perhaps I should call you Harold Bratton?" Oscendale stood still and watched the man turn slowly round to face him. He was bareheaded and had no equipment other than a bayonet that caught the pale light of the midday sun.

"How did you know I was here?" replied the man.

"Well, nobody's seen you for a while and I know what you've been looking for in this wood so it seemed only logical to put the two together."

"So you know about the diamonds?"

"Yes. You see, I also have a copy of the map."

Bratton frowned. "But Bill Vincent said he had the only copy."

Oscendale shook his head. "He had the only accurate copy

– the original. Mine was drawn from memory by the German officer who gave it to him and he made an error."

Bratton stared at the ground. "If it hadn't been for them bastard Germans I'd have had the lot." He paused. "Thing is, I've been back to the spot and the rest of it has gone. Funny that. Have you taken them?"

"I found them, yes, and I've passed them on to the authorities."

Bratton grimaced. "You what? You honestly think they'll put them to any decent use? All they'll do is use them to prolong this bloody war!"

Oscendale kept calm as Bratton's right hand became more animated, gesturing wildly with the bayonet as he spoke. "They weren't your diamonds, Bratton. They belong to someone else."

"Some rich bastard, you mean? Someone who spends more in a day that I ever seen in a year?"

"Maybe. But it's still someone else's property and you had no right to it." Oscendale felt he was being forced into defending an indefensible position, adopting moral high ground that he did not necessarily agree with.

Bratton helped him out. "Don't really have many rights the likes of us, do we, sir?" sneered Bratton. "I mean, you're not a proper officer, not a toff like, are you?"

Oscendale was tiring of the pointless exchange. "Come on, Bratton. Give me the bayonet and let's get all this sorted out, eh?"

For a moment he thought Bratton was weakening, then he spoke again.

"Why couldn't you leave his watch with him, sir?" The voice was taut and full of emotion. "Our mam gave it to him last year. I didn't want it."

"And that was your mistake," said Oscendale. "If it hadn't been for the watch I wouldn't have known."

Bratton slumped against the remains of a tree.

"You saw your brother die, didn't you?"

The man sobbed. "He was there, close to me, on the other side of the shell hole, staring right at the bastards and then the liquid fire. The bloody flame-thrower set him alight. He was burning right in front of me. And the smell..." His voice trailed away into the surrounding silence.

"And so you joined the burial detail to bury your own brother. But then a thought occurred to you. You took his identity tags but you left the wristwatch."

"What else could I do? I knew someone was on to me. I could tell from the looks of the others. I thought if people believed I was dead then no-one would follow me. I'd be free to start a new life. In a while I'd desert and be gone." Bratton fell silent, reflecting on what he had so nearly been. "But at least *I* buried him, not some other blokes."

"So it was you who put his body in Denby's grave."

"It was easy. Just sent those idiots Chadwick and Cooper away and dug it deeper. They never dig 'em deep enough, anyway. That's why the bits fly into the air when the shelling starts."

"And you thought you'd be safe, impersonating your brother?"

"People always said we looked alike. It's not much of a crime, is it?"

"Well that rather depends on your point of view. And the fact that you killed Corporal Howells."

Bratton's eyes widened now. "Vincent shot Howells."

"No, he didn't. Howells woke up as soon as the first shot was fired, the one that killed Sergeant Jackson. Vincent didn't

305

have time to reload so he used his bayonet. But it takes precision to kill a man immediately with a bayonet and Vincent wasn't precise. That's why he kept looking back at the hut as he ran towards you. He thought Howells was following him. You went back into the hut after Vincent killed himself and you shot him."

"He would have died anyway. Why would I want to finish him off?"

"Because Vincent told you something before he died and you realised that Howells knew as well. The only way to keep the secret safe was to end his life before he spoke to anyone."

"And what did Vincent tell me?"

"Oh, I think he'd told you quite a lot before that night. You were certainly aware that Jackson and Howells had it in for him, but you didn't know why."

"Those sods were blackmailing him and when he refused to pay them any more they had him demoted."

"But it was only as he lay dying in front of you that you found out what the secret was, didn't you? It was the map. Vincent gave it to you and passed all his guilt over to you."

"They're my diamonds," said Bratton, his eyes widening.

Oscendale saw the bayonet start to rise. "Yes, but like I said, I don't have them any longer, if that's what you're thinking. They're with the authorities. I'd like to say 'proper authorities' but I'm not so sure they are." He paused for a moment then asked, "When I discovered the box of diamonds, you had been there before me, hadn't you?"

Bratton nodded dumbly.

Oscendale continued, "So where are the ones you took? You must have taken some that night."

The last dreams of Bratton's world collapsed before him

and he sank to his knees. "So it was all for nothing: Vincent, Jackson, Howells, Josiah. Even this bloody wood wasn't worth the cost," he said.

"It's all worth something, son. If not, then what's the point? Look around you. These dead men all thought it meant something to take the wood otherwise they wouldn't have enlisted, and wouldn't have walked across the valley to die here."

Bratton paused and followed Oscendale's sweeping arm. The dead watched them as silent witnesses to their debate, ready to vote one way or the other. Bratton's eyes were caught by three torsos that stood upright in the ground, red pools of blood around them like macabre bathing rings. They had been digging a trench when a shell fell and had ended up digging their own graves – from which they now protruded as if on Judgment Day. In a shell hole two signallers lay as if sleeping, their bodies seemingly undamaged yet their insides crushed by concussion blasts. The horror of it all flowed into and onto him like a huge black wave and he knew it was the end.

Before Oscendale could reach him, Bratton plunged the point of the bayonet deep into his neck. His eyes rolled backwards and a jet of blood pumped from his severed artery. He flopped to one side and lay still while the ground around him became saturated with red. Above him the trees sighed with despair at yet another young man's death and Oscendale raised his head to the heavens. He bent down and took Bratton's identity tags from his bloody neck, stood over him for a moment and then turned and walked away.

CHAPTER 59

13th July 1916

THE RAIN TEEMED down outside as Oscendale watched a military policeman check Kathleen's travel warrant at the barrier. The steel-grey clouds above and the dampness of the wooden building merely added to his sense of gloom and foreboding. This was the journey he had dreaded. Going home was always a mixed emotion. There was the sense of excitement as he thought of the possibilities of what he had proposed to Avate. But there was also the feeling that he had moved on from what he was pre-war. Everyone had, he supposed, and he was not the only one who would never be the same again, but a return home now just filled him with sadness.

When he had told Kathleen that he was returning to Barry to tie up the loose ends of the case, she had insisted on coming too. She had more leave due than she knew what to do with and as it was only for two days and she couldn't really get to Belfast and back in the time, it made sense for them to have some more time together after all the distractions of recent events.

He had nodded and agreed but felt once more that unnerving sense of being cornered. He had chosen not to become involved in a relationship as close as this one for some time, and he wanted to set the pace, to decide how quickly things progressed, and the more she pushed the more he felt like running away. The trouble was he liked her too much to tell her they were moving in a direction he felt uncomfortable with.

So here they were at a dismal train station, their paperwork being checked and rechecked and he wasn't sure how he felt anymore. Bratton's death had upset him more than he had thought possible. The young man would not have been executed, he was sure of that. Howells was dying anyway, and, given the traumatic experience of seeing Vincent shoot himself, this would probably have swayed the court in his favour. Add to that the nightmare of burying his own brother and he could have expected a reduced sentence on the grounds of neurasthenia.

The shriek of the train whistle broke into his thoughts and he shook his head involuntarily.

"What is it, Tom? That boy's death again?" Kathleen asked, slipping her arm through his.

"Mmmmm. Time to move on, I think," he replied and took her case as they made their way to the platform.

Barry was a grubby, bustling, burgeoning town which had grown from a docile hamlet of a few cottages to a sprawling conurbation of terraced houses and shops in just a few short years. The reason was the docks and everything in the town centred around them. The ships came and went by the dozen and were filled with coal from the seams in the Welsh valleys to be exported around the world. The demand for the black gold to serve the war effort had been huge and the town had boomed. *A valleys town by the sea*, Oscendale always thought.

It was yet another town much affected by the sorrow of the increasing death toll of the war. The names littered the local papers each week and the surnames were repeated as a never-ending sea of gloom washed across the streets of terraced houses.

And now there was another name, that of Harold Bratton.

When Oscendale had looked at his enlistment papers and seen he had lived in Barry, he had sighed and shaken his head, amazed at the symmetry of it all.

The Bratton family home was built of solid working-class brick, reflecting the characters of the souls who inhabited these streets that ringed the docks. Life was hard for these people. Oscendale knew that well enough from his own father, and this was not the time for subtlety or grace.

Mrs Bratton was a matronly figure who answered his knock at the door wearing her apron, and he knew this was no affectation of toil. The woman had probably risen at dawn and would work until long after dark to ensure the smooth running of the household for her husband and sole remaining son.

"Yes?" she asked without politeness or reserve and he knew it was because he was intruding into her finely tuned litany of tasks.

"Good afternoon, Mrs Bratton. My name is Captain Thomas Oscendale, Military Foot Police. I have a few questions regarding the recent deaths of your sons, Josiah and Harold. May I come in?"

There was no question of a policeman being kept on the doorstep, military or otherwise, not with inquisitive neighbours around, and he was soon seated in the front parlour, the place reserved for solemn occasions such as these.

The drawn blinds had indicated to him that the woman was aware of her sons' deaths, but she had shown no emotion as she stood aside to let him in.

"First of all, can I say how sorry I am at the deaths of your boys, Mrs Bratton. I know it must have come as a great shock to lose both of them." He knew his platitudes were stiffly conveyed but he was never at ease discussing family loss.

The woman sniffed but he couldn't be sure if this was an expression of grief or of disdain. She merely nodded in acceptance.

Before he could get any further the front door opened and slammed and a voice shouted, "Iris! I'm home."

"In the parlour, Bert," the woman replied and Oscendale saw more confidence come into her eyes, as if reinforcements had just arrived.

"What you doing in there? Have we got visitors or something?"

The man who followed the voice into the room was dressed in the shabby, dirty clothes of a docks worker, his greying moustache and lined face speaking of years of hard physical work. He removed his cap and looked at Oscendale.

"Oh, it's you, Mr Oscendale. Come to arrest me again?"

Albert Bratton. Oscendale remembered the man. He had arrested him once for drunkenness. *Well, well, well.*

"Hello, Mr Bratton. No, not if you've done nothing wrong. It's about your sons."

Bratton surveyed Oscendale's uniform. "Joined up, have you? Not enough criminals in Barry now, eh? Thought you'd chase them over to France and nab 'em all there?"

"As it happens, this *is* about a crime, Mr Bratton. A crime one of your sons committed."

"The only crime they committed was getting bloody shot by the Germans!" Bratton's voice was hostile and he glared with resentment at Oscendale.

"Look, Mr Bratton, I can understand you're upset but I need to ask you a few questions."

"A few questions? That's all you bloody coppers ever do. Well I'd like a few answers. Like when are my boys' bodies coming home so we can bury them properly!"

A great cry came from Mrs Bratton and Oscendale turned to see the woman with her face in her hands and her shoulders jerking with the effort of breathing.

"They were the two most precious things I had in the world," she sobbed.

Bratton slumped into one of the aged armchairs and fell silent.

"Did Harold write home to you often?" Oscendale asked after a while.

"Course," replied Bratton. "We looked forward to the letters from both of the boys. But that's all gone now, hasn't it?"

"Did he ever mention a man named Vincent, William Vincent?"

Bratton frowned. "Vincent? Yes, Harry was in the same company as him. Used to mention him from time to time. Why?"

"When was the last time Harry wrote to you, Mr Bratton?"

"Just before he... Just a few days ago. And a package arrived yesterday. As you can imagine we haven't felt like opening it yet."

"Package?"

"Yes. He used to send letters but we got a package this time. Must be a few of his personal effects. I can't bring myself to open it."

"Could I see it?" Oscendale asked.

Bratton hesitated and looked across to his wife. She looked up for the first time since her husband had entered the room and nodded.

Bratton led Oscendale along a dark hallway to a small kitchen whose walls were running with the condensation generated by a pan of water that was about to boil dry on the stove.

"Damn," said Bratton, turning it off. "She's in such a state with this news that she's not herself. She's going to burn the bloody house down one day."

A brown package lay on the kitchen windowsill. "May I?" said Oscendale.

"Yes. Probably best if you're the one to open it. I... I'll go back to see Iris." Bratton's face revealed his compassion for his wife and he left the room.

The package was wrapped in brown paper and stamped with a military postmark. Oscendale carefully unwrapped it. Inside were a letter of condolence and several of Harold Bratton's personal items. Opening his wash roll, which contained his shaving and washing kit, a small paper packet dropped to the floor. Oscendale picked it up. The contents felt hard and moved between his fingers. Glancing over his shoulder to ensure that the Brattons were still in the parlour, he slipped the packet inside his tunic.

CHAPTER 60

13th July 1916

OSCENDALE SAT ON the dockside mooring post and gazed across the oily water to Barry Island. The rows of tightly packed houses, built to be rented to the dockworkers, glared back at him, their untidy, scrambling lines crawling up and down the contours of the hills. The docks around him were alive with the hustle and bustle of a busy port.

He opened his palm to reveal once more the collection of diamonds he had found in the packet that Bratton had sent home to his parents. It was their way out of the hand-to-mouth existence they found themselves in and through which they would struggle for the rest of their lives. And not just their lives. Their remaining son would follow the same course and the whole cycle of deprivation, coupled with hard work and hard drinking, would shadow his descendants as well.

Oscendale pondered on the way that fate dealt out fortune. If they had opened the brown packet their lives would have been changed forever. As it was, he had removed the packet of stones and slipped them into his pocket before Mr Bratton had re-entered the kitchen. They would never know how close they had come to wealth beyond their dreams. The stones would be added to the others he had recovered, passed through the hands of various departments and disappear into the wealth of the government.

"Well, how did it go?" Kathleen appeared at his side and stood over him, her back to the dock.

He opened his hand once again and the morning sun caught the jewels, their brilliance flashing in the light.

"A package from the Front that would have changed their lives," he responded.

Her eyes gazed at the jewels and then shifted to his. Her hand went to her handbag and brought out a pistol which she aimed directly at his forehead. A quizzical look came across his face and he wondered whether this was not all part of a mad, bad dream and that really he was back in France not in this nightmarish scene.

"Give them to me, Tom," she said quietly. "Do it without fuss and you won't get hurt."

He knew it was a lie. As soon as the bright stones were in her hand she would shoot him. The noise of the shot would be lost amongst the noise of the docks. She would walk quickly away and his lifeless body would be dismissed as another drunken sailor sleeping off a good night in the 'Chain Locker' before someone got closer and realised there was blood seeping from the hole in his head.

"I don't understand. Why do you want it, Kathleen? You've never struck me as the mercenary type." He was confused, bewildered. What was going on here?

"Tom, there are wider issues in this war than you will ever realise."

"Try me." He had no idea where this was leading. Was their relationship all about this? Had this been what she had wanted all along? Walking, talking, loving. All to this end?

The gun wavered for a moment as she pondered whether to kill him now or in a few seconds. He would like to think that something would affect that decision, something of the nights they had spent together, the closeness they had had for the past few months.

"This war is not about German imperialism, Tom. It's about the British and their bullying attitude towards other countries."

"Yours?" he ventured.

"Yes. Our politicians tried the peaceful way but the British weren't having it. Now it's time for some direct action."

"But you've tried that. The Easter Rising in April was a bloody disaster, you know that."

He had noticed that Kathleen was standing near a wire hawser that snaked along the quay. He had also noticed a snap of movement along its length some twenty yards away. If he prolonged this discussion someone might spot the snagged cable and approach to rectify the problem.

"So it's to be sold to buy more guns. Don't you think that you and I have seen enough killing? For God's sake you don't want to watch more men die, do you?"

The compassion flickered across her face but was quickly gone.

"This is different. This is for *my* country and the issues are not the same."

"It's always the same. Don't fool yourself. When did you decide to do it?"

And the look told him everything. He cursed himself for being so blind. He had allowed her to get under his skin and it became a torment. She had used him from the beginning. He had foolishly shared parts of the case with her and she had accompanied him back to Barry to kill him and take the diamonds.

"But you couldn't know I'd find anything in Bratton's house."

The cable twitched again and began to tauten.

"I must admit it was a bonus. I thought I'd missed out

completely when you handed the other lot in and I'd have to shadow you for longer. But now my job is done. Don't think it wasn't good while it lasted, Tom, but it's over now."

She raised the pistol a fraction and as she did so the cable broke free from its obstruction and whipped along the dockside. It lifted from in front of her feet, flew into the air and caught Kathleen flush under the jaw. She was catapulted backwards into the dock. The gun flew harmlessly into the air and her body sank lifelessly into the black oily water.

Oscendale rushed to the edge of the quay and stared hopelessly into the water, hoping to see her rise to the surface. After several minutes he knew it was over. She had certainly been rendered unconscious when the cable struck her and could have even been dead already before she hit the water.

Life went on around him. No one stopped their work, no shouts of alarm were heard and Kathleen Morrison became yet another body to sink to the bottom of Barry's Number One Dock.

"Mr Oscendale. Forget something did you?" Albert Bratton could not disguise his contempt as he opened his front door in answer to Oscendale's knocking.

"Yes, Bert, I did," Oscendale replied with a sigh.

"What?" said Bratton belligerently.

"I left something in your kitchen. Can I fetch it?"

With a resigned shrug, Bratton stood aside and gestured for him to enter. "Yes, go in," he said. "Get it quick and shut the door on your way out. You coming here has upset Iris again, not that I think she'll ever get over it anyway. So just get whatever it is and leave us alone."

With that Bratton disappeared into the front parlour to comfort his grieving wife.

Oscendale made his way into the steamy kitchen once more. From his tunic he drew out the packet he had taken earlier and removed all of the diamonds except two, then he replaced the small packet inside Harold Bratton's last posting home to his mother and father.

As he passed the doorway to the parlour Oscendale said, "By the way, there was nothing in Harold's packet that will be needed for evidence. It's all yours now."

There was no reply but he heard the couple talking quietly to each other and left them to their sorrow.

As Oscendale closed the door of number 7, Dock View Road and stepped out into the July sunshine he felt as if the world was welcoming him anew.

They were the two most precious things I had in the world.

CHAPTER 61

14th July 1916

THEY SAT IN the *estaminet* and Avate placed two glasses of red wine on the table. Oscendale watched his for a while, unable to bring himself to begin while Avate looked at him.

"It's over now, Tom. Over," said Avate at last, gesturing to the untouched glass.

"But is it? Is it really over?" Oscendale replied. "There are wrongs here that can't be righted. I doubt if the families of Jackson and Howells would agree. And what about the Vincents or the Brattons?"

"They'll all carry on in one way or another," said Avate patiently. "They won't forget but they'll get through it. The families of Jackson and Howells, and even Harold Bratton, will be told their boys died in action. There's no need to tell them the truth."

Oscendale reached for his glass at last and took a large mouthful.

Avate continued. "I'll read your report in good time but I must admit I'm not sure what it's going to say. There's an awful lot that's gone on here and I'm puzzled as to how it all holds together. For instance, how did Vincent get hold of the map?"

Oscendale's eyes left Avate and focused somewhere in the distance. "My guess is that he and Karl Muller met somewhere on the battlefield. I must admit I have no idea where but my guess is sometime in 1914 when the Germans first fought us in this area. For some reason Muller gave his old friend the map. Perhaps he thought he wasn't going to come through it."

"And Vincent knew what it was?" asked Avate.

"Yes. He knew that the map was genuine and that there was something buried in Mametz Wood of great importance and certainly of great value."

"And he had to wait two years to get it?" said Avate, shaking his head.

"That was the thing that ate deep into his soul. Mametz Wood was in enemy hands so he had to wait until after the war was over or for an opportunity to get near it. After all, he could hardly set off on an expedition into German territory."

Avate contemplated this information then added, "So he discovers the Welsh Division are planning to be in the area and requests a transfer, citing personal reasons or something. Seems unlikely."

"He pulls some strings somewhere. Don't forget, he's an old soldier. He knows the ropes and probably had friends in many low places. Call in a few favours, fill in some paperwork and Bob's your uncle, he's transferred to the Welsh Regiment. Of course, our intelligence people were on to him by now, having intercepted the letter from Muller to his home in Swansea. That's why Vedmore tried to warn me off."

"But how did Jackson and Howells find out about his plans and begin blackmailing him?" said Avate.

Oscendale shook his head uncertainly. "I'm not sure about this bit. They may have known half the story for some time but as the day for the attack got closer, Vincent couldn't take the risk of being found out. Perhaps they found out about the irregular nature of his transfer or perhaps he boasted about something when he had been drinking."

"So he killed them?" asked Avate.

"No. He killed one of them – Jackson. Howells woke

up when he heard the shot, although Vincent had tried to muffle it with a pillow. That's why the witnesses only heard one shot. Howells was in the next bunk. Vincent panics as he had planned only to kill Jackson and then blame Howells. So he stabs Howells, severely wounding but not killing him, and runs out of the hut. He expects to get clean away and probably join the group of deserters we rounded up in the woods when we caught Price. But he had a backup plan if he failed. He'd thought all this through pretty carefully."

Avate frowned. "The stick he used to push the trigger?"

"Exactly. It was preferable to being shot for murder by a firing squad so he had made it ready. Imagine his horror as the man he encounters standing on guard duty is Harold Bratton, a young man he had befriended. He can't bring himself to kill young Bratton so he decides to kill himself. In his final few seconds of life he attempts to right a wrong by giving the map to Bratton in the hope that he will understand its significance and be lucky enough to survive the forthcoming attack and be able to retrieve it."

"An awful lot of ifs, Tom," said Avate sceptically.

"I agree but with a treasure hoard that valuable it was worth taking the risk."

"Hang on," said Avate raising a finger. "You said that Vincent only killed Jackson. So who killed Howells?"

Oscendale smiled sadly. "Harold Bratton. Unfolding the piece of paper that he has just been given, he sees at once what it is. Something clicks inside him and he goes to the hut to see what Vincent has done. He sees Jackson is dead. By now the other men are awake and he tells them about Vincent. They run out of the hut and he is left alone. Howells has been bayoneted but is not yet dead. The others assumed he was still in a drunken stupor. Bratton knows that Vincent had attempted to kill both men for a reason so in gratitude to Vincent and to clear the coast for himself he finishes Howells off with his rifle. Then he joins the others outside."

"Good grief!" said Avate. "Then we move in, think we have a murderer who subsequently commits suicide and really a second crime has occurred. The killer then is back with his unit and free to carry on with his life. How about the bloody *Boche*? How the hell did they know what was going on?" Avate was clearly becoming exasperated at the events of the case as Oscendale was unfolding them.

"Again I am taking an educated guess here of course, but I think it's fairly close to the truth. The German officer who was captured during the trench raid had a map similar to, but not the same as, that carried by William Vincent, plus a letter to Vincent. We will never know for sure because he didn't have the correct identification on him, but I think he was Karl Muller. Vincent knew Muller was in the area too. Got the information from two members of his regiment he interrogated in May. Unfortunately for Muller he was captured by our lot and when I took his map he knew the game was up. The jewels were going to pass to either Vincent or us."

He paused as Avate let out a low whistle. "Muller! But why was his map incorrect?"

Oscendale leant forward onto the table. "Because he had drawn it from memory some time after he gave it away. I don't think he had it in his possession for long before he gave it to Vincent. Then time passed and it was only when he found himself in this area again, as he had in 1914, that he attempted to redraw the map as he recalled it. Unfortunately for him he placed the spot on the new ride rather than the old one."

Avate interrupted. "He was here in 1914? As part of the first German offensive, I suppose. So how did he get hold of the original map in 1914?"

"From one of the Comte's servants. I think the servant stole the map from the Comte and probably killed him too when he saw the writing was on the wall. He soon realised he had no chance of escaping with the goods so he traded the information to the Germans in exchange for something. His life maybe if they caught him stealing some food or drink."

"And the second man? The one who stole your map?"

Oscendale took another drink from his glass. "German Military Intelligence, I suspect. Far too cunning and resourceful for an ordinary Hun soldier. Fortunately, it was the wrong map anyway and the Germans got back the map they'd lost which was no good to them; they ended up digging in the wrong spot. But Intelligence were involved on both sides. Our lot were alerted that the Huns were searching for something in Mametz Wood, perhaps by one of our spies. Unfortunately, an innocent woman had to die in a bungled attempt to obtain the map. It was reported that Catherine Jaulard was friendly with William Vincent and someone in Intelligence without any intelligence assumed that the love note he had passed to her was in fact the map when his body was searched and no map was found. A pretty poor job actually and a great pity."

"And Bratton? He was the one who found the box before you did and opened it?" Avate enquired.

"He remained behind in the wood after the attack on the tenth had petered out and went to the spot using Muller's original map. When he returned to our lines he became suspicious that people were onto his secret. Who, if anyone, I'm not clear. So he took advantage of his brother's death to attempt a switch of identities. Nearly got away with it too.

If it hadn't have been for Millbourne's burial party we might have missed it."

"Why didn't he take all of the jewels if he found them first?" asked Avate.

Oscendale paused then said, "I think the German patrol that nearly did for me disturbed him before he could remove anything."

Avate nodded in comprehension but he knew Oscendale had yet to reach the most painful part of the story. Silence fell between them for a moment or two. Then Avate said quietly, "And Kathleen Morrison?"

Oscendale stared at the floor. "I had no idea," he began. "I really had no idea. She fooled me from the start. If it hadn't been for a stray ship's cable she would have had some of the diamonds and I'd be the one rotting at the bottom of Barry Docks."

"Don't be so hard on yourself, Thomas," said Avate soothingly. "She was well trained, first by her own people and then by the Germans."

"I know but I let her get under my skin. It won't happen again," Oscendale said and downed the rest of his wine.

Leaning back in his chair as Avate went for refills, he watched the wide variety of human beings go about their business, this way and that, in the rest of the room. Any one of them could hide a dark secret, he decided, then brushed the thought aside and turned his attention to the second glass Avate had just placed in front of him.

After he had finished the wine, Oscendale stood up and placed his cap on his head. Avate looked up, surprised. "Off, Tom? I thought we were here for the evening."

"Thank you for the drinks, sir, but I have one more part of this case that I need to resolve."

Avate frowned with curiosity. "You didn't mention anything else in your report. Is there something you're not telling me?"

Oscendale looked at Avate. "This is a civilian not a military matter, sir. It will be quickly resolved."

Avate nodded and turned his gaze to the rest of the room as Oscendale left.

CHAPTER 62

14th July 1916

THE CANDLES BURNED on the large château table and the chatter of after dinner small talk filled the air, as did the pungent odour of cigar smoke.

Oberst Markus Sollner relit his cigar and turned to the man seated on his left.

"So, Bernhofer, any news on the agent you were running?"

Bernhofer lowered his empty wine glass to the starched white tablecloth and noticed a drop of red wine which had flowed to its base begin to stain the pristine linen. This was the moment he had been dreading.

"No, *Herr Oberst*. She has not been heard from for some time. I can only assume that she has been compromised."

"So the operation was a failure. The British have the jewels to buy even more armaments from the Americans and we must go on scraping the bottom of the barrel."

"It would appear so, *Herr Oberst*."

"And this policeman, what was his name?"

"Oscendale."

"Ah yes, Oscendale. This British policeman has outwitted the combined minds of several members of Department IIIb. He has recovered the jewels and has compromised, as you put it, one of our agents."

Bernhofer could add nothing. He was acutely conscious that the conversation around the room had muted in response to Sollner's rising tones. The reply was left to Stoltz who leaned forward from the other side of the table.

"At least we know we have one man who can penetrate British lines and return with information, *Herr Oberst*. He could be of use to us again." He finished by looking at Bernhofer who stared back with hatred.

Sollner nodded. "Yes. Perhaps there will come another time when we can use him. In the meantime, gentlemen, can I remind you that we have a staff meeting at 9 a.m. tomorrow morning to discuss our next response to the British offensive."

He rose and the other officers around the table rose in unison. Stoltz smiled at Bernhofer who turned away. *Next time*, each vowed, *it will be my turn*.

CHAPTER 63

14th July 1916

THE CAFÉ WAS empty at this late hour. Oscendale entered and saw Laurent sitting alone at a table. *Perfect*, he thought, as he approached the man. Laurent looked up with his usual malevolent look, suspicion burning behind his dark eyes.

"Good evening, Monsieur Laurent," said Oscendale pleasantly. "Mind if I join you?"

Laurent merely shrugged, which Oscendale took to be a sign of indifference, so he pulled back a chair and sat down.

"I understand Madame Jaulard's funeral is tomorrow. Will you be attending?"

"Of course. Although I didn't know Madame that well. I was just an employee."

"Oh I don't think that's true, Monsieur Laurent. I think you knew her very well. You see, I thought that the British officer called Price murdered Catherine Jaulard and that threw me for a while but then I began to realise that there was no reason for him to kill her. He could have found out what he needed to know by questioning her and I don't think that an honest woman like Catherine Jaulard would have attempted to deceive the authorities. So I began to wonder who had the motive to carry out such a terrible deed. Then I recalled our conversation outside here the other night. You made it perfectly clear that you have no particular affection for British soldiers. But I think that you did have a particular affection for Madame Jaulard. So much so that when you suspected she was having an affair with a Tommy, which by the way, wasn't true, you went to her house to confront her with it.

The café owner here tells me that you had left late that night, or should I say morning. You had been drinking and playing cards with your friends. I think you decided to pay Madame Jaulard a visit on your way home, which coincidentally takes you right past her front door.

"She, of course, was getting ready to see someone, probably the British officer I have just mentioned. She opened the door to you because she was expecting a visitor. You told her what you thought; she denied it and told you to leave. Whether it was the drink or lust, you forced yourself upon her. You realised that someone else was arriving soon so you killed her to make it look like the second caller had done it. When the British officer arrived, for that was who she was expecting, he knew he was in a very difficult position so he tried to bluff it out and nearly succeeded. He must have tried to save her, getting blood on his overcoat as he did so, and she tore a button from it in her death throes."

Laurent had watched Oscendale throughout and, as he paused, the man looked confidently across at him and said, "A very entertaining story, Captain Oscendale, but you have no proof."

Oscendale smiled crookedly. "I was never quite sure about you from the moment I met you. Played the role of the loyal employee far too well. But you see it goes further than this. We've checked and the Comte de Mametz never actually made it to England as you claimed. In fact he has disappeared. I don't think there ever was another thief – only you. I'm also willing to wager that you killed him and buried his body around here somewhere. You took the map and planned to use it but the Germans got hold of you and you used it to save your skin. You're a coward as well as a double murderer. The thought of those diamonds, inaccessible in a fortified wood must have eaten away at you for the past two years. So close and yet so far away. You probably overheard Vincent talking about his infatuation with Madame Jaulard in this very place and decided she was nothing but a trollop. Yet it made you insanely jealous. What you didn't know was that Vincent had your map on him at the time."

Laurent's face changed and grew malevolent. "He had the map?" he hissed.

What was it Loram sometimes said? Wait for the other man to make a mistake. He always will.

"Yes," replied Oscendale. "He would have had the diamonds and Catherine Jaulard. You'd have lost both of them."

It was like pulling a trigger. Laurent snapped and tipped the table over. Oscendale had been waiting for the moment and leapt backwards as the table crashed to the floor. There was a blur and Laurent held a knife pointing towards him.

"Put it down or I'll blow your bloody head off." Loram's voice echoed around the empty café. Laurent turned to see the sniper pointing his rifle at him from the doorway. As he did so the café door opened and Inspector Valère entered with two gendarmes. Laurent let the knife fall to the floor and raised his hands slowly in the air.

CHAPTER 64

15th July 1916

NORTH SHOWED LORAM into the office and announced him. Oscendale looked up from his typewriter.

"Morning, sir. You asked to see me?" said the NCO.

"Ah, Loram. Yes. I wondered whether you were interested in a new career. Or whether you were happy risking having your head shot off by a German sniper every day?"

Loram grinned. "A new career, sir? Didn't realise there were many career opportunities for men like me in the British Army."

"Well, normally there wouldn't be but I need an assistant. Someone with initiative." Loram raised an eyebrow. "And someone who can bale me out when I overreach myself," Oscendale added. "I know from your record that you were a copper in civilian life so you know what I'm talking about."

"Yes, sir."

"Well?"

"You mean would I rather work with you or stand in a bloody trench for days on end with the Boche shelling and shooting at me? Oh, I'd have to think about that, sir." He grinned again and nodded.

Oscendale stood and the two men shook hands.

When Loram left, Oscendale opened the window and looked down onto the square below. The usual hubbub of noise and bustle of military traffic was playing out its daily scene. In the distance the guns were rumbling once again and his eyes caught those of a fresh-faced soldier who looked up at him from the ranks of khaki below him. Oscendale looked away. At the moment he could not meet the eyes of any of the men being sent up the line. One more death was too many.

EPILOGUE

7th July 2007

JACK OSCENDALE SMILED to himself and wondered what his father would have made of the fact that the secret was still safe. He ran his hand over the cold, white stone and noted the pitting where the rain had done its work. Small drops of water had gnawed away at the stone, like tiny insects on a piece of wood. Raising his head, he looked around the cemetery at the rows of silent sleepers lying in their well-tended beds, their lives cut so agonisingly short.

A shadow fell on the ground and he noticed that the light had begun to change. Steel-grey clouds had gathered overhead and the first drops of rain tapped on the back of his outstretched hand. The wood called to him now and he left the cemetery, quietly closing the gate behind him as he went. *To keep the tourists out or the dead in?* he wondered.

He began to climb the slope to the cover of the dark mass of trees that frowned at him as he approached. The rain was now falling heavily, making the ground more slippery and he lost his footing more than once. As he reached the edge of the wood a white flash lit up the darkness within and was closely followed by a deep growl that seemed to shake the earth beneath his feet. For a moment he wondered whether he had ignored the warnings about abandoned ordnance at his peril and that he had become the latest victim of the Great War. Then the lightning flashed again and he raced the final few steps for the sanctuary of the wood. The black mouth opened and swallowed him up.

He was alone now and the darkness closed in around

him without comfort or warmth. A cold sense of evil was all around him and he shuddered as his mind began to imagine the ghosts of the past watching his intrusion into their pain. Memories stirred amongst the trees.

Walking a few steps, he stopped at the sight of a rusting shell, its base pointing directly at him from the spot where it had landed ninety years before. He attempted to skirt around it but saw another, then yet another. His mind began to play with his senses and as the thunder rumbled overhead he became part of the past and closed his eyes to feel the horror of what had happened here.

He could hear it now, the roar of battle from long ago, and imagined the scenes his father had described for him when he was a young man. He was here now, with him, a part of all that had happened. But he could escape, if he went no further.

Opening his eyes again, Jack Oscendale chose the present not the past and carefully retraced his steps out of the wood until he emerged once more into the storm. Rain lashed down on his uncovered head and he slipped and slid down the slope to the road.

He turned around only once and saw the wood still brooding on the hill, contemplating his intrusion into its edge. The evilness of the place finally overcame him. He shuddered, hurried back to his car and was gone.

Let the dead rest in peace, he decided.

If they were able to.

The Dead of Mametz is just one of a whole range of publications from Y Lolfa. For a full list of books currently in print, send now for your free copy of our new full-colour catalogue. Or simply surf into our website

www.ylolfa.com

for secure on-line ordering.

TALYBONT CEREDIGION CYMRU SY24 5HE
e-mail ylolfa@ylolfa.com
website www.ylolfa.com
phone (01970) 832 304
fax 832 782